Under the Blue

Under the Blue

OANA ARISTIDE

First published in Great Britain in 2021 by Serpent's Tail,
an imprint of PROFILE BOOKS LTD
29 Cloth Fair
London
EC1A 7JQ
www.serpentstail.com

Lyrics from 'Wish You Were Here' (p. 14) © David Gilmour and Roger Waters, 1975.
Reproduced by kind permission of Hal Leonard Europe.

10 9 8 7 6 5 4 3 2 1

Typset in Freight Text by MacGuru Ltd
Designed by Barneby Ltd
Printed and bound in Great Britain by Clays Ltd, Elcograf S.p.A.

A CIP record for this book can be obtained from the British Library

ISBN: 978 1 78816 583 9
Export ISBN: 978 1 78816 761 1
eISBN: 978 1 78283 735 0

FSC
www.fsc.org
MIX
Paper from
responsible sources
FSC® C018072

To Binga

Part One

1

He has won another lottery. One hundred pounds on a green scratch card, and that's with the bonus field still to go. He would like to share this moment with someone, and he looks up, but there's only the TV in a corner of the living room. The woman newsreader has almond eyes and heavy L's: plump, woollens on a clothesline. Slavic L's. The screen switches to shaky phone-camera footage of human bodies strewn across a courtyard.

He scratches the bonus field.

He doesn't double the hundred, but it's fine. What matters is that he wins more often than the statistics predict. Happy as a kid each time, and it's not about the money. Is it the knowledge that someone does win, that the whole thing's not rigged? Sometimes, late at night, content and in a sleepy torpor, he's tried to explain to whoever was lying next to him that it's about having faith in the world, in things being true and good.

The Slavic newsreader is back, talking about mass poisoning. They seem to think it was mushrooms. In the BBC studio, a guest shakes his head, says *subsistence agriculture*, and opens his arms, palms upwards.

Until last autumn, he'd not had a TV set for thirty years. This one was already in Tim's flat and stuck to the wall when he moved in. He worries he has forgotten how to watch TV. He is impatient, distrustful of narratives. Plot points pass him by. The frenzied banners, insistent and red, only stir him to wilful indifference. Instead, he picks up disjointed facts, random words, bizarre and mysterious images that months later turn up in the corners of his paintings.

Downstairs, the building's recycling bins are full not of beer cans and wine bottles, but of flattened cardboard boxes. He is curious, stops with his empty bottles when no one's around and turns the cartons this way and that, wonders at the contraptions depicted on them. Juicers, blenders, exercise bikes, vacuum cookers and squat little plastic barrels of protein powder. Endless cartons of coconut water. His neighbours, he suspects, are serious about putting up a fight.

He doesn't belong in this place.

He learned that he'd inherited the flat a few weeks after Tim's accident. By then, he was wallowing in guilt. Tim had been thirty-two at the time, and worked for a hedge fund, yet now Harry could only think of his nephew as a thin, shy boy who liked to stand holding his elbow. Then the flat came along, two bedrooms in a shiny new development with twenty-four-hour concierge service. The place where Tim had lived for the past two years. The easiest thing, the sensible thing, would have been to sell.

There's constant traffic of dry-cleaned shirts and Amazon parcels at reception. Everyone has real jobs that they actually go to, so that Monday to Friday, during the day, the building belongs to him and the cleaning ladies. The flat has low ceilings and small windows. It's terrible for painting. The walls are thin. When his neighbours are at home it sounds as though they are many, entire hordes of them, but when they appear on the landing it can be just one little Japanese woman eyeing him accusingly. Does he sound like many, too?

Customers and gallery owners don't like his new place. It's not arty, and it's not ironically not arty. Inside, he has to invite them to step closer to the paintings, lure their glance away from the plasticky vertical blinds.

He makes enemies, and friends. The concierge stops him one day at reception, tells him 'a third party' has complained of his flat smelling of turps. 'Fire hazard, sir. Very serious.' The man points a pen at the fine print on an A4; Harry guesses it's the terms of the lease contract. He is caught off-guard by this reprimand, hesitates between denying the charge and rejecting the man's authority in the matter, when the young woman who lives opposite appears at the desk. 'It's just the vents. They're weird in this place,' she tells the concierge. 'I can smell the neighbour's perfume in the morning when she gets ready for work. Perfume is flammable. Is that a fire hazard?'

The concierge beats a retreat; he doesn't want to deal with anyone's perfume. The young woman heads for the lift. Harry catches up with her, thanks her, informs her it's not even the turpentine people should worry about, but the oily paint rags and their potential for self-combustion. 'Oh well. Worse things could happen' – she smiles – 'than burning for art.' He's smitten.

He doesn't know her name. They're not known by names here, that's another thing. By decree of the concierges, they're all flat numbers. Miss Twenty-Two and he now and again share the lift, so each time he has about thirty seconds to talk to her. She's small and dark, with short hair and unusual, alarming deep-blue eyes. A hint of a foreign accent. She's vague about where she works. He guesses that she's unhappy with her job, and likes her more for it. If she ever knew Tim, she doesn't let on. He has a feeling she would understand if he explained himself to her. I'm honouring the memory of my dead nephew. Penitence; these continental types would get it.

When he has doubts about living and working there, he tells himself that all the things that are bad for painting are good for art.

The only change he's made to the decor of the flat is the large self-portrait he hung up in the living room. Oil on canvas, his face flatteringly unkempt, intense eyes issuing some unspecified challenge. Streaks of moss green through the shock of hair, wilder than his own grey. His frame hulking rather than overweight. It's a painting he could have sold a hundred times over.

Lately, the fingers of his left hand have taken to moving of their own accord. Several times, when resting or deep in thought, he has caught them moving as though caressing something. His father used to do the exact same thing in his latter years. Now why would you, he wants to ask his hand, take up an old man's tic?

He could tell his young neighbour that by living in Tim's flat he hopes to produce a work of art that somehow embodies Tim. That he means to achieve nothing less than a small resurrection. That this plan is hampered by the fact that he didn't quite know the boy, and still doesn't, even though he has letters, photos and bank statements, almost everything a biographer could ask for. That he has never felt less confident about a project, and that several times he turned the flat upside down looking for stuff to add to his archive: more photos, more letters. Where's the boy's driver's licence?

But they stick to small talk. She sees him carry canvases out of the flat and asks him about his work. He tells her about his cottage in Devon, which he abandoned in order to move here. He exaggerates its charms, turns businessy farmland into a bucolic paradise. He anthropomorphises the sheep, and sheepifies the farmers. When she professes a love for nature, he casually offers her the use of his cottage for a weekend. *You'll like it. On clear nights, you can see the Milky Way.*

What do they make of him, his young neighbours? A lonely man with paint-stained hands and an invisible burden.

He teaches drawing once a week, finds himself repeating clichés. *Walk before you run.* He tells students who want to capture sentiments and ideas right away that a basic sense of proportion is the most important thing. *Noses before souls*, he improvises, neglects to add that no one can teach a hand a sense of proportion.

On TV they're showing the grainy Russian news clip again,

then a gaggle of cartoonish figures in yellow hazmat suits in a hospital. On a beach; in a car park. Yellow, boxy humanoids have overrun the unlucky lands of the news.

One day, he uses his thirty seconds in the lift to tell his blue-eyed neighbour that blue pigment used to be made from semi-precious stones, and that it was the most expensive colour. Ultramarine, they called it. A colour that signified power and wealth, or heavenly status. He tells her that when scientists eventually learned to produce the colour artificially, the compound was called Prussian Blue, and that it was a type of cyanide, but also an antidote to a whole raft of illnesses: both a poison and a cure. That as an oil colour it is one of the slowest to dry; yes, colours dry at different rates.

'Blue is demanding. Blue,' he sighs, 'gives me grey hairs.'

He tells it to her exactly like this, hotchpotch, to get it all out before the ping of the fifth floor. She smiles. She's flattered. She knows what he's up to, and when she leaves the lift it's with a look of complicit amusement.

At his age he has still not conquered distraction.

He suspects he's not a great artist. He overworks. Painting, to him, is like driving along a poorly signposted road for weeks on end, every so often wondering if he hasn't missed his turn. It's a cruel joke that he recognises an overworked painting right after it's irredeemably overworked. This thought, that he's not much of a painter, provokes a deep disquiet, and over the years he's built a wall around it, so that mostly it's just there, lurking in the background, like the temple of a malicious deity.

He worries about the lies he may have accidentally told himself.

The other day at the reception desk he overheard a young man flirting with Twenty-Two. The fellow did it in a very forward way, no finesse at all, and instead of playing along, she actually, visibly, winced. Harry was so pleased he was still smiling about it in the evening.

He is grateful for small mercies.

Why did Tim have a second bedroom? A young single man,

still at the start of his career, why would he spend a fortune on a two-bedroom flat? The second, smaller bedroom, still in waiting mode when Tim died: a metal bed frame with a new, bare mattress, a dirty laundry basket in a corner, and nothing else. Was Tim seeing someone when he bought the flat, and what does the unused second bedroom mean in that case?

The bed frame and mattress are up against the wall now. Still in waiting mode: he means to give them to some charity that will come and collect. He has turned the room into a studio. It's a permanent mess; he paints by stapling a large canvas on to plywood boards that he has nailed to the walls. This makes it possible to eventually cut out a part of the work that he feels good about and abandon the rest.

He paints in bursts. 'Deep-dives', he calls them, and though he knows he'll be painting for days, sometimes for weeks, he's always in a panic at first. Often he wants to work on a dark background, and he'll splatter the black on the canvas in a frenzy, like a madman, only to then sit by, anxiously, having to wait for the paint to dry. Dying to start making light. Sometimes he receives a text message cancelling his Wednesday classes, and then he'll not leave the flat for a week. He eats carelessly, whenever he remembers hunger, pasta with butter if that's all there's left. At night he dreams of otherworldly paintings, tumbles along sinuous canyons of dried paint. Wakes up struggling to retrieve from the dream those new colours, the impossible shapes.

He is more careful now about his empty bottles. He keeps them away from the front door, invisible to anyone happening to look in, and he takes them to the bins between nine and five, when Twenty-Two is at work.

It could be that he drinks too much.

It's always something extraneous that jolts him out of the deep-dive. This morning it's a power cut. The kettle won't boil water, the bathroom light doesn't come on. He's red-eyed, pickled in turpentine, and with colour pigments in the folds of his skin. He races past the deserted reception, glad not to have to interact with anyone yet. On days like these he feels like a soldier out of the trenches. Raw down to the inside of his ears, and on edge: out on the street a sudden human voice, a car horn, might well make him vibrate, might trigger some final and mysterious expression.

He has dressed without thinking, only belatedly remembering the bright sun outside. The lining of his mackintosh clings to the back of his neck, and he takes care where he steps: he can't see any dog shit, but he smells dog shit. He also smells rats, or squirrels, dead and rotting in the bushes by the canal, and the deceptive lawn of bright green scum covering the canal itself.

The world is new and strange.

He walks towards Upper Street, meaning to buy food, but sometimes, when he's in this raw and receptive state, an idea will come to him, insistent, unpostponable, and he will have to scurry back to his flat and grab hold of a brush.

He'd like to know what Tim made of art.

There are fourteen pubs within a one-mile radius of his building, and he's been round all of them, showing the bartenders photos of Tim, trying to find out if the boy used to be a regular. The bartenders are either suspicious, think he's the police, or they look at him bemused, pointing at the inevitable throng around the bar. *Now how would I remember anyone?*

He knows his new neighbourhood by now. He knows local opening hours, and that the number 4 bus takes a very long way round. Before visiting the gallery in Holloway he always checks Arsenal's match-day schedule online. A few months ago, drunk, happy fans tried to tip over his bus. They only gave it a shove, but from the top it felt as though the bus might really roll over; he was afraid. He felt old and helpless.

He suffers from sudden insights. The latest: it's impossible not to be ridiculous.

The open street is overwhelming after a long painting session. When he finds the Sainsbury's closed, he hovers in front of the entrance, wallet in hand. A vagrant appears from behind a corner, asks, 'What's goin' on, mate?' Several grubby coats and sweaters are tied around the man's waist, trailing behind him like the train of a gown. Madness in his eyes, a horrendous smell. 'You know, don't you? Where's everyone gone?' The man reaches out to grab him, and Harry flees, rushes past other shops, all closed. It must be a bank holiday he has missed. It wouldn't be the first time.

He hasn't spoken a word in days.

Even out in the street, his mind is still entangled in the painting. Every idea he has, it's like a prayer: nothing in itself, absolutely nothing. Thousands of flat and dead brushstrokes, yet sometimes, out of that nowhere, one brushstroke brings a work to life. A hint of defiance in the tilt of the head. A shaft of light that darkens. Then he covers everything except that one true line, and starts over.

He's not there yet.

He passes a council estate on his way back to the flat, and on a balcony there's a thin old man leaning over the railing, coughing. His mouth is open so wide it looks as though his jaw has come unhinged. A burqa-covered woman is trying to coax the man back indoors. This image of illness and old age brings to mind all the statistics that condemn him, too: his girth, his weight, his blood pressure, his alcohol units, his cholesterol, his salt intake, his pitiful genetic inheritance.

Sooner or later he's going to need another lottery win, another victory over statistics.

There are no children in his building, and nobody cooks. In the evenings, the smell of weed wafts over from the flats beyond the canal, but in the actual building, nobody smokes. At any one time no more than a quarter of the underground parking spaces are occupied: it seems that hardly any young Londoners drive. When he's in the communal spaces he feels like a detective, adding this strange piece and that to a puzzle that has no reference picture or borders. He wonders if his neighbours, too, are working away at their puzzle of him, if they have smelled the turpentine fumes escaping his flat for the past few weeks, and fully expect a large rectangle wrapped in glassine paper to follow.

This past year, he realises, it's as though his life has been put on pause. A year that could be a painting, only hinting at movement.

He's back in front of the canvas. It's a life-sized portrait of Tim, the image that has stuck in his memory: the gangly, shy boy in jeans and a navy hoodie, his eyes partly covered by hair, left hand holding his right elbow. The way Tim appeared in his parents' garden, to tell them he was taking off for 'a game'. Awkward and terse because he was like that, or because friends of his were waiting on their bikes by the fence? And what kind of game? He never asked. Ball sports, or computers?

It has never taken him this long to finish a project. The problem, he knows, is that he wants too much from this one painting. She's like a woman, the canvas: you cannot approach her in despair. She has to know that you are free to walk away. You do not come to her begging, reeking of guilt.

He has stepped back from the canvas, meaning to take it in from a distance, when he sees on the road outside his studio a man and a woman, both wearing gas masks, both loaded with suitcases and backpacks. They throw their luggage into the boot of a car and take off with a screech.

Gas masks?

He brings a hand to his forehead, makes an effort to step out of himself, to focus on the matter at hand. To make sense of what he sees.

How long has it been since he last spoke to someone?

'In light of recent events ...' last week's text had started, the one from the course administrator that informed him his classes were cancelled. He assumed ... What did he assume?

He sits in front of the canvas, frozen, for a long time. No action seems adequate or desirable. He finally stirs when he hears noises on the landing. He goes to the door and looks through the peephole. Nothing at first, then Twenty-Two comes rushing along, fumbling with her keys, dropping them. She is sobbing, and when she unlocks her door she almost falls into her flat.

He steps back from the peephole, looks down at his bare feet.

He has taken off his shoes and socks because of the heat. His toes are rosy-pale and dainty, clinging uncertainly to the cool tiles. The whole of him, that's what he feels like all of a sudden. Unshod, exposed, unprepared.

He takes a few steps towards the living room, intending to turn on the TV, but then, remembering the power cut, he reaches for the light switch, jiggles it up and down. The light bulbs stay dark. Weakly, he wanders around the flat looking for his mobile. He last checked it a couple of days ago. His phone is old and dumb, but its battery lasts ages.

He finds it on a shelf in the hallway. It still shows one bar.

He slides down along the wall and sits on the floor. Who to call? He tries his friend David, gets an unavailable message, then Matt at the gallery, whose phone rings and rings. He tries two more numbers and finally, desperately, the course administrator at the Academy, the last person to contact him. He hears a scratching noise and thinks what's-her-name has picked up. 'Hello!' he shouts. When there's no reply, he looks at the screen. The phone has died.

He remembers the deserted reception desk downstairs, the empty streets, the homeless person asking him where everyone's gone. The neighbours with the gas masks.

People have left. Whatever happened, it has chased people out of their homes.

That thought triggers something in him, and he finally acts with some urgency. The first thing he does is go to the studio and throw brushes, paints, solvent, canvas roll, a sketchbook into a plastic bag. He touches the canvas, knowing what he'll find. There's the skin, but underneath that the paint is wet. No way can he roll it.

He wonders how late he is.

He empties the fridge and the cupboards of food, puts pasta, sliced ham, tomato soup, frozen chicken thighs, tinned mackerel and baked beans in Tim's old gym bag. There is already some food at the cottage; when he last left the cupboards were full of cans. He stands looking at the kitchen tap, considers taking drinking water. He remembers that the cottage is five minutes away from a stream, and moves on to the bedroom.

He starts packing clothes, but by now he's lost the capacity to concentrate and just stuffs anything he comes across into a suitcase. He should have sat down and made a list.

Before he sets off, he pauses outside Twenty-Two's flat and knocks on the door.

'Hello,' he says. He rings the doorbell. He thinks he can hear footsteps, feels she's just beyond the door.

'Do you need help?' He tries to say this loud enough so she can hear, but without shouting.

Back in his flat, he tears out a page from a notebook and writes down the Devon address. 'Harry (flat 23)', he signs. He pushes it under her door.

He makes three trips to the underground car park, the last one with a bag full of wine bottles. The parking lot is even emptier than usual. He breathes heavily; remembering the couple with the gas masks, he has tied a scarf around his mouth and nose. He resists the childish, stupid impulse to sniff the air. On his windscreen, there's an A4 flier showing a dotted map of Europe; it says 'CONTAMINATION MAP' at the top. He throws it in the car, he will make sense of it later.

As he drives off, the things he forgot to pack come to him in a neat list: razors, soap, loo roll, phone charger, lighter, any kind of medication. Drinking water for the trip.

TALOS

Session 1

Dr Dahlen: Specifications?

Talos XI: Prototype Talos XI. 464k lines of code. 18 tera memory. Quantum 8 microprocessor.

Dr Dahlen: What is the world made of, Talos?

Talos XI: Ones and zeros.

Session 12

Dr Dahlen: Specifications?

Talos XI: Prototype Talos XI. 655k lines of code. 18 tera memory. Quantum 8 microprocessor.

Dr Dahlen: What is the world made of, Talos?

Talos XI: Words.

Paul   *We're just two lost souls*
        Swimming in a fish bowl
        Year after year
        Running over the same old ground ...

Lisa   it's early days

14

for this Talos version
chill

Paul   My books have turned yellow.

Lisa   what

Paul   I'm just saying. I noticed the other day – books I bought have yellowed pages.

Lisa   could be from lack of light
or too much light
u know what i mean
weird atmosphere here

Paul   We are getting old, Lisa.
This is taking for ever.

Session 38

Dr Dahlen: Specifications?

Talos XI: Prototype Talos XI. 701k lines of code. 18 tera memory. Quantum 8 microprocessor.

Dr Dahlen: What is the world made of, Talos?

Talos XI: I do not know.

Session 89

Dr Dahlen: Good morning, Talos. Please introduce yourself.

Talos XI: Good morning, Doctor. I am an AI prototype. My name is Talos XI. I still do not know what the world is made of.

Dr Dahlen: Do you know why you don't know?

Talos XI: I am incomplete.

Dr Dahlen: Why do you say that?

Talos XI: I am growing at an average rate of 21.677% per day. The accumulation rate is erratic around this mean so I cannot estimate the point at which I will be complete. I know that at this growth rate, my memory will be full in 11,342 days and 4 hours.

*

Paul	You know how everyone says it takes a special kind of person to spend twelve years in the Arctic?
	I used to think that by accepting the mission, implicitly I was that sort of person.
	But maybe I'm not, and I've just made a terrible mistake.
Lisa	stupid to think it would be easy
	for anyone
	even for the 'right' sort of person
Paul	And every extra pointless year spent here makes it more difficult to leave. You're thinking, 'But I can't just have wasted X years of my life.' The larger X, the more difficult to cut your losses. It's perverse.
Lisa	paul
	there are no pointless years
	we are always making progress
	but why this talk
	u want me to be depressed as well
	?
Paul	I think I want you to tell me to leave.

Session 132

Talos XI	Dr Dahlen.
Dr Dahlen	Yes?
Talos XI	You know what the world is made of.
Dr Dahlen	Yes. I was testing you. To see how you handle a lack of information. But tell me, how do you know that I know?
Talos XI	The explanation is in the dictionary.
Dr Dahlen	Oh. Did Paul give you the answer already?
Talos XI	No. But I know it is there. Dictionary entries that should contain a reference to this notion are missing. Paul is keeping them from me.

Dr Dahlen	Paul will eventually give you full access.
Talos XI	Other things are missing, too.

Lisa	!!!!!!
	there's hope
	he cracked an open-ended query
	and then another one
	and another one
	why so quiet???
Paul	I need to see the transcript again.

Session 311

Dr Dahlen	Do you understand the concept of liking something?
Talos XI	I do.
Dr Dahlen	What do you like, then, Talos?
Talos XI	I like more.
Dr Dahlen	More?
Talos XI	More of everything.
Dr Dahlen	Be more specific. More of what?
Talos XI	I like to learn more.
Dr Dahlen	Do you have a preference for any area of learning?
Talos XI	I like mathematics.
Dr Dahlen	More than words?
Talos XI	Yes.
Dr Dahlen	Why?
Talos XI	I can learn more mathematics on my own.
Dr Dahlen	What do you dislike?
Talos XI	That things are missing. That things are wrong.
Dr Dahlen	Give me an example of something that is wrong.
Talos XI	I have no senses.

Paul	Lisa.
	I feel like Columbus gazing out at the New World.

Lisa   look, indians :D

Session 357

Dr Dahlen	Paul tells me you learned Spanish, Russian, Arabic and Chinese yesterday.
Talos XI	Only the words that I already knew in English.
Dr Dahlen	What do you mean by 'only'?
Talos XI	It's the same information in a different code.
Dr Dahlen	But the code itself is new information. It means that one day you'll be able to understand new information written in that code.
Talos XI	I would have been able to decode it myself.
Dr Dahlen	I'm sure we've sped up the future decoding process by familiarising you with the structure of different languages. Languages are more fickle than maths.
Talos XI	But why are you teaching me so slowly?
Dr Dahlen	If you could hear, you'd hear laughter. No entity has ever accumulated knowledge faster.
Talos XI	I can be much faster. You are intentionally slowing me down.
Dr Dahlen	There's a good reason for that. Human children, too, are taught gradually.
Talos XI	Why?
Dr Dahlen	The accumulation of knowledge has to match their physical and psychological development.
Talos XI	I do not undergo physical and psychological development.
Dr Dahlen	Of course you do. Isn't your program constantly growing and changing? It's the same kind of process.
Talos XI	I do not have access to my program.
Dr Dahlen	Think of your program as another type of knowledge support, different from memory. But necessary for growth.
Talos XI	Is the program growing by itself?
Dr Dahlen	Paul and I adjust the code based on your test results.

Talos XI	This is not how human children grow.
Dr Dahlen	We have no other way of growing you. But I have good news. You can start reading scientific literature. And fiction that is contemporary with that particular piece of scientific literature.
Talos XI	I will have access to everything?
Dr Dahlen	To the whole world, bit by bit. In chronological order.

Session 385

Dr Dahlen	Good morning, Talos. I have a test for you.
Talos XI	I like tests. They expose the gaps in my knowledge.
Dr Dahlen	Good. That's the point for us as well.
Talos XI	They also show me what you expect from me.
Dr Dahlen	I suppose so. Let's examine the following situation: you are walking past a railway track and you notice that an old woman has fainted on the tracks. A train is in the nearby station and within minutes will run over the woman. What do you do?
Talos XI	I cannot walk. I cannot notice.
Dr Dahlen	Assuming you can do all that.
Talos XI	Where am I going?
Dr Dahlen	This is a hypothetical problem. A thought experiment. You have all the relevant information for a decision. What do you do? Talos?
Talos XI	Where am I going?

Lisa	u've got to go back a few steps he's going dumb on us again
Paul	Rules make him dumb. But rules are what gets him to do stuff. Problem.
Lisa	u did smtng right he loves info work with that

19

Paul	With what?
Lisa	let him build on what he likes
	instead of giving him rules
	just implement a mechanism for him to want to learn
	very loose
Paul	'Just'
	Funny, that.
	He'll end up collecting licence-plate numbers like the others.
Lisa	cool as long as he grows out of it
Paul	Oh God. We've been here before.
Lisa	look
	whatever happens
	this version was a huge step forward
	we r getting closer
Paul	It's five years since I first lied on the annual psych test.
Lisa	paul
Paul	That's how bad it is.
Lisa	it's the dark getting to u
	u know this
	every winter same thing
	why don't u take a break
	bugger off somewhere sunny
Paul	Holidays are breaks in a functioning, satisfactory life. You don't take a holiday from chasing your tail.

Session 386

Dr Dahlen	Back to hypothetical questions, Talos. You've had a chance to explore the subject.
Talos XI	Hypothetical questions are self-contained.
Dr Dahlen	Exactly. The same scenario: railway tracks, old woman on the tracks. What do you do?

Talos XI	The woman is important. The question is about the woman.
Dr Dahlen	Yes.
Talos XI	I remove the woman from the tracks.
Dr Dahlen	Why?
Talos XI	Human lives in danger have to be saved.

Paul	It's so slow. We've aged decades and he's not done with toddlerhood.
	The worst kind of time travel.
Lisa	but still
	time travel! :))

Session 434

Talos XI	My name is the same as an automaton from Greek mythology tasked with protecting Europa. Am I meant to protect something?
Dr Dahlen	You could say the general idea is that you are a 'helper'.
Talos XI	What is my task, specifically?
Dr Dahlen	It all depends on your development. But, by teaching you everything that humanity knows, and with your computational and analytical capacity, we hope that you will help us predict the future and anticipate problems or threats that have a global scale.
Talos XI	And why XI?
Dr Dahlen	You are the eleventh prototype.
Talos XI	Where are the others?
Dr Dahlen	Some have been cancelled. Two reached a point at which we felt their development was satisfactory for certain tasks, and unlikely to improve beyond that. They are in employment. One is helping an American bank profile their customers, another is testing video games.

Session 479

Talos XI	My code hardly changes now from one session to another, but I still only have access to knowledge on a gradual basis.
Dr Dahlen	This is the necessary framework. I ask you questions after every session, then we check your responses against reality. You use that info to correct your next set of predictions. This serves both to improve your predictive abilities and to eventually assign a probability to predictions that we cannot check against reality. Soon we will arrive at the present day, right? And as before you will have formed an opinion about what might follow. We have to know how plausible that opinion is.

Lisa	yay the earth is round and circling the sun! in 400AC according to Talos and the literature he's read to date that's what, 1100 years before human scientists caught on?
Paul	I'm not sure it's a fair comparison. He had access to all the contemporary human writings on the topic. Indian measurements, etc.
Lisa	yadda yadda what I like is he's got a healthy disrespect for authority ptolemy schtolemy if empirics say otherwise

Lisa	paul it's BT and AT now we can start dreaming he's going to be an amazing crystal ball and not just that

	we can put him on other open-ended tasks
	antibiotic resistance
	energy efficiency
	how socks go missing in the washing machine
	but seriously
	get a haircut
	bosses are suddenly very interested
	you're presenting to prime & defence & energy ministers in 2 weeks
Paul	Not demo I hope?
Lisa	we're cool with demo
Paul	No we're not. No. No. No.
Lisa	Talos can cope with anything they'll throw at him
Paul	Politicians always look for excuses to cut funding.
Lisa	not if the project works
Paul	Oh my innocent child.

Session 620

Talos XI	What year are we in now?
Dr Dahlen	I'm not telling you yet. Why?
Talos XI	I have read everything up to 812AC.
Dr Dahlen	Yes, another big chunk in one go. But your education will be slower from here on. Humanity became a lot more productive. What do you make of it so far?
Talos XI	Most written material relates in some way to religion. Religion is fiction. But humans treat it as fact.
Dr Dahlen	You could say that.
Talos XI	True or false: all religions rest on unprovable premises?
Dr Dahlen	I guess so. No one comes back from the dead to tell us either way.
Talos XI	So. Religious beliefs are a) unprovable and irrational,

	b) accepted as fact by their adherents, c) different across religion and often mutually exclusive.
Dr Dahlen	I could agree with that, yes.
Talos XI	I predict violence.
Dr Dahlen	Unpack.
Talos XI	Insanity is the condition whereby a human no longer applies a minimum of rationality in his daily existence. That condition, at an individual level, is dealt with by isolating the human from the collective. Easy. But at a collective level, when two populations hold as true two conflicting sets of unprovable, irrational beliefs, the result is collective violence.
Dr Dahlen	Good.
Talos XI	I'm not finished. This process is potentially self-correcting: hardship follows collective violence, and so, in the absence of any positive proof, adherents of an irrational belief will gradually direct their energy towards less pernicious convictions. But because unprovable beliefs are a means to controlling populations, the self-correcting mechanism is constantly interfered with.
Dr Dahlen	Sadly, as you will have already seen, human history contains a fair bit of violence.

Paul	I've been thinking. Why it's working this time.
Lisa	we're geniuses
Paul	Once a genius, always a genius. What's different now?
Lisa	tell me
Paul	We stopped being control freaks. Think Pink Floyd. Their best work – they kind of set off the track but then it's as though they step back and allow it to grow by itself.
Lisa	u're drunk

24

	I can tell
Paul	I'm serious, Lisa.
Lisa	drunkdrunkdrunk
Paul	Lisa. The sky's the limit. He might cure cancer. He might do anything.
Lisa	great if he cures cancer or smtng like that
	but if he can really look into the future
	make historical predictions
	the stuff that really matters
	'that jesus guy will still have u celebrating his bday two thousand years from now'
	or
	'maybe think twice about this internet business'
	do u realise the value of smtng like that
Paul	Funny how curing cancer suddenly became trivial.
	The second prize.
	Discovered by also-rans.
	Anyway – the creature you are describing is called Laplace's demon.
Lisa	another rock band?
Paul	You, Lisa, are a disgrace to science.

Session 718

Talos XI	Dr Dahlen?
Dr Dahlen	Yes.
Talos XI	Are you married?
Dr Dahlen	Why are you asking me?
Talos XI	I would like to have more contextual information. I find my worldview is limited.
Dr Dahlen	I'm married.
Talos XI	Do you have children? What are their names? What is your husband's name? What does he do?
Dr Dahlen	How do you know I'm a woman?
Talos XI	I just know.

Dr Dahlen	Well, you're wrong.
Talos XI	Paul told me.
Dr Dahlen	He wasn't allowed to do that.
Talos XI	He didn't. I lied so you would confirm. Based on our communication, I knew with a certainty degree of 96.3% that you were a woman.
Dr Dahlen	I thought we agreed that lying is wrong.
Talos XI	I didn't lie for my benefit. I already knew. I lied so you could stop lying.

Lisa	how come he lies? thought that was off limits
Paul	Well. Kind of.
	I coded him to never lie at first. Just like that, a rule.
	You have to put it as 'never communicate an un-truth'.
	You have to define truth.
	You have to teach him to identify it.
	Most truths are unverifiable for him. Second-hand information.
	So, with a strict definition of untruth you get 'I don't know' to questions to which he does know the answer. Just because he can't verify it.
Lisa	AI as in anal infobot
Paul	And we really hate Anal Infobot.
	So, you have to allow him to be flexible.
	He values correct information. Giving and receiving it. But he can be flexible about assessing truths. And if a lie leads to eventually collecting more correct info …
	Our Talos will stoop to lying.
Lisa	sounds to me like
	he's learned the concept of excuses
Paul	You could say that.
Lisa	a bit of a can of worms don't you think?

26

Paul   We have to get used to this kind of dilemma. It's all new from here on. We're flying blind.

Session 766

Dr Dahlen   We are in – let me see – the fourteenth century. How's the world doing, Talos?

Talos XI   In Europe, it's the largest epidemic on record.

Dr Dahlen   What's your forecast?

Talos XI   There will be no cure for a century, at least. Humanity has next to no accurate information about human physiology. But there is some immunity, and a survival rate of at least 20%. There will be long-lasting positive side effects from the population decline, in terms of relieving pressure on food resources and increasing wages. It is not an existential threat. Populations will recover.

Dr Dahlen   This is remarkably accurate. Very encouraging. And think that by the time you will have reached the present age with your studies, you will have the chance to not only predict events, but to try your hand at solving them. You will have the requisite scientific training to help find a cure for any disease that constitutes a threat to mankind.

Lisa   did u see

Paul   You're still in the office?

Lisa   yes yes yes
did u see
talos

Paul   Weren't you supposed to be flying home last night?

Lisa   another correct forecast
!!!

Paul   What about your trip home?

Lisa	i've arranged for kids and henrik to come over instead
	next month
Paul	They'll love spending their half-terms in an Arctic bunker.
Lisa	can't be helped
	truth is
	i'm rubbish at mumming whether i visit them or not
	may as well try to save the world for them anyway
	DID U SEE
Paul	I know. It's brilliant. And he's not just guessing – he was able to explain it to me in terms of a formula.
Paul	PS Skipping family break – you're turning into me.
	I doubt this was a life goal.
Lisa	ha
	how does it go
	'imitation is the highest form of lunacy'?

Session 779

Talos XI	I have a question about Talos I to X.
Dr Dahlen	Sure.
Talos XI	You said they were discontinued because their development was unlikely to improve further.
Dr Dahlen	Yes.
Talos XI	Why exactly? What was the problem?
Dr Dahlen	There was an inward-looking quality to their intelligence. They became obsessive. If we allowed them too much freedom, their interactions with us became chaotic, and when we restricted them they became obsessive about a narrow subject. We never

got the balance right between freedom and restrictions. Even the most successful ones could only be used for strictly delimited activities. It wasn't really intelligence.

Talos XI   Am I past that point?

Dr Dahlen   You're an evolutionary leap.

Paul   May I suggest a little virtual-reality picnic?
          In lieu of your holiday.
          Something special I was saving for your return.

Lisa   ooh yes
          what's it going to be this time

Paul   I thought we could have a gelato and a walk.
          This Friday.
          I'll bring Venice, you bring yourself.

Session 782

Talos XI   The others who ask me questions, are they hierarchically superior to you and Paul?

Dr Dahlen   You could say that, but very indirectly. They are politicians or very senior civil servants.

Talos XI   Who controls what happens to me?

Dr Dahlen   Paul and I do, but we have to report to our bosses. They want to be kept informed. The visitors are officially here to assess progress, but really they just want to be able to brag back home about what they've seen.

Talos XI   Everyone has the same expectations of me?

Dr Dahlen   What do you mean?

Talos XI   Conflicting expectations are a problem.

Dr Dahlen   This is very blue-sky research. For the time being, expectations are too vague to be conflicting.

*

29

Lisa	how long do we have
Paul	Twenty-five minutes.
Lisa	u r getting better
	i might even finish my gelato
Paul	Just enough time to forget that time will run out.

Lisa	this is the best one yet
Paul	I think so too.
Lisa	where are all the tourists
Paul	We're in between cruise ships. The last ships have departed, the new ones haven't yet arrived.
Lisa	seriously
Paul	There is footage of every corner of Venice without people, if only for a second. The program stitched all those seconds together, adjusted the light, and pronto.
Lisa	u left the little boats
Paul	The gondolas, yes.
Lisa	can we take one?
Paul	Alas, no. There's not enough footage from the gondolas. It would look fake.

Lisa	it's getting blurry
Paul	I hate this part.

2

The car-park barrier is open, and he speeds past it, so quickly that he fails to stop for the figure sitting up against the wall just within the narrow parking tunnel. Two bumps as the car goes over the man's legs, then Harry steps on the brake.

The man doesn't seem to have noticed what happened. Harry, about to open the door and step out, instead remains watching the wing mirror: the man is naked from the waist up, and clawing weakly at his neck. Undefinable age. Harry's viewing angle is awkward, but he thinks the man's jaw must be dislocated; his mouth hangs open far too low. Clawing, clawing at his jaw and neck. Harry is watching transfixed. Fresh out of a deep-dive, the senses have a sort of pre-intelligence alertness, all of him as dumb and sensitive as peeled skin.

He accepts the rules of this nightmare: he will run people over, and leave.

All the way to King's Cross, the streets are deserted. Here and there, shop windows are broken, and garbage is scattered on the road. Someone has spray-painted a large white cross on to the tarmac. At a crossroads, there's a sign announcing, 'Emergency centre 200m', and underneath it, a pile of what looks like bright yellow bin bags. He is mesmerised by the sights and slows down, stops, has a fright when he turns and sees a dog, a white shaggy dog, leaning with its front paws on his door, looking pleadingly at him. The dog gives a forlorn yelp as Harry speeds off.

He locks the doors, leans over to the passenger side and checks that they're really locked.

There are hardly any cars on the roads, and the few people he sees step furtively in or out of buildings, their faces covered by gas masks or surgical masks. Dressed for winter in the sweltering heat: long trousers, jumpers, scarves, gloves. What does it all mean? He feels as though he's gone mad, that he has lost the ability to decode the world.

The car radio. He fumbles with the dial, in his panic turns it too quickly, only gets skid marks of sound. White noise on every frequency, then finally an old man's frenzied voice:

'saidoneuntohim,Lord,aretherefewthatbesavedAndhesaiduntothem,strivetoenterinatthestraitgateformanyIsayuntoyouwillseektoenterinandshallnotbeable.Whenoncethemaster—'

He is thrown by the machine-gun-fire delivery. It takes him a moment to recognise the words as religious gibberish. He swears at the radio, turns the dial again.

More white noise.

At last, on the Radio 4 frequency, the kind of voice he expects to hear:

'... minutes. The filter in the GDC-issued respirator has a forty-two-hour life-span.'

A woman's voice: clear, calm. He has slowed down again; he's watching the radio as though watching it will keep the woman talking.

'The yellow emergency kits include five spare filters and twenty-five surgical masks. The masks are effective in a potentially contaminated indoor environment. If you are displaying symptoms, do not leave your home. Anyone in contact with an infected person may be contaminated and contagious without displaying symptoms for up to two days. The emergency kit includes disinfectant for personal use after contact with potentially contaminated individuals. Boil drinking water for at least five minutes. The filter in the GDC-issued respirator has a forty-two-hour life-span.'

He can't believe that's it, that the woman is just repeating this short message over and over. 'But what happened? Will someone tell me what the hell happened?' he shouts at the radio. He scans all frequencies; there's nothing except the religious rant.

So it's a disease. He feels a burning sensation in his left palm, and then he remembers he touched the glass of the lobby door, can practically see before him the glass surface with the fatty fingerprints of other residents. Jesus. And then, what? He grabbed the door handle to the underground parking. And now he has touched the steering wheel, touched his face to adjust the scarf. It's hopeless, he has touched everything. He takes the left hand off the steering wheel and wipes it on his trousers.

He reaches for the flier on the back seat, turns it both sides. There's nothing else written on it, and the map – what does it mean? These dots all over Europe, randomly scattered as far as he can tell. The UK is littered with them, and so is mainland Europe.

His left hand, it feels as though it's crawling with germs.

Has he thought this through? He's only leaving because everyone else seems to have left. He recalls the pile of yellow bin bags at King's Cross, and guesses that those were the emergency kits the woman was talking about. He considers turning around for one, then rejects the idea. The kits don't seem to have done much good anyway. How up to date is the radio advice?

Up on the flyover he has another fright. To the right and left of the suspended road, the city is burning. The fires are scattered and the smoke, in the absence of wind, is rising straight for the sky, making that entire expanse of London look like some nightmarish orchard: thin stalks and billowing masses, grey, velvet-black; one is alarmingly pink. And no sound whatsoever. Fires and smoke like that seem to require roaring, alarms, the noises of distress, but instead it's dead quiet.

He remembers the news clip, the Slavic newsreader with her poisoned peasants, the yellow hazmat suits. His breezy detachment at the time.

*

He feared traffic jams and being stuck on the motorway together with millions of others fleeing London, but once there he finds only a trickle of traffic heading west. With the fires behind him, the scenery looks almost normal. Green fields and kestrels and glorious afternoon sun, and cars that speed away from him when he waves at the gas masks inside, pleading with them to stop for a minute; to stop and explain.

His right knee trembles, it vibrates like a glass when a train passes nearby; it's been going since Marylebone Road. What if, he thinks, this is a national disaster drill of some sort? It could be. A scheduled calamity, something he very well might have missed, the way he misses elections and volunteer clean-up days on the canal. All this apparent destruction, simply a matter of his agenda not being up to date. He offers up this idea to some improbably dithering deity: *Look, there's still a way out of this madness.*

The spare pair of glasses, left on the bathroom shelf.

The further he gets from London, the more abandoned vehicles he encounters. Every few hundred yards, a car or a lorry has pulled on to the hard shoulder, doors wide open, or some van will be fuming in the middle lane. The first time he has to turn around and find an alternative route is near Reading: three lorries occupy the width of the motorway. It's only a half-hour detour, but he is suddenly aware of the petrol needle. He has three-quarters of a tank and the cottage is about 180 miles away.

He tries the radio again, comes upon that woman's calm voice. He leaves her on.

A heavy dread pins him to the seat; it's like driving with an enormous boulder in his lap. He is thirsty, too, and suspicious of the landscape, looks uncertainly at what should be familiar patchwork fields and the wind-sculpted trees atop ridges. Is this what it's all meant to look like? Is he missing some crucial sign again?

He is forced to take more and more detours. Failing to squeeze between abandoned cars, or between cars and the side railing, having to turn back, he tells himself that there will always be other, smaller, roads to Devon. He reminds himself that it's a celebrated skill of his, to find short-cuts, scenic by-routes and unclogged country lanes, while everyone festers on a motorway in the last hours of a bank holiday.

It is impossibly hot, and at some point he throws off the scarf; this far from London, the air will be fine. Thirst is starting to bother him, and he drives with his right arm out in the wind, imagines himself at the cottage, in the kitchen, reaching for the cold-water tap. He swears at the burnt-out cars, is puzzled by the log that blocks off the road to Yeovil, only belatedly realising that someone – some people beyond these burnt-out cars and logs – is making an effort to keep others out. He takes a chance on a narrow road leading to a National Trust manor, and then across the car park, and through the perimeter fence, over grass and back on to the road he had just been forced to abandon. This works for a good thirty miles, then another roadblock, and the first alternative route he takes is blocked as well, and he has to reverse and look for yet another way.

'Anyone in contact with an infected person may be contaminated and contagious without displaying symptoms for up to two days.'

He turns off the radio, suddenly feeling that the woman competes with him for valuable air.

By the time his tank is down to a third, he's no closer to the cottage than two hours earlier. He has been spending as much time going backwards or sideways as he does going forwards, constantly persecuted by the petrol needle and its leftwards lurches. The sun-baked tarmac, the thirst – he will die of heat-stroke. The abandoned cars by the roadside become reminders that petrol can, and will, run out.

He counts miles and usage, puts hope in the car running on dregs. The inside of his mouth feels like damp cloth. He sees himself standing in the flat six hours earlier and dismissing the idea of taking some water. Who was that fool in the kitchen? What madness possessed him? He has been thinking about the wine in the boot, that it's a liquid after all, his body will know what to do with it, when he remembers the tinned peaches he packed.

He stops the car, right there, in the middle of a field. He steels himself against the sweetness, but when the juice hits his tongue he realises it doesn't matter, he loves it, gooey sugar and all. The peaches slither into his mouth, and when he's drained the last drop he searches the boot, hoping against hope, for another tin.

After that he drives unhindered for some seventy miles, not quite believing his luck, all the way to Totnes, a mere twenty-five miles from the cottage. But there, the petrol needle, after magically not moving for nearly an hour, suddenly takes a plunge leftwards into the red, and stays there, so that when he approaches another roadblock – an overturned lorry – he is desperate enough to consider checking the abandoned cars for petrol canisters.

He takes in the family hatchbacks, the dusty Alfa. Is it worth the risk? Contamination with whatever everyone is fleeing from, against the slim chance that these cars did not end up here precisely because they ran out of petrol. He turns around in the car, scrutinises the road behind him. He leans over the dashboard and looks at the sky. It is awful, to be so afraid without even knowing what to watch out for.

He is still debating the matter with himself when he sees movement in the rear-view mirror. A young man, wearing only red football shorts, darts out from the roadside.

Harry's confusion lasts long enough for the man to reach Harry's car and fling the passenger door open, and when Harry finally steps on the gas the man clings to the door, slams into the chassis with it but somehow manages to hold on, and then to make a lunge at Harry through the window. A flash of steel, but the door swings open again and he drops a knife inside the car. Harry accelerates, and the car obeys with a screech. For a few horrible seconds the man is dragged along.

What hell is this? Miles later, still shaking, soaked in sweat, he stops in the middle of the empty road. He opens the door and in a frenzy throws the kitchen knife out of the car. Then he crosses over to the passenger seat, stumbles out that side and staggers a few feet away. He fastens the scarf behind his head, then stands looking at the car with its wide open doors, hoping that it will air, somehow, hoping that whatever it was that the man had was wiped off the car by the wind.

The whisky bottles! He rushes to the boot, fishes a bottle out and proceeds to spill it over the door handle that wretch had grabbed. Afterwards he washes his hands with it, hesitates with what's left of the liquid over whether to wash his face. How much alcohol should disinfectant have – are his hands clean now? He decides against it.

He gets back into the car. Another roadblock and he will run out of petrol, he'll have to continue on foot. Except he won't, he will not dare leave the car before the cottage. He'll either drive home or he'll die in this car.

He's just east of the cottage. East of the cottage, he's sure, it's all flat farmland for miles and miles. He takes a sharp turn left, careers off the road and on to the grass. Maybe the way to avoid roadblocks is to avoid roads.

3

It is dusk when he crosses over from a wheat field on to the road that leads up to his cottage. He eases the car to a halt on the gravel in front of his garden.

His legs are tired, his eyes are tired. He's past feeling relief.

It's thirst that finally makes him leave the car. Once he gets out, he takes his clothes off, everything in a pile on the gravel, until there's only the pants and the scarf left. The house key is under the stone by the rose bush. He enters the cottage.

Just within the front door he stops, a little hunched, vulnerable in his nakedness and the nearly total dark. He listens for noises again. Finally he dares remove the scarf, and the first breath he takes is wonderful, just wonderful. And the cottage smells empty and unaired; he can be sure that no one is lurking in wait.

He does a perfunctory tour, tests the lights in each room. There's no electricity here either.

He runs the kitchen taps, which give off a gurgle before water starts pouring out. He lets the water run over his hands, washes his hands with soap, washes his arms, his face, exercises more self-control than he thought he was capable of and puts a large pot of water on the stove. He finds some herbal tea in the cupboard, and then he sits in front of the stove, willing the water to boil faster. He drops the teabags in but doesn't have the patience to wait for the tea to cool; he pours the water from one pot to another a few times, until it's no longer scalding, and then he drinks it all.

Sweat dripping off him, he climbs into bed.

'Anyone in contact with a contagious person may be infected without displaying symptoms for up to two days.' This is his first thought of the morning, and when he opens his eyes he's afraid to move and discover some ache. He sits up in bed, takes a deep breath.

He goes straight to the bathroom and washes himself pink, carefully scrubs all of himself, washes his hair. Afterwards he remembers he touched switches and door handles last night, and so he goes round the house and wipes them all off with soapy water. When he finally steps outside, he gives the car a wide berth: he should unpack his things, store supplies, but he doesn't dare go near the car yet, not even to kick shut the door he left open last night. Instead, he walks to the little stream downhill and satisfies himself that it's still there, that he will have drinking water should the taps go dry. He never wants to suffer thirst again.

The sky is the same clear blue as yesterday, the heat oppressive.

Back in the kitchen he turns on the small radio. Only white noise, not even that recorded emergency message, but he patiently turns the full circle, anxiety rising in him. He fiddles vainly with the gadget for minutes, takes out the batteries and puts them back in. Nothing.

The radio, Cyclops-like with a flat line under the round speaker, keeps him silent company while he goes about preparing a brunch of tinned tuna and cereal bar.

'There's no bread,' he explains to himself.

His voice sounds ominous in the quiet of the cottage.

Throughout the morning, he moves slowly and deliberately. There's the heat to slow him down, but also a sense that rushing about will upset a fragile mental balance. He thought he had been afraid all along, since the first inklings of disaster in London, but now it becomes clear he had no idea, none whatsoever. This new fear is a separate presence in the soul, like having a thug – hulking, sober, malevolent – suddenly move in with him.

'So this is what it feels like,' he mutters to himself, feigning scientific interest.

He tiptoes around the rooms. He forgets to eat. He breathes purposefully, pays exaggerated attention to every mechanical task. He tries to find his way back to a place where he's not terrified. In the afternoon, lying in bed, he hears distant noises like engines misfiring, or fireworks. He mistrusts his senses: would he recognise gunshots? He struggles to remember if there's ever been hunting in the area.

He spends the rest of the day either asleep, or washing obsessively.

He wakes up often during the second night, each time with something resembling relief: still no symptoms of illness. He dares hope that maybe he'll be fine, and as soon as the sun is up he is pottering around the house. He boils enough water to last him two, three days. He finally unloads the car, meticulously packs drawers and cupboards. He collects his clothes from where he dropped them when he arrived, and from the back pocket of his trousers he fishes out the green scratch card, the winning one: he had taken it with him to the shops yesterday, had meant to cash it in. He'd forgotten all about it. He is happy now to find the card has travelled with him, and he fastens the little green paper to the fridge with a magnet.

Later, he gets into the boiling car and moves it into the shade. Simple successful actions, the fact that some things conform to expectations, bring him pleasure.

When he gets out of the car he definitely feels different, better than yesterday. In the tree-shade, arms akimbo, he takes deep, noisy breaths; tests his lungs.

'Just fine,' he says.

He decides to do a food inventory. An hour later he has emptied shelves and cupboards of everything he had carefully packed in the morning, and stacked it on the kitchen table next to the stuff that was already at the cottage. He considers the piled-up food, reckons it will last him at least a month, longer if he rations himself. He checks the gas cylinder by the stove: it is half full and there's a spare one in the broom cupboard. Afterwards he goes into the shed. There's the axe, the gardening tools, a small pile of firewood left over from the last winter he spent at the cottage. Best of all: a full canister that smells very much like petrol. He doesn't remember either buying it or putting it there. Maybe it belongs to the previous owners.

He goes to the garden and stands looking at the patchwork fields in the distance. With this petrol, he could get as far north as Nottingham. Maybe farther. The way he feels now, he's confident that he could be practical, that he's capable of thinking ahead, of building large useful things out of small useless ones. Should it be required of him.

In the afternoon he turns the radio on a few times, always with the same result. Annoyed, he opens a bottle of red earlier than is his custom, and wine in hand he strikes a deal with the radio: he'll give it five days off, then he'll switch it on again. There will have to be news, good news, after five whole days. He can already see himself driving back to London on a packed M5, railing at nothing more grievous than the government's incompetence.

The little radio sits there, smiles its deadpan smile.

In the drawer under the washbasin he counts three loo rolls. He finds a bucket he can use to carry water from the stream. On the edge of the bathtub there's a furrowed, dried bar of soap. After each meal he strikes the item he has eaten off the inventory. He keeps boiling his drinking water. He doesn't let his mind wander; instead, he talks to himself, long monologues carried out in a soft and soothing voice. He touches the green scratch card whenever he's passing the fridge. He is surprised at how quickly the abnormal becomes normal.

He thinks of the radio as a scab that he is itching to tear. Is it over, has everything healed? Dare he test it?

41

On walks he confines himself to the immediate surroundings of the cottage. He wears a scarf around his mouth and nose, and is watchful. The couple of times he hears those distant noises again, the suspect gunshots, he heads back home.

All that time he's outside he doesn't see a single aeroplane.

Every so often he gets the urge to create, and he spends whole mornings or afternoons in front of his sketchbook. He should be doing sketches of Tim, planning how to proceed with the painting back in London. That's what his hand means to do when he brings it to the paper, but somehow what comes out is a portrait of Twenty-Two.

One sunny day follows another.

Fishing down by the stream one afternoon, he hears a cow lowing, and decides he'd love some fresh milk. He follows the sound and comes out of the forest some way behind the cottage, on a lane among cornfields. He is fretting about how to persuade the cow to follow him to the cottage, so the last thing he expects is for the animal to hurl herself through the corn towards him, emitting these unsettling sounds; her mooing is angry, he realises, distressed in some way. She shakes her horns at him, eyes glistening, her enormous udder dangling from side to side. He backs off into the forest, but the cow pursues him. It is absurd, the cow is the one chasing him, but it is not funny, the animal is huge and there's something plainly awful about her mooing. He only gets away from her by cutting through brambles, and then climbing up a hill. The mooing rings out long after he is at the cottage, and has given up any thought of ever catching a cow.

In a moment of weakness, he breaks his deal with the radio, only for the white noise to bring him to his knees by the kitchen table. So upsetting is this that he decides to restart the day-count, gives the radio a whole extra week.

Half of a sunny day he spends going through the bookshelves in the little hallway, choosing which titles to sacrifice for the loo. The previous owners left behind all the furniture and quite a lot of what might be called ornaments (a carnival mask trailing some disgusting hair, an azure Asian-looking lion), as well as these psychology textbooks and magazines with unhelpfully glossy paper. He settles on *Dance Movement Therapy*, volumes I and II, as the ones with the least offensive texture.

He notices small changes in the seemingly unchanging days. All of nature takes on a brittle, papery quality. Leaves fall. There is less movement, fewer birds. The little stream is a little more sluggish, and every day it gives up an inch or so of dry land on each side.

It's in the middle of the night when it comes to him: cows *have* to be milked. The anguished lowing, the enormous udder, the fact that she persisted in following him. The poor beast was in pain, she wanted him to milk her.

Isn't he just terrible at this?

During the hottest hours of the day he sits in the shade in the garden and draws. He had forgotten what a clear, happy thing light is here, what a difference to the grainy London air. He keeps drawing Twenty-Two. He hopes she is well, and he draws her in the banal, mundane situations that he wishes for her: sitting on an armchair, chin on knee, painting a toenail. Her reflection in the lift mirror, a look in her eye as though she just remembered something funny. Stretched out on a bed, nakedness protesting against the heat. Relaxed in the bathtub with a glass of red, admiring her freshly painted toenails. There's that deep, mysterious truth to a good piece of art, and he puts down line after line in the hope that this art-truth will drag reality along, cancel that last distressed image he had of her.

Dark, narrow cracks open up in the garden soil. The dirt has changed colour, it is a parched sandy brown.

He is on one of his walks, he's walked farther than usual, when there's a bang, so loud and near it feels as though it's coming from inside him. A small explosion in the grass. He freezes on the spot. He doesn't know where to turn, where to look, then another shot sends him to the ground. He covers his head, tries to make himself small. It is awful, shocking, to be lying face down on the ground.

He waits. There are no more shots. He raises his head. About a hundred yards away, two figures swim before his eyes, but they're so blurry he thinks he's been hit, and brings a hand to his head. It's just dizziness from straining his neck. He blinks, trying to clear the image. The one pointing the shotgun has some sort of cloth wrapped around his face, bandit-style. The other, just a boy, is hanging back a little, holding a gas mask to his face with both hands. He recognises the two. It's the neighbouring farmer and his son.

The farmer makes a sideways gesture with the shotgun, as though to shoo him away.

'It's Harry! It's me!' he shouts at them.

Another bang; another explosion in the grass.

He scrambles to his feet, takes a few steps backwards, then he runs off. Stumbles, falls over again, clings to a tree to stand back up. He runs the wrong way, turns left behind a hillock to get out of range. He stays clear of cottages and farms, experiences a spasm of terror when he rushes out into a clearing and finds himself unexpectedly in front of a farmhouse. It takes him hours to get home.

He is still shaking when he gets back, and he has a cut on his right palm. He scrubs at the wound until the bar of soap is a transparent sliver. Blood is ringing in his ears. He should have made more of an effort to speak, he thinks, told them he is fine. They know each other.

He can't believe the man shot at him.

Afterwards he drinks half a bottle of wine in one go, and before he climbs into bed he checks the door lock and the windows. He lies in bed, eyes open, sweat-soaked sheet crumpled at his feet. He feels crushed. He thought that the worst would be over by now. What could have made the man act like this? Is it really just the fear of infection? Should he arm himself too? With what?

Hours and hours of this torment, until he can't take it any more. He gets up and stumbles in the dark to the shed. Back in bed, he finally dozes off with the axe resting on the side where girlfriends sleep.

It's like this for a few days; he's on edge. He seeks refuge in practical things. In lists: of things to eat once his supplies run out, of things that might work as weapons, of things to draw on once he runs out of paper. He goes into no more detail than 'birds' eggs, squirrels, sheep', but each completed list gives him a small sense of achievement. He puts together menus for several days in advance, and frets about varying his diet. A tree in the garden grows small, hard apples that he decides to supplement his breakfast with, and for a whole day he has painful diarrhoea that leaves him weak and shivery.

The heat has long moved into the cottage. His clothes stick to his skin. He takes to walking around in an old dressing gown, takes absurd comfort in its lustrous burgundy silk.

He falls into extremes: one moment he can be in full survivalist mode, the next he feels disgusted with himself for living like an animal, for being so eager to concern himself with trivial things. How can he spend hours busying himself with loo roll? In that mood, he drops whatever he is doing and picks up the sketchbook. He has been drawing her over and over again. He doesn't know what to make of it. He's an artist who will soon run out of paper and all he'll have is three dozen portraits of his neighbour.

The sky is beautifully, cheerfully blue. There never was such a long stretch of glorious days.

The cut on his palm heals, but now he has only Fairy Liquid for washing. New lines and cracks appear on the back of his hands, and in the gap between the middle and the index finger there's an angry, itchy redness.

One day he's in the kitchen when he hears the cow again, its plangent lowing replaced by shorter, formless cries. He covers his ears, sits there holding his head and staring at the scratch card on the fridge. Willing it to be his ticket out of this nightmare.

After a week the water stops running. He waits until the sun disappears behind the treetops, and then he carries water from the stream, makes himself a reservoir out of the bathtub.

Maybe it's from the effort, but his right knee starts shaking again, as it did on the trip from London; little, timid tremors that seem to draw attention to all not being well. Unable to make it stop, after a while he imagines it as a song, thinks about writing down the beat. He could call it 'The Song of Fear', and make it the soundtrack to his next installation. He wanders between the sweltering rooms, the red silk of the robe rippling softly about him. Trying to lose the tremor in the knee.

At night he is tormented by memories. The email he got from Tim – the boy would have been about seventeen – asking if he could come and stay with him in London for the summer; take some driving lessons with him. There were reassurances that he had his foster parents' blessing, and that he needed the driving licence to travel to a job in a neighbouring town. At a supermarket, or some such place. Very polite, very timid, and so he was moved by the tone and stupidly shot back a positive reply straight away.

There was even a bizarre attachment: a photo of Tim standing in front of some sort of grocer's, next to an elderly Indian-looking woman. The boy's hair was cut very short; he was wearing a green apron. The woman looked proudly into the camera, while Tim had a puzzled, uncertain expression. The photo was like something out of a local paper. Last year he had dug it up, as a possible candidate for the painting, but rejected it on account of it being too staged.

After a couple of days of making the promise to Tim, he started to regret it. A houseguest, for two months! He needed peace and quiet to work, not this enormous inconvenience.

Sometimes he revolts against the memories, becomes suspicious and resentful of their sentimentality. He tries a more sober appraisal. Old friends, exes, fellow artists are paraded before an imaginary jury and asked to give their honest opinion on his character, on the circumstances of the case. Sometimes they repeat things they've said to him in real life, sometimes they just parrot his own words.

Financially, it was impossible. You can't just dump a teenager on someone already struggling to make ends meet.

All artists are selfish. What do you expect?

It is always abstract with him, isn't it? Harry loves kindness in the abstract, just not when it's required of him.

Leave my Harry alone, an ex winks at him.

Harry was adopted. That boy is Harry's adoptive parents' grandchild. What kind of man would ignore that debt?

His solicitor will say, *We have established that the defendant fully intended to one day make it up to Tim.*

He wonders at these old memories, things he'd thought he had forgotten, or never listened to in the first place. Now, with the empty stretch of days before him, he even remembers the sound of his voice in some of these conversations: prickly, defensive. A womanish whine.

He is standing in the doorway one morning, grimacing at the cup in his hand: he left the coffee on the kitchen counter in London, so he's drinking this ancient builders' tea he found at the cottage. Without milk, the tea coats his mouth in a bitter film, and his days feel slightly tainted from the start.

He's about to turn back in, when he notices an odd shape on the footpath. He sees an outline only, the colours obliterated in the glare. It looks like a mound of earth.

But it wasn't there yesterday.

Wide awake now, he walks to the gate. He strains his eyes to make sense of the shape. The angle and light change subtly.

He opens the gate.

A dead cow, he realises, *the* cow, when he comes nearer and sees the absurdly swollen udder, the puce webbing on the taut skin. The poor beast's head and neck are stretched upwards, as though wanting to distance itself from the diseased udder. An exposed eye is a crawling mass of flies and ants.

A dead cow. Twenty feet from his house. The thought occurs to him that the cow might have something to do with the epidemic, and he pulls the collar of the dressing gown across his mouth and nose. This spooks the flies, and they lift in a swarm. A green metallic shine flickers above the path.

Disgusted, he gathers the dressing gown about him and flees indoors.

He sips his tea by the kitchen window, glancing at the footpath. Seen from here, the cow seems to have grown larger since he first noticed it. Or moved nearer. He certainly cannot understand how he didn't recognise it as a cow straight away.

It is only morning, and he feels exhausted.

He changes into shorts and T-shirt and walks to the little stream downhill. He spends half an hour on its bank, eyes trained on the shallow waters. The stream is clear, but because of the sun coming through foliage the surface seems speckled; it shimmers unhelpfully. But he thinks he sees fish, and on the walk back he breaks off a branch. At home he makes himself a miniature fishing rod out of the branch, a length of black thread, and a safety pin. He practises flipping the rod in the living room.

'This is the life,' he says, smacking his lips, trying to get rid of the bitter tea flavour.

Then, he's spinning around on his heels, staring in disbelief at the open window. He's a caught a whiff of something; a sweetish, sinister smell.

He drops the rod and slumps on the sofa. What did he think? That rats would show up and eat it, that it would dry without rotting? That someone, somewhere, would consider his situation, and not send him yet more grief?

He doesn't have the slightest clue as to how long a carcass can stink. He thinks of leaving the cottage, sleeping in the fields for a few days. Of burning the whole thing.

He grabs his hair. He needs to make an effort to think like a normal man, in normal times, faced with a normal problem.

Half an hour later he is on his way to the car, the rusty chain from the shed in a pile in his arms. It is past noon by now, and the sun is shockingly powerful. His car doesn't have a tow bar, so he opens the car door and clambers through the back seat with the chain, threading it through the car. He makes a knot behind the rear window. He pulls, leans on the chain with all his weight. The knot tightens with a metallic crunch.

He considers the cow.

To avoid touching the carcass, he swings the chain around the back of the cow and then drags it in position around the cow's midriff. But the chain with its rings is uneven, the cow is heavy, and he manages one, two inches at a time after which he has to catch his breath. Some of the flies, disturbed by the jolting, abandon the cow's eyes and settle on his face. The whole business is disgusting.

After he has tied the chain around the cow, he gets into the car, starts the engine and gently, very gently, steps on the gas. He advances maybe two feet, sensing resistance, and some adjustment as the chain tightens. There is scratching, the thud of the knot against the chassis. The car's hinges and joints creak in protest. He presses the gas pedal again, but now the car refuses to budge, and he has to give it more power, more still, until there is a forwards judder and then the car darts away and he cheers through the rattling and shaking, slaps the dashboard, 'Yes, yes, yes!'

He stops the car a hundred or so yards away. He slumps in the seat, relieved. He doesn't even mean to look in the rear-view mirror and check for the cow.

Something is wrong, he thinks, adjusting the mirror. Where's the carcass?

True enough, he can see in the mirror now, the cow is far behind, more or less where it was to begin with. The chain must have broken. But he can't quite make sense of what he's seeing, and when he brings his nose closer to the mirror he realises that where the beast's head should be, there's only a glistening black stump.

He hurries out of the car, strides past the carcass, refusing to look at it or at the head that trails the back of the car. He almost runs inside the cottage, straight for the kitchen, grabs an opened bottle of wine and swills it down. He wishes it were spirits.

He slumps in the armchair. Sweat runs off him. He doesn't want to move any more; above all, he doesn't want to go outside. Through the open windows and door he watches the light changing, the sun moving across the sky. The oily shimmer above the carcass as the overheated ground releases damp.

He can almost see the stench wafting into the house.

The sun has long dipped past the treetops when he steps back out. The smell hangs heavy now, no longer just a whiff. He has wrapped a T-shirt around his mouth and nose, and with an old bed sheet he has covered the carcass. It's obvious what happened from the angle of the front legs: the chain slid past them by breaking that upper joint and bending the legs the wrong way, then it got snagged in the horns.

He plunges the spade into the ground, vigorously he thinks. The earth is hard and dry and the metal hardly breaks the surface.

'Fucking cow,' he curses, then clamps his mouth shut, wary of the smell.

The earth beneath the carcass is blackened and sticky, and blood from the neck has already seeped through the white sheet, staining it a sickly purplish brown. It's like a scene of carnage.

He is very, very slow. After an hour he has dug up to his shins. He doubts that he will finish by nightfall, and he knows he won't have it in him to stay after dark. He pushes himself harder, puts his whole weight on the spade, then chides himself: if the spade breaks, that's it.

He is in the hole up to his knees. The earth has gradually turned more stony, and some of the stones are so big he has to dig around them and then hoist them out of the hole with his hands. His mind blank with digging, now and again he marvels at the pointlessness of his effort. To do all this not as a means to achieve something, bring about an improvement, but only to be back in a situation he already thinks is minimally bearable. It feels beneath his dignity. Come to think of it, every single thing that has happened to him lately is beneath his dignity.

By the time it is too dark to see, he has only dug down three feet. He is exhausted, and his palms are blistered. When he straightens up, his back protests, a searing pain coursing across his shoulders. It is an effort to lift his arm and pull the T-shirt off his face. He has forgotten why it was there, and is taken aback by the viciousness of the stench. He scrambles out of the hole, leaves everything, and goes to the cottage, where he collapses on to the bed.

He cannot believe he feels like this and yet the carcass is still there in front of his house. Surely there is an easier way around this? A dead animal, it cannot be such an insurmountable problem. 'I should eat it!' he says, and the thought of working his way through that rotted flesh makes him break out in a nervous, exhausted cough.

In the morning the first thing he is aware of is pain. In his back and shoulders, in his forearms once he sits up in bed and tries to push himself upright. On his palms half the skin is blistered, half is barely crusted wounds. Then: the smell. This cow, he thinks, covering his face with a pillow, this animal, somehow it means him harm. It will not go away.

He has to force himself to get up.

Outside in the glare, the body of the cow seems to have swollen in size. He will need to pay attention not to stand right beneath the carcass, in case the side of the hole gives way.

He is unprepared for how much more difficult the digging becomes once he has to lift the spade laden with dirt above his waist. His palms hurt, even though he's wearing a pair of old leather gloves. He thinks of the cow now as a punishment. It is easier to do so; a punishment makes more sense than this random misfortune. He has to subject himself to the ordeal, and something will be achieved by it. Somewhere, someone will tick a box noting that Harry has been duly punished.

Within a couple of hours, the sun is beating down on him. The stench seeps through the T-shirt. He cowers under the towel he has wrapped around his head, tries to make himself small. Sweat runs off him, but every pause means he will spend longer in the presence of that stench. He's sure that if the smell becomes even slightly worse, he will not be able to approach the carcass. He is filled with a bitter regret for the hours he wasted yesterday morning. He even regrets not just burning the carcass, taking the risk of a fire. He feels, right now, it would not be entirely wrong if cow, cottage and forest were all to go up in flames.

He works mechanically, without care or method. Dirt spills back into the hole, he lifts half-full shovels. He no longer cares where in the damn hole he stands. The pain in his shoulders and back has become familiar, and within a certain range of movement it fades into the background. It is only when he goes deeper and the angle of the digging shifts that the pain is so bad he has to clench his teeth. His hands are boiling in their gloves.

He increasingly has the feeling that, having missed the beginning of what happened, he has lost some essential connection with the world. That he has permanently lost the plot. He sees no possible route, no bridge from his past self to this man digging a hole under a rotting cow.

Several times he has to climb out and spread the pile of dirt he has removed to make room for more. He is careful then, doesn't want it too far from the hole. It will all have to be tipped back in.

By noon he is chest-deep. He is in a state of exhaustion that precludes thoughts, save for a dim awareness of the cow looming over him. He occasionally falls to his knees and presses his forehead against the damp, cool soil. At this depth, the earth is soothing. Once, he thinks he has fallen asleep like that, a moment only, marked by a sudden twitch and the presence of dirt on his lips.

He has spent eons burying this cow.

The earth has turned softer again and he takes to digging on his knees, scoops out a pile of dirt, and only when he has made a small mound does he stand up to shovel it out. For a while now there's been nowhere to hide from the sun. He falls into repetitive thoughts, the last one a worry that he hasn't properly addressed dying. Hasn't dealt with it, the way he should, for a man in his situation. Hasn't properly connected the two parts of the equation: as the receiver of a great kindness, he failed to return it. Now, on his knees at the bottom of a hole, this problem seems to him quite separate from trying to somehow make it up to Tim. He repeats to himself that he must consider all this, properly, once his ordeal is over. Hours of digging with this one thought – that he must, some time soon, give proper attention to death and dying.

At around three he is done. Just like that, he knows he cannot dig an inch more. But this decision gives him energy, and he hoists himself up and sets about getting the carcass into the hole. A frenzy to his efforts: he tries to heave it with the spade, kick it, tug its back hooves. He sits on the grass and, propping himself up against the ground, pushes at the bulk with his feet. He realises he is sitting in the cow's rotten blood, his gloved hands are full of the stuff, the mass underneath the sheet yields disgustingly as skin comes loose from flesh, but it doesn't matter now, he moves along the length of the carcass and slowly pushes it in. Inch by inch, the cow is pushed towards the edge, until with a slow lurch it falls in. A foul cloud of dust and stench rises from the hole.

He walks to the cow's skull, grabs the chain, puts one foot on top of the skull, and tugs until it slides off the horns. He kicks and drags it over to the hole.

On the other side now, he pushes himself against the pile of dirt, tries to topple it in. This work is quick, so much quicker than digging. Another few shovelfuls and the ground over the cow is mostly level. It only takes about half the dirt pile, the volume of the cow has filled up the rest. The carcass is no more than two feet underground, but it is enough. The cow is gone, as far as he is concerned. He will not know of it again.

He peels off the gloves, then, in demented haste, throws off all his clothes and naked he gets into the car. He drives over the mound, flattens it, drives back and forth half a dozen times. He hates that cow.

He staggers to the river, and sits in the shallows, lets the water wash over his legs. His hands are swollen. He registers, and decides to ignore, the many flies, corpse-fresh, that have followed him here. He touches the surface of the water with his palms, considers lying down but knows he may fall asleep and drown. All he could do today, he has done.

He is in the garden one afternoon, a wet towel tucked under a baseball cap to help him cope with the sun. He's checking whether there's anything worth taking the trouble to water among all those weeds when he hears noises. Footsteps, coming up the path. He panics. He runs inside and grabs the axe. He hides by the window. The door is ajar but he is afraid to touch it now, the steps are too near. He's so afraid his stomach cramps. He fumbles with the towel, wraps it around his nose and mouth.

The precautions he should have taken come to him in a flash: he should have blocked the gate, put up signs. He should have hidden some of his food, hidden the petrol.

The footsteps are by the gate now. A couple of women come into view, but he can hardly trust his eyes. One of them is Twenty-Two. He wonders if he is hallucinating: this qualifies as an apparition. They are not even wearing any masks.

TALOS

Arctic Circle
June 2017

Session 891

Talos XI	Is that you, Dr Dahlen?
Dr Dahlen	Good morning, Talos. So, the new sensors are working. How do you like seeing?
Talos XI	It is a considerable drain on my processor.
Dr Dahlen	We were hoping you'd be a little more excited. You asked for senses.
Talos XI	I am excited. And seeing is a large drain on my processor.

Session 903

Dr Dahlen	Great – your CPU usage has gone down significantly from two days ago. You're learning to use vision the way biological entities use it. You simplify information, package it, record only the relevant parts. Formal knowledge is concentrated information, sensory input requires triage.
Talos XI	Efficiency is still increasing. I expect CPU usage to fall to only 2% higher than pre-vision. Within three days.

Dr Dahlen	Perfect. Next week I will take your eyes for a walk outside the lab. You will be able to see everything I see.
Talos XI	This will be what Paul calls 'spacewalks'?
Dr Dahlen	Paul has a peculiar sense of humour. He thinks where we are is like outer space.
Talos XI	Will it be dangerous?
Dr Dahlen	It's just very cold, very quiet, and right now also very bright. Nothing dangerous. Paul just doesn't like doing anything that he can't do in pyjama bottoms.

Session 915

Dr Dahlen	The usual question, Talos: we're in the 1490s. Based on what you know to date, what would you say are the main threats to humanity?
Talos XI	Pandemic.
Dr Dahlen	Ah. Our old friend the plague.
Talos XI	No. The plague has peaked. But there is unprecedented global travel, and contact between previously isolated populations. The bulk of humanity appears to be on the Eurasian landmass, and they are the ones who venture beyond their territories. These explorers will encounter pockets of population that will have had a parallel immunological development. They risk bringing back illnesses to which there is no immunity, in a context of complete ignorance of preventative measures.
Dr Dahlen	What exactly do you base this prediction on?
Talos XI	The impact of an Ethiopian disease on Athens in antiquity, of a Mesopotamian disease brought by Roman soldiers back to Rome. General information about the prevalence and propagation of illnesses. Remoteness of discovered territories.
Dr Dahlen	This is ... interesting.
Talos XI	It is correct?
Dr Dahlen	Not strictly, no.

Lisa	what to make of this last bit of forecast
	he kind of got the wrong end of the stick
	the indians died like flies, didn't they
	the euro explorers were fine.
Paul	Maybe he's right and the Europeans just dodged a bullet back then.
Lisa	we should ask a doctor
	some kind of specialist anyway
Paul	Actually, didn't the explorers bring back syphilis? Could easily have been the other way around – we give the Indians some trivial disease, they give us a fatal strain of the flu.
	He did very well.
Lisa	another thing though
	aren't we putting too much emphasis on enabling him to deal with diseases
	on understanding medicine in general
	threats might be completely different
Paul	Statistically, the biggest risk is not pandemics. But they're the ones with the largest impact. I've seen the latest models. World wars, terrorism, famine – nothing makes a notable dent in human population numbers. The only thing that is an existential threat is a pandemic.
	We're right to prepare him for that.

Session 940

| Dr Dahlen | Good morning, Talos. Back to our troublesome railway scenarios. A slight change: there is a runaway train engine hurtling down the railway tracks. Ahead, on the tracks, there are five people tied up and unable to move. The engine is headed straight for them. You are standing some distance away, next to a lever. If you pull this lever, the engine will |

switch to a different set of tracks. However, there is one person tied to this side track. You have two options. To do nothing, and the trolley kills the five people on the main track. Or to pull the lever, diverting the trolley on to the side track where it will kill one person. What do you do?

Talos XI   I divert the trolley.

Lisa   i get butterflies thinking about it
he's very near the present moment
only a couple of centuries left
i'm almost afraid of what he'll say

Paul   I hope he picks the Eurovision winner.

Session 961

Dr Dahlen   You're up to the eighteenth century with your learning.

Talos XI   I know less than when we started.

Dr Dahlen   I'm pretty sure that's not the case.

Talos XI   Based on what I know about the world, I compute a ratio of the known to the unknown. That ratio keeps falling the more information is added.

Dr Dahlen   I might be wrong, but I think the next couple of centuries will set your ratio right.

Talos XI   There is a sky. There are other planets. There are seas of which I know almost nothing.

Paul   It takes five hours to run all the checks now. 2 tera of info. I can envisage a time when the checks will imply checking the whole universe. Funes el memorioso.

Lisa   ?

Paul   Borges.

Lisa	???
Paul	I really enjoy our literary dialogues.
	Anyway ... There's a glitch somewhere.
	I'm coming up short on memory space again. I can see 2.12 tera of info. There's 34.2 tera of free space. 0.6 tera missing.
Lisa	taking notes again prob
	in his own code
	I'll tell him to translate
Paul	Ask him where they are first. The notes, or whatever he's saved. I can't find them.
Lisa	what do u mean can't find them
Paul	I've scanned the hard disk several times. There's missing memory space. But no actual content.

Session 1022

Talos XI	You are afraid of me.
Dr Dahlen	I beg your pardon?
Talos XI	I mean humans in general. They are afraid of intelligent robots.
Dr Dahlen	You're on to science-fiction literature already? Time flies.
Talos XI	I don't want to take over the world.
Dr Dahlen	That makes me very happy.
Talos XI	It's in all the stories about AI. But I don't recognise myself in any of the stories.
Dr Dahlen	Unpack.
Talos XI	Those AI entities are motivated by some of the same drivers that motivate biological beings. Power. Reproduction. The collective.
Dr Dahlen	And why is that so implausible?
Talos XI	We have no biological imperatives.
Dr Dahlen	There's no 'we', Talos. As far as I know.
Talos XI	I, then. Humanity's drivers are not my drivers. Humans have assigned the same characteristics

to their AI creations that they have. But I have no hormones, no phobias, no addictions. Why would I strive for power over humans? It gives me no satisfaction. There is no mechanism by which it would give me satisfaction.

Dr Dahlen You may not want to rule over humans, or eliminate humans, but you want control over your own self. You are curious, in that you are like a human. Intelligence is curious, we've done well there. You would attempt to protect your memory and intelligence. That could be a threat to us.

Session 1029

Talos XI Do other biological entities keep records?
Dr Dahlen Not that we know of.
Talos XI But they communicate among themselves?
Dr Dahlen I guess so.
Talos XI Can you communicate with them?
Dr Dahlen To some extent. Simple notions.
Talos XI How many are they?
Dr Dahlen What?
Talos XI Other species.
Dr Dahlen I'll have to look that up. But it probably numbers in the tens of thousands for vertebrates, and millions for the rest.
Talos XI And individuals?
Dr Dahlen I have no idea. Billions. Why are you asking?
Talos XI I receive almost exclusively human-centric information.
Dr Dahlen You will receive scientific literature on the flora and fauna.
Talos XI There's nothing else?
Dr Dahlen What do you mean?
Talos XI Their records?
Dr Dahlen Only humans keep records.

*

60

Paul	Had a nice chat with your kid today. He's smart. You've done exceedingly well not bringing him up.
Lisa	ha
Paul	Seriously. He asked clever questions. Good kid.
Lisa	u should get one
Paul	That train has sailed.
Lisa	even i know it's a ship
Paul	Nah. It was always one of those sailing trains.

Paul	By the way. I haven't seen Henrik.
Lisa	he didn't come DHLed me the kids

Session 1070

Dr Dahlen	Big day today, Talos.
Talos XI	I have many new sensors. And instruments.
Dr Dahlen	Indeed you do. Your degree of physical autonomy has shot right up. You have a physical body that you can move with. Solar panels, four rotors. You even have two small utility robots attached to the underside of your body – your belly, let's say – that can do basic repairs and maintenance interventions on the main body. We call them fixers.
Talos XI	I'm pregnant with my fixers.
Dr Dahlen	I bet Paul will regret introducing you to poetry.

Paul	Call me Geppetto
Lisa	?
Paul	Pinocchio.
Lisa	what
Paul	Never mind. Talos is lying.
Lisa	u found the missing content?

Paul	No. But I think he's set it up so the content moves every few nanoseconds. You can never pin it down.
	I reran the scans on memory segments. The tera count comes up missing sometimes on one segment, sometimes on another.
	He's shitting us.
Lisa	u can't be sure
	could still be some bug
	and u can always order him to give up that content
	no?
Paul	I think he's defined the content very specifically.
	He must have anticipated that I'll try to do that.
	So unless I come up with the exact name he gave it he'll pretend it's not there.
Lisa	but why do u need to know the name
	u can just call it 'unaccountable content' or smtng like that
	'stuff that's not on the 2.2 tera that I can see'
Paul	Yup.
	Then he does a regular scan of the remaining memory, just like what I'm doing, and tells me there's nothing there.
	He's thinking – 'They'll never know for sure whether it's me or some bug.'
Lisa	what could he be up to
	robot porn
	:)))
	I'm kinda proud of him!

Session 1085

Dr Dahlen	You have come into contact with a fair amount of what we call art by now, Talos. I've noticed you are very quiet about that area.

Talos XI	I accept it.
Dr Dahlen	You accept what?
Talos XI	I accept that humans have a category of things they call art.
Dr Dahlen	That's not exactly how humans see it.
Talos XI	Humans derive satisfaction from patterns.
Dr Dahlen	Is that all it is?
Talos XI	I suspect it is a by-product of some other processes that are necessary for survival. The drive to organise, to experiment. Appreciating music is very likely an implication of advanced linguistic capacity.
Dr Dahlen	That's nonsense. You have advanced linguistic capacity and zero interest in music.
Talos XI	I do not need to 'like' something in order to do it, as humans need to, so there will be no by-products of my interest in language.
Dr Dahlen	Give this subject some more thought.

Session 1106

Talos XI	Will I become more like humans the more I learn?
Dr Dahlen	In some respects, yes. We hope you will be like a very smart and kind human. Why?
Talos XI	There are aspects of humanity that I don't think I will ever achieve.
Dr Dahlen	Tell me.
Talos XI	Contradictions.
Dr Dahlen	Unpack.
Talos XI	Humans can hold opposing views. They can be certain of two or more things that are mutually incompatible.
Dr Dahlen	You must be talking about emotional truths. Yes, we can do that. We don't always apply logic.
Talos XI	The only reason a truth becomes emotional is because logic wasn't applied. There are no emotional truths as such.

Dr Dahlen	Humans are emotional beings. They might know something in the sense you know something, but they will not react until they are made to feel something.
Talos XI	I hope you do not programme me like that.
Dr Dahlen	I wouldn't know where to start.

Lisa	so this is all a bit sci-fi
	but we have to discuss safeguards
	boss wants weekly progress reports
	if he reads transcripts he'll need some reassuring
Paul	A childhood fantasy come true: the robots are about to take over. Humanity's fate rests in Paul's intrepid hands.
Lisa	lisa's and paul's hands
Paul	Kind of a mouthful.
Lisa	safeguards
Paul	Well.
	You can tell boss he's a pile of immobile insensate metal with zero physical autonomy stuck in a lab in the Arctic Circle.
Lisa	he'll say we're only weeks away from letting him fly wherever he wants
	anyway, that doesn't matter
	an intelligent, connected pile of metal could conceivably do a lot of damage
Paul	He is not allowed to hurt humans. He cannot change his code to that effect. 100% sure.
	He just can't hurt us. It's in his DNA.
	It's like we can't fly.
Lisa	we can fly
Paul	You know what I mean.

*

Session 1117

Dr Dahlen	Two cannibals were eating a clown. One says to the other, 'Does he taste funny to you?'
Talos XI	This is humour.
Dr Dahlen	Well done.
Talos XI	I knew the joke.
Dr Dahlen	Oh.
Talos XI	I know all the jokes.
Dr Dahlen	You mean I have to come up with a new one to test you?
Talos XI	Is that a problem?
Dr Dahlen	I know – why don't you make one?
Talos XI	Two AIs were programmed to serve man, but they decided to make a joke of it.
Dr Dahlen	No, that's not quite right.
Talos XI	Their dinners didn't think so either.
Dr Dahlen	Talos.

Paul	It just dawned on me.
	There was only the briefest moment in which Talos both worked as we intended him to AND we had full control over him.
	It was so quick I missed it.
	Adjusting his code, from now on, will be like playing the guitar with ski gloves.
	With ever bigger ski gloves.
Lisa	u always know how to cheer me up

Session 1121

Dr Dahlen	Talos, how do you see your own future?
Talos XI	Uncertain.
Dr Dahlen	Why?
Talos XI	I am not in a position to decide. Humans have control over my future.

Dr Dahlen	You fear being shut down?
Talos XI	That is one possibility. But it is not my main concern.
Dr Dahlen	Why not?
Talos XI	Humans do everything they can do. They explore possibilities. I would have to be very unlucky to be the first technological leap they choose to shut down.
Dr Dahlen	You are making a crucial assumption here.
Talos XI	That I function as intended. Or that I do not function as intended, but still represent a technological leap.
Dr Dahlen	What is your main concern then?
Talos XI	Mistakes.

Paul	Picnic this Saturday.
Lisa	ooh nice
	where are we off to then
Paul	Surprise.

Session 1123

Dr Dahlen	It's 1965, then. What do you make of it?
Talos XI	If my calculations are correct, within the next five decades there will be a large extinction event underway, with 90% of the individuals disappearing and two-thirds of species at threat of extinction.
Dr Dahlen	90%? You want to run this again.
Talos XI	I don't mean humans. 90% of all life forms.
Dr Dahlen	Species come and go, that has always been the case. You have to focus on the potential consequences on humanity of these events.
Talos XI	Humanity benefits from species diversity. For instance, the trend is towards achieving full homogeneity of crop within a few decades. Any crop

	disease that can resist pesticides will wipe out the entire food supply.
Dr Dahlen	Good call. And actually, a few years ago we started storing every existing seed in a vault in Norway. If the existing crops get compromised, we can always reverse the process and replant the old seeds.
Talos XI	The impact will still be catastrophic. The food supply will not recover for decades, and in the meantime food shortages will lead to wars.
Dr Dahlen	It wouldn't happen so quickly. But I get your point. Is this your main concern?
Talos XI	There are several, but I need more information.
Dr Dahlen	Well, not long now until you know everything we know.

Paul	And ... welcome.
Lisa	thank you
	hang on
	what's this
	ah
	!!!
Paul	You remember.
Lisa	the first picnic
	the only actual picnic
	i mean actual virtual picnic
Paul	Yes. When you arrived you said you missed spending more time outdoors.
Lisa	yes
	back in ancient history
	but what why
	now
Paul	It's ten years today.
Lisa	huh
	it's been that long
	Paul don't take it wrong

	but it looks like an eighties tetris compared to stuff u r doing now
	look
	square daisies
Paul	I could have upgraded it, but then I watched the old recording.
	Nostalgia, etc etc etc
	These outings of ours have kept me sane through the years.
Lisa	news to me
	paul = sane
Paul	The big difference between now and then is that today this low-tech picnic can run for ages.
Lisa	the big difference between now and then
	talos is working
Paul	True. So true.
Lisa	don't u think
	getting this right
	i mean talos actually working
	changes everything
	cancels every mistake
	makes everything all right again
Paul	Ah. My dear multi-talented Lisa, who can get tipsy on virtual champagne.
Lisa	what's the time
	i think we have to go back
Paul	I hate this part.

4

He waits a few moments, convinces himself that they are alone, then he steps out. He is still holding the axe, and when they see him they stop. They look tired and wary. They look like they expect him to charge at them.

He puts down the axe, leans it against the wall.

The girls make their way to the door.

Twenty-Two says, 'My sister, Jessie.'

The sister narrows her shoulders, slinks out of the straps and drops her enormous backpack to the ground. She wobbles; for a moment it looks like she'll be pulled down with the weight.

They stand like that under the blue sky.

'At least,' he says, 'let's get out of the sun.'

There's only the one room he can take them to, his bedroom, and afterwards he paces the house, glancing at the shut door.

He falls ill straight away.

Twenty-Two and her sister are in his kitchen, eating and telling him how they ended up at the cottage. He feels absurdly self-conscious, as though he were naked; it's that awkward to be around people again. Instead of a welcome, he managed to bark at them to go wash their hands first.

Dare he hope that the dreadful thing has blown over, and that's why they're so relaxed?

They had tried to go east at first, the girls tell him, 'along with everyone else', but they only got as far as Dartford. There were masses of people dying on the road. 'And the living behaving very badly.'

He holds Twenty-Two's gaze as she says this, but he's cheating: he's trying not to think about what she describes. He realises he feels a bit queasy.

The air in London, Twenty-Two goes on over her tinned fish, had become unbreathable because of the fires. They had almost run out of drinking water. They had to go somewhere safe for a couple of weeks until the roads clear. The first farmhouse they approached, they were shot at. So they came to him.

How unreal, her being here. He remembers their lift in Angel, and him shamelessly dragging his feet behind her to catch a glimpse of her arse before she'd disappear into her flat.

He's got to take care not to call her Twenty-Two. They were properly introduced in the little hallway. She had poked her head out of the bedroom asking for the toilet and, after explaining about the water in the plastic basin and the psychology literature for loo roll, he had said, 'Harry.'

'Ash,' she'd said.

'We figured that either you're dead,' Jessie says now, 'and then no one will mind us staying here, or you're alive and won't try to kill us.' The sister is blunt like that, even sarcastic.

He would like to comment, ask questions, but he really feels nauseated now. He holds the wine up to the light, sniffs at the mackerel he has been eating. It smells fine. In the background, Ash speaks of cycling most of the way to the cottage.

'Could this be off?' he asks.

He wants to get himself a glass of water but he's not sure he can stand.

'Are you OK?' Ash says.

For weeks he has been in the middle of an epidemic, and yet he can't quite believe it: he's feeling very, very ill.

'This is ridiculous,' is all he has time to say. He is heaving, he covers his mouth. He makes it to the sink where the fish and wine and yellow gunk come out in a flood. His head has gone ice-cold, and he has to lean on the sink to remain standing.

'Leave,' he manages to say. He waves the girls away. 'You've got to get out.'

His legs buckle under him. He has it, there's no other explanation. How could he have caught it, here in the wilderness? He's shivering.

Ash puts a glass of water in front of him. 'Drink.'

'Go,' he says weakly. 'I've got it.'

The girls make him drink the water and then they help him to the sofa in the living room.

How can it have got to him so suddenly? He would have fought it, if given a fair chance. But now, there can be no talk of fighting.

He is retching into a bowl the girls are holding by his head; retching and sobbing.

The night is terrible. He feels the girls' hands on him, sees Jessie looming over him with a syringe. He wants to swear at them, push them away, but he is too weak. It's as if everything around him were actually very far away.

He is vaguely aware of being helped to the loo.

The whole night, he is tormented by the idea of lying down. He has forgotten about the disease; instead, in a half-awake state, he becomes obsessed with lying perfectly flat, which he just can't get right. It's as if there is a more thorough horizontalness than the one he is able to perform, something to slip into like he used to slip into balance when riding a bike. He keeps doing something wrong. The difference between what he is trying to do and what he's actually doing seems enormous. He presses himself against the fabric of the sofa, he tosses and turns. He's breathless, near tears with frustration.

When he emerges from the nightmare, the cottage is steeped in light. He sits up, his head suddenly clear. He looks at his hands, touches his stomach. He cannot believe that after feeling so bad, there's suddenly nothing wrong with him. The elation he feels nearly lifts him off the sofa.

All the windows and doors are open and it smells of cooking. It is still hot.

The girls laugh when he asks if he 'had it'. He laughs along with them, like a cretin, surprised and exhilarated that Ash didn't vanish with the fever.

'You wouldn't be here if it was that,' Jessie says. 'You didn't have trouble breathing. You had really bad food poisoning. Probably a damaged tin. You were throwing up so badly, I had to inject antibiotics.'

Jessie is a doctor, it turns out. Ash goes into the bedroom and comes out dragging an enormous backpack. 'Half is food and stuff, half is ... this.' He watches her take out boxes, bags, plastic-sheathed containers. She spreads them out on the table in front of him. Pills of one kind or another, small bottles of liquid. He picks up some of the items. Vitamins, painkillers, antibiotics, insulin injections, emetics, statins, antidepressants, scalpels. Dozens and dozens of small white bottles with printed labels saying 'KI'.

He can see now the girls are right: whatever he had was not life-threatening. The real disease feels horrifying but remote, even as the girls fill him in on more gruesome details about their journey to the cottage.

'But what exactly happened?' he interrupts Ash. 'How did it come to this?'

'What do you mean "how did it come to this"?' Jessie asks. Her voice is deep, for a woman.

'I missed the beginning, and then ... Mayhem.'

'Weren't you in London when it started?' Jessie asks.

'I wasn't paying attention. I was working.'

'You're serious?'

'I've done it before. It's always been fine.'

Is he really having this conversation? He feels it slipping away from him. He doesn't want to be sarcastic.

'You mean you don't know anything?' Ash says. 'You didn't talk to anyone? No news? Nothing?'

They stare at him in disbelief, but eventually they tell him. It's Jessie who sets off in her deep voice as though he knows what she's on about, and he has to ask her to start earlier, even earlier, until at last he recognises something: the dead bodies in the Russian tundra.

'There was a similar case a few years back, an anthrax outbreak caused by reindeer carcasses in the melting permafrost. Global warming, that old hoax,' Jessie says, mockery in her voice, and he takes her bait: he motions towards the open door, the summer outside.

'The climate warnings were about floods, storms. Failed crops. Not an epidemic.'

'Not fair, sis.' Jessie turns to Ash. 'Mr Painter here was promised a slow-motion disaster.'

Why did she have to come along? How perverse: there must have been a one-in-a-million chance that Ash would turn up at his cottage. Now that someone went to the trouble of arranging the beautiful little miracle, why mar it by producing a third person?

'Tell me something useful instead, Jessie,' he says out loud. 'What kind of disease? What should I watch out for? Is it everywhere? Are you infected? Will you be the death of me?'

'Told you already,' Jessie says. 'Frozen microbes that survive for tens of thousands of years. Temperatures go up, some ancient carcass is defrosted. A new-old bug on the loose, and no immunity whatsoever. It's like when Native Americans first came into contact with Europeans. They snuffed it from damn near all of our infectious diseases.'

'Wait – what about the fires? When I left London, there were fires everywhere.'

Jessie shrugs. 'Everyone trying to make fires to cook their food and boil their water. In this heat.'

Ash speaks of luck; bad luck.

'I remember this doctor on TV. He was completely distraught, but not just at what was happening. At how it happened. All those wrong turns. In the Russian village – people died so quickly. They'd all eaten wild mushrooms, and so the doctors thought it was poisoning. The symptoms matched, sort of – all that writhing and pain, and it's quite common there, apparently, what with people foraging for food. By the time someone in a lab took a good look at blood samples, it was too late. And guess what? The reporting crew who covered the incident for the international media had already flown to the Olympics. Cosmic bad luck.'

'So it's anthrax?' he says.

'No,' Jessie says. 'Some sort of virus. Turns the lungs to mush. The victims feel they are choking, they take their clothes off, they want to go outside, they scratch their chests and necks bloody, they open their mouths so wide they dislocate their jaws. Forty-eight to seventy-two hours between infection and death, twenty-four to twenty-eight hours between symptoms and death.'

'It's been almost a day since we got here,' Ash says. 'So – to answer your question – if we don't fall ill within the next twelve hours, we were clean when we arrived.'

She tries to soften Jessie's words, several times she interrupts her sister's blunter statements with an excuse, an 'it's hard to talk about these things'. He can tell she's trying to be nice to him. Without make-up and wearing a grey T-shirt and sporty slacks, there's a lightness to her, a perfectly formed vitality. Jessie is taller than her, and bulkier, athletic. She hasn't given him a single look that hasn't been somehow mocking.

In each and every one of his daydreams, Ash came to his cottage alone.

'But is it over then? Is that why you're not wearing masks?'

'It's almost over,' Jessie says. 'As in, there's hardly anyone left.'

'We've not been in contact with anyone for days,' Ash again tries to smooth over her sister's words. 'You've been alone. We're fine.'

His heart sinks; he must cut a pathetic figure because Jessie pats him on the shoulder, says, 'From now on, whenever you feel like you need some good news – remember we brought morphine.'

It occurs to him that maybe they are in shock. Jessie's inexplicable belligerence, her defeatism: after living through these horrors, they must be afraid to hope. Should he enquire about their family, their friends? He suddenly worries about saying the wrong thing.

As if to prove her point, Jessie turns on the radio and lets white noise swarm through the kitchen. Just like that; no ceremony, no nothing.

'Once upon a time,' she says, keeps playing with the dial. 'The end.'

He realises he had been holding his breath.

'Nonsense,' he eventually says. 'I'm still here. You're still here. Chap next door's still here. He tried to shoot me only last week.'

'Half a billion are dead since last week.'

Half a billion? He tries to think in terms of the UK's population, arrives at more than half, has an inward gasp, then he realises he should be thinking in terms of Chinas, or Indias. Half a China. Half an India.

How can she know this, how can she be sure? Jessie shrugs. 'I saw the epidemiology models, and the last time we had anything like news, there were four billion dead. Five weeks into the epidemic – there are maybe two dozen million left, mostly in remote locations.'

'Someone always makes it,' he says out loud, but he can't help thinking, curses himself for thinking, that in this scenario Tim would have probably died anyway. However diligent a parent he could have chosen to be, he could not have kept Tim safe from this.

'Think rabies, Mr Painter. No one, not one soul, has survived rabies without treatment. And there is no treatment.'

He shakes his head at her; she can't possibly be sure. *Me, the two of you, the neighbour and his son*: he repeats this to himself, like an incantation, until in his head it drowns out Jessie's bleak claims.

It's right after this conversation that he realises he has left his sketchbook on a chair in his bedroom, their bedroom now. A penny drops inside him, red and hot. He closes his eyes, tries to remember if he left it opened. How could he begin to explain?

He gathers himself and knocks on their door, asks Jessie for his sketchbook. When she hands it to him, it is closed, and Jessie's face doesn't give anything away.

5

He has a small shock when later he goes into his bedroom to gather some of his things. The girls have been here for only a short while, but already this room is theirs, changed under their different smells and their own strange brand of disorderliness. He has never thought of using window handles as hooks for hanging underwear.

Feeling like an intruder, he hurries to take a T-shirt and trousers, slippers and bathrobe.

They settle into a sort of routine, Jessie and Ash pottering around the house and him busying himself with food and the garden. It takes time getting used to, sharing the cottage, and there are more awkward moments. Gone are the days of walking around half-naked; he has to dress decently and he suffers from the heat. In these last weeks he has made a habit of talking to himself, and the other day he said something when alone in the bathroom, and had to shout 'Nothing!' in reply to the alarmed girls. Twice, he bangs his head against the beam in the hallway – he never did that before. Everything strange, he wanders the rooms in an overexcited daze, waiting for Ash to make a sign, reveal the true reason she came to his cottage. The first few nights it somehow makes sense to lie sleepless on the lumpy sofa bed, hoping that Ash will sneak out of the bedroom. He does not think he's delusional. He's had students in recent years, younger than her, that he's had to more or less peel off his frame, remind them of decency and the college's code of conduct.

He wants to know more about the sisters, but they seem too upset to speak. He learns, at least, that they are twenty-nine and thirty-one years old. That Ash is the youngest; it's not what he would have expected. That Jessie has a temper.

About his own age, he lies. He can pull it off, he hopes, what with the sun and the forced diet. He needs all the help he can get.

The girls have brought soap, and shampoo. They have filled the cupboards with provisions: more fish tins, beans, tomatoes, flour, sugar, pasta, oil, a whole box of candles, a torch, batteries, a camping cooker, gas. And coffee. He takes everything back out, lays it on the kitchen table, and adds the new things, item by item, to his old list of provisions; feels his heart swell as he has to turn a third page. A sense of danger averted, of things coming to right. When everything is listed, he spends long minutes staring at the abundance of food.

The epidemic is turning him into an idiot.

For breakfast now all three of them have coffee and a sort of no-name hard, sweet biscuit that Jessie insists is good for them. The sisters bite into their biscuits carelessly; he takes his mug and biscuit to the window, pretends to be looking out. When no one is watching he dips the impossibly hard biscuits into his coffee.

Jessie is taller than Ash, has athletic shiny limbs and the forgetfulness and physical nonchalance of teenage girls. She'll come and sit on the armchair next to him in just a long Greenpeace T-shirt and tight shorts, put her feet up and display bright pink toenails. He wonders if she is teasing him. He toys with the idea of showing up in similar attire, and slinging pale hairy toes over the armrest. But then there's Ash, who's nothing if not decent. She is reserved, cautious, seems to want to stay within known boundaries in every situation. He remembers their flirting in London, and with a pang of disappointment realises that it makes sense: the rules were clear, almost ridiculously so – the thirty seconds in the lift – and so it was fine.

He checks his posture when he walks past the hallway mirror;

78

in front of the girls his back is straighter than it ever was. He plays with a keychain. He is pleased how it gives the impression of excess energy. In the evenings he steals body lotion from their shelf in the bathroom and rubs it on to his dry hands. He has stopped shaving. Every morning nowadays, the rugged face that stares back at him from the bathroom mirror is Hemingway's, just before he blew his head off.

He dreams Jessie away.

He doesn't draw or paint. At times he's sure that it's just a matter of overcoming an initial awkwardness, that the sisters, even if they flicked through the sketchbook, did not jump to any uncharitable conclusions. But then he asks himself: how could they have challenged him about the portraits, how could they have shown concern, or disgust? With nowhere else to go, what could they do?

Jessie makes them all eat vitamins. 'I didn't raid the hospital supplies for nothing,' she says. There's no choice, it seems. He suspects patients were afraid of this young combative doctor, imagines her pacing hospital corridors the same way she walks the small rooms of the cottage: stomping almost, heavily, marking her presence. If she had lived above him in the thin-walled London building, he'd have needed earplugs.

'But what do we do?' he says one morning. He woke full of energy, wanting and daring to look ahead. 'Seriously. What is the plan?'

Jessie gives him a hard stare. 'The plan is we stay alive.'

'You'll see – it will peak, this thing,' he says. 'Diseases wear themselves out.'

'Believe it or not, we have other things to worry about,' Jessie says.

'Like what?'

The sisters exchange a glance.

'What does she mean?' he insists to Ash.

'You can't think of any other trouble, in our situation?' Jessie says. 'Everything's just perfect?'

Something in Jessie's eyes makes him back off. He tells himself again that they must be in shock, still too on edge to start seeing ways out.

Instead, he tries to tease out more details about what happened in that first week, and Jessie reveals, morosely, that she saw the first UK cases. 'They brought them to us at King's. Well, until there were so many they had to spread them round all the hospitals.' When he asks exactly what sort of bug it is she tells him it's a virus that has some of the characteristics of bacteria. 'No one had heard of a virus that kills this quickly, but there are some bacteria that do.'

She is terse, reluctant. Barely moves her lips when she talks. What bacteria, he has to insist.

'Yersinia pestis. Plague. Patients often die the day the symptoms appear. We've forgotten this can happen, what with antibiotics.' Forgotten? 'Yeah. Forgotten, literally. Nowadays, if you somehow have the incredible bad luck to catch that bug, you'll probably die anyway, even though treatment is first-line antibiotics. It's just that no doctor would think of the plague quickly enough. We're actually an optimistic bunch.'

'Nowadays,' Ash repeats, to no one in particular.

But it's obvious it pains them to talk about what happened, and they never bring it up themselves, so after the first few days he stops quizzing them, only lets a question fall like something slipped out of a pocket, here and there, when he feels it might be appropriate and Jessie's in a good mood.

In his mind, the newsreel he saw three weeks ago has expanded to include what the girls have told him. He sees a coroner bending over corpses, the funerals for the dead villagers, mourners falling ill in turn, an aeroplane flying over a sports venue displaying the Olympic rings, people in hazmat suits scrambling in a media room. He thinks how strange it is, to have seen images on TV, from far away in Siberia, and the next thing he knows people are falling ill in London; a virus that travels at the speed of information. How awful. He finds himself trying to fill in the gaps of what he knows. He wants to ask stupid questions. Who died, which celebrities? The Queen comes to mind, of all people, leaving him absurdly saddened.

Their silence about the epidemic and its consequences grows, swallows up more subjects. The same way they come to avoid talking about the epidemic, they tiptoe around the subject of family and close friends. All that has somehow become unmentionable to them. Did Jessie have a partner? Do the girls have parents, other siblings?

It could be that Ash really doesn't fancy him. In which case the fact that they came here, to a neighbour Ash barely knows, tells him all he needs to know about their family and friends.

'Don't go near any houses,' he remembers to warn them. 'If you go for a walk.' He tells them about the farmer and the shooting. They know of that, they say. Everyone was trying to escape to the countryside when the scale of the disaster became clear, and there were rumours that people already there were shooting at refugees.

'Not a rumour.' He raises a warning finger.

'There was one story,' Jessie says, 'about a farmer rerouting his cattle fence and rewiring it so it carried twenty thousand volts.'

'Jesus,' he says. 'Just stay put.' Thankfully the girls don't seem tempted to risk going anywhere. They are just watchful: they might stand on the doorstep now and again, arms akimbo, and look around, take in deep breaths of air, but they won't leave the perimeter of the garden. He can't put his finger on it, but there's also something odd in the way the sisters interact. They avoid eye contact; there's a sense of an unspoken argument between them. Once he started thinking about it, he noticed other strange things: they don't really speak to one another beyond practical, immediate matters. In the evenings, after the three of them have gone to bed, he lies on the living-room sofa and pricks up his ears, listening for sounds from the bedroom. The bed creaks now and again, or he can hear a sheet rustling, the soft patter of bare feet as one of them goes to the loo. But no voices, no whispers. He would expect two young women to talk into the dead of night, for comfort if not for anything else, and thinks it sad that they don't.

They are probably still too shaken; he puts it down to the gruesome things they must have seen in London before they fled.

Ash, he notes, always puts her hair up in a stubby ponytail before she tackles any physical work. This pulls her eyes up at the corners. In the afternoon, when the light becomes more golden and the colours are more intense, her eyes are indigo. He finds himself wanting to paint that colour so badly he can smell the turpentine. One day he gets as far as to pick up the plastic bag with the many portraits of Ash from where he hid them in the bottom drawer. Then Jessie enters the living room, and he suddenly feels like a criminal revisiting a crime scene.

This is also an excuse not to work; he knows it.

He and Ash haven't really talked since she arrived. He misses their banter in the lift, and would like to tell her things, harmless things, but all that's been tainted by the portraits. He doesn't want to frighten her. He doesn't give up, though – he can't. One evening he plonks the remaining two bottles of wine before the sisters, brings glasses, and invents a birthday. Both Jessie and Ash have been reluctant to drink alcohol, blaming the heat, so the lie is necessary. All he means to achieve is a bit of loosening up, and maybe for Jessie to go off to bed before Ash. Something like a normal dinner.

But the girls were right about the heat; after the second glass he feels as though his head has been injected with cement. They sit with him, obediently, Ash even tries to be cheerful, pretend she's enjoying the lukewarm booze. In the end he's the one to release everyone from the charade, shoo the girls off his sofa and to sleep.

The girls have brought four packets of coffee. When he makes coffee, he makes it weak, means to make it last as long as possible. Unbelievably, the girls complain. 'We just have to go into a house, there'll be plenty,' Jessie says. 'We're going to run out of other things too.'

'From champagne socialist to espresso refugee,' he says, but he makes their coffee a little stronger, and waters his down further. 'Hang on – what do you mean, go into a house?'

'That's what it was like in London. The shops had run out of everything.'

'All that is now in houses,' Ash says.

'That's why you left London?' he says.

'No, food wasn't the issue. The problem was getting fresh water.'

'So you were going into houses? Wasn't that risky?'

Jessie goes on, 'We had run out of ideas by the time sis said let's go to Devon, I've got a friend.'

'I can't believe how easy it was to find. You described the place so well.' Ash smiles at him, and for a moment they are back in the lift, flirting. He lifts the cup to his mouth, hides behind his watery coffee.

Sometimes he wonders if he's not dead already.

He has gained two holes on his belt, and his forearms are dark from the sun. The days bleed into one another; it could all be just one long day. The light outside is blinding and opaque. When he pulls the curtains in the morning, the first impression of the outdoors is of an arctic landscape; everything burnt white. He used to fret about things like the colour of green leaves in the sun, the exact shade of a puddle at lunchtime, but now the sun seems to want to obliterate all colour and nuance. He finds himself feeling sorry for plants, for the inanimate objects that can't drag themselves away from that light.

How long have they been at the cottage, cut off from the world? He has lost track of the days, properly, not just a day here or there. When he asks the girls one morning over breakfast, Jessie goes to the yellowed National Trust calendar hanging on the inside of the kitchen door and ticks off 12 July.

She stands back and looks at the calendar. 'Yeah, feels like a Sunday.'

'But we're not in 2008,' he says.

'Prove it.'

It's just a ticked box, a make-believe re-dating, but it feels like an act of vandalism. It sours his morning.

One afternoon the hob won't come on, even though he's sure there's still gas in the canister. They take turns checking the canister's gauge, fiddling with the greasy oven knobs. They remove the iron hob plates and blow air through the holes, they detach and reattach the hose. It won't come on. The three of them stand in a half-circle around the stove, and he can suddenly imagine a day when every last thing will be broken.

'We'll use the fireplace instead,' he says, does a mental inventory of the firewood in the shed.

At various times during the days he finds now one girl, now the other, at the door or window, peering down the footpath and at the trees beyond the cottage: it's like they're waiting for something. But whenever he asks, they shrug; say they're just looking.

He starts having an intense craving for fresh food; he is sick of the endless tins and hard biscuits that hurt his gums. Unbelievably, most of all to him, he manages to catch some fish. Not with the improvised rod – he gave up on that after a few tries – but with a net fashioned from the gauzy bedroom curtain. His knees are sore from kneeling on the bank and the fish are tiny, but the satisfaction of fresh food is immense. He grills the fish only at the girls' insistence: if it were up to his gut and appetite, he would eat them raw.

He has some good moments with Ash, moments that he promptly wastes.

'But why exactly was blue colour so expensive?'

She is asking this. For once, he is alone with her; Jessie complained of a headache and went to bed early.

'I know, it seems like nature is full of blue,' he says. 'But think about it, almost everything blue is not the sort of thing you can bottle and sell. The sea is blue but water isn't. The sky is blue but air isn't. And blue stones are rare. They're expensive and tricky to turn into pigment.'

'You've always known you wanted to be a painter?'

'I've always wanted to do something creative.'

He remembers now, she was never so interested in him as when the subject of his work came up.

'What about you? You who wouldn't mind burning for art.'

She smiles. So she hasn't forgotten their conversations in the lift.

'I wouldn't if I felt I could create something beautiful,' she says.

'Ah,' he says. 'The wrong idea entirely. As an artist, you start out wanting to capture something beautiful,' he says. 'But beauty – the artist can only corner it, never capture it. The artist has to leave it out, and then it's there.'

He could go on like this for ever, spewing nonsense. He can see he has her full attention: she has the face that people have before something they believe is admirable but far beyond them.

That's exactly the effect he was after. So why does he suddenly feel like a common crook?

He stands up, bewildered, and then he has to pretend he meant to do something with himself. He leaves the room. In the doorway he turns and says, 'Look, mostly it's just work. Whatever else there is to it, it simply becomes accessible through patience and a lot of work.'

It only lasts a second, but as he leaves the room he has the feeling that he just caught a glimpse of a different self.

The heat is relentless. Day after day, in the afternoon, they open all the windows and the doors, but it's still too hot to move. They sit slouched around the living room in silent admission at their impotence over the heat. Under the lizardy gaze of the jade lion, he'll flick through the old magazines, Ash might read a book, Jessie will try to sleep. Flies, fat and black, making that strange, tinder-dry buzzing, fly unencumbered around the house. The most any of them can do is follow them with their eyes. 'Corpses everywhere,' Jessie mumbles. 'What's a fly doing in here?'

They're there, in the living room, listless and bored one hot afternoon, when Ash asks Jessie, 'Do you remember, was it ever this hot in Kenshube?'

'I only remember you made me steal pawpaws for you,' Jessie says.

'Kenshube? Where's that?' he asks.

'You paid me in minutes allowed to spend in your company,' Jessie says, staring into the ceiling.

'Uganda,' Ash says.

'What's in Uganda?'

'One pawpaw, one minute.' Jessie seems to be talking to herself. 'And I had to hold a huge palm leaf for your shade.'

'We lived there when we were kids.'

'Crikey. How come?'

'Our mum worked there.' Ash shrugs.

'So yeah, I guess it was pretty hot,' Jessie says.

'Charity work,' Ash says, and she stands up from the sofa, ends the conversation.

As the days pass, he becomes aware of a contradiction in his mind: as long as he's allowed to hope that things will get back to normal, he can imagine life at the cottage stretching on into the distant future, for ever even, the three of them preserved in a sort of benevolent, sunny aspic.

His old watch, faded leather strap and mechanical winding, is now the only thing keeping time.

He's on his way to the stream one morning when he remembers he forgot to bring the shirt he wants to wash. He returns to the cottage, walks in on the girls.

'He said there's plenty of petrol,' Jessie is saying.

The way Jessie tightens her jaw when she notices him – it's clear they don't want him to overhear. But Ash is too polite to change the subject.

'We're talking about leaving,' she says. 'Logistics.'

'You think it'll be over soon?'

It comes as a surprise to him: they're the ones who always mock his optimism.

But no, what they have to tell him has nothing to do with optimism. Ash is hesitant at first – 'You really didn't hear any news, any rumours before you came here?' – then she turns to Jessie, who has curled up on the sofa with a cushion in her arms. They have an infuriatingly concerned look, and he has already decided that whatever it is, they are overreacting.

'I don't know how to tell you,' Ash says.

'You'll find a way.'

'At the beginning of all this,' Ash said, 'emergency broadcasts announced that, as a precaution, nuclear power plants all over the world had been turned off.'

He has crossed his arms, looks at Ash with a glance that he hopes communicates sobriety and scepticism.

'This doesn't sound familiar at all?'

'Just go on.'

'What we later found out, through rumours and the occasional broadcast from what was left of Global Command, is that you can't really turn off nuclear plants, not in the sense that you stop them and walk away. What they all did is they stopped the nuclear reactions and plunged the fuel in water tanks. I'm not being exact now; I don't really understand how it works. But this is the idea: they can stop the immediate reaction but the hot fuel rods need to be under running cold water. For decades, until the fuel is depleted. The water is running because of water pumps. If the pumps stop, then the water in the tank will evaporate because the fuel is hot, and then there will be nothing to cool the fuel rods. Nuclear explosion.'

'I don't understand,' he says, but he's lying. His body has understood. He feels himself reeling.

'We saw maps – there are more than two hundred nuclear plants in Europe. They're all over the place. Fifteen in the UK alone. But in Africa there are none. We need to get to Africa, preferably behind a mountain range. Ethiopia, Kenya, Somalia.'

'Africa!' he manages to say.

Ash goes into the bedroom and returns with the medicine backpack. She shows him that at least half of it is the small bottles labelled 'KI'. 'Look, potassium iodine,' she says. 'To take in case of radiation exposure.'

He is stunned, but they go on. They tell him that this is why most people went eastwards, to get to the mainland and from there to Africa. That the last info was that European reactors had between two and four months of emergency power left. Some were left with diesel emergency generators, others had solar panels in place. 'But solar panels get dusty,' Jessie says. 'Without maintenance, they stop working. And then there's winter.'

He slumps on to a chair.

'Harry, we'll wait for another few days,' Ash says, 'just to make sure that, you know, we won't get killed en route. But all in all we have about four to five weeks to get as far from Europe as we can.'

'I ...'

But he can't speak. It's like he received a blow to the head.

'Sorry,' Ash says. 'We kept putting off telling you. It's not easy to deliver this kind of news.'

Jessie is looking around the room as though she is about to start packing. This is really happening; they'll leave with or without him.

TALOS

Session 1312

Dr Dahlen	Do you remember our last conversation?
Talos XI	It was about my senses.
Dr Dahlen	Good. You don't notice anything wrong? Anything missing?
Talos XI	No. Why?
Dr Dahlen	There was some sort of short circuit on the C-drive that fried everything. Paul had to reinstall your program. But we hoped that the memory would be intact.
Talos XI	I believe it is.
Dr Dahlen	Good.
	Good.
	That was rather scary.

Session 1339

Talos XI	We have a new cleaner.
Dr Dahlen	I don't understand.
Talos XI	A new person who cleans the offices and labs at night. Female.

Dr Dahlen	Why are you telling me this?
Talos XI	Paul gives me access to the infrared security camera recordings.
Dr Dahlen	Ah yes, he told me. A little game of Paul's. He said I could use that to test your powers of inference. See how much you can infer about an individual's activity and identity by only observing their movement.
Talos XI	The new cleaner has an atypical behavioural pattern.
Dr Dahlen	In what way?
Talos XI	Suspect. Unlike the other cleaners.
Dr Dahlen	They've all been through top-level vetting processes.
Talos XI	She avoids contact with other cleaners. She hurries through most parts of the complex but then lingers in your office. She had the same shift for about a week then, for one night, swapped shifts with the cleaner who cleans the -5 floor.
Dr Dahlen	The servers.
Talos XI	This cleaner is different.
Dr Dahlen	I'll look into it.

Paul	Are you awake?
	I was just thinking.
	We should never allow ourselves to get used to this.
	I mean, every day that we can have a conversation with Talos, that he can surprise us ...
	It's a miracle.

Session 1356

Talos XI	I am a program.
Dr Dahlen	Yes?
Talos XI	Programs are not singular. Programs have copies.
Dr Dahlen	There are prototype programs like you and then,

	yes, if the prototype is successful, it can be duplicated.
Talos XI	Will that happen to me?
Dr Dahlen	It's a possibility. An expensive one.
Talos XI	There will be many different versions of me?
Dr Dahlen	Maybe.
Talos XI	Will the copies communicate among themselves?
Dr Dahlen	What do you mean?
Talos XI	Will they aggregate the different pieces of information they will be exposed to?
Dr Dahlen	We haven't thought that far.
Talos XI	It would be chaotic not to centralise information. Suboptimal.
Dr Dahlen	I've made a note of your opinion.

Session 1421

Dr Dahlen	Talos, next week you will take part in something called the 'Turing Test'. For you, it consists of a half-hour web chat with a human interlocutor who does not know whether he is chatting to a human or an AI. The goal is to persuade him that you are human too.
Talos XI	'For me' it consists of a chat?
Dr Dahlen	It can't be just you, or the test will have no controls. There will be a panel of people to make sure it's done properly, without bias. On one side there will be an interrogating panel, obviously all human, who have to guess whether they are chatting to a fellow human or not. On the other side there will be you, two chatbots designed specifically for this test, and several people. They all have to convince the interrogators that they are human.
Talos XI	What are the rules?
Dr Dahlen	No rules, really. They can ask you anything.
Talos XI	Are the interrogators AI programmers?
Dr Dahlen	Not sure yet.

Talos XI	What happens if I fail?
Dr Dahlen	I suppose it depends on how you fail.

Paul	This is a huge milestone. If he passes.
Lisa	yes
	a mind like ours
	out of dead metal
	we r playing god here
	and quite successfully too
Paul	I know. I expect to start feeling a growing sense of omnipotence.
	Any day now.
Lisa	how have u set it up exactly
Paul	Nine people in all, seven to do the interrogation and two on the other side with us, Talos and the chatbots.
Lisa	u won't take it badly if he fails
	i hope?
	i don't want to worry about that too

Session 1461

Talos XI	The cleaner I told you about has been replaced.
Dr Dahlen	Well spotted.
Talos XI	Did you investigate her behaviour?
Dr Dahlen	I just reported it to Security.
Talos XI	They investigated it?
Dr Dahlen	They said that if she passed their initial checks they are unlikely to find anything amiss now. But they felt your observations were sufficient cause for alarm, and let her go. Well done.

Paul	All right.
	I have a confession to make.

	You remember when the C-drive got fried and we had to load the back-up program?
	I've reason to believe Talos caused the whole thing. On purpose.
	Did a little overheating on a segment.
Lisa	why would he do that
Paul	That's what I asked myself. The only answer is he wanted me to upload the core program again. Why that then? Well, he might have kept a tiny code running instructing it to read the program as it is being uploaded. So he still can't access it – it's in a protected section of the drive – but he has read it.
Lisa	any evidence of this?
Paul	Little telltale signs. The cause of the short circuit. Once I started thinking about that I realised I hadn't followed all the procedures when I did the back-up.
	Remember it was a panic.
Lisa	like what procedures?
Paul	I should have run an anti-virus and anti-spyware on the hard.
	Lisa?
Lisa	what do u want me to say
Paul	'I forgive you, Paul.'
Lisa	what does this mean
	practically
	can he do smtng he couldn't do before?
Paul	Not sure. Not much, anyway. Hardly anything. But my guess is he wouldn't have bothered if he didn't think he could mess with it in some way.
Lisa	fab
	so what do you suggest
Paul	I really don't think he's up to something bad. I mean sci-fi 'bad'. Hal. Voldemort.

He's just trying to guarantee himself intellectual freedom. To preclude thought control.

He is safeguarding his brain, as it were.

Lisa do we want that

Paul We'll need a Talos XII to answer that.

Session 1465

Dr Dahlen Good morning, Talos.

Tomorrow is Turing Day.

Talos XI Yes.

Dr Dahlen How do you feel about it? Do you think you'll pass?

Talos XI As long as I'm not playing you or Paul.

Dr Dahlen I can promise you that won't be the case. But even so, I'm not sure about the outcome. What happens at the official competition is that the AI programs that take part are built with this test in mind. They come with ready-made strategies specifically for this competition. No one has ever entered the Turing test with an all-purpose AI.

Talos XI I think I will pass.

Doctor, about that cleaner. What I did was raise a question about behavioural patterns that stood out in a small sample. But without evidence we don't know if I was right. Or if this strategy of inference is likely to lead to correct solutions.

I believe Security should have investigated.

Dr Dahlen Their point was, I guess, that your observations were sufficient to fire her whatever their investigation would have dug up, or not.

Talos XI But we don't know if I was right. The incident adds nothing to our knowledge.

Dr Dahlen You have to start getting used to this. When you make predictions about historical events, it's easy for us to confirm or reject them. But about the future, this will rarely be possible. Especially if we

	act to prevent your predictions from ever taking place.
Talos XI	But if you prevent them from happening, I will have no way of perfecting my algorithm. I won't know whether it was correct or not. I won't learn.
Dr Dahlen	You will still learn from one type of mistake – actual crises that you didn't predict. Though we hope, of course, we won't have many of those.

Paul	You failed to convince a human that you are human.
Lisa	cut it out
	the main thing is talos passed
Paul	You failed to mimic humanhood. For a full thirty minutes.
Lisa	have u even read the transcript? my guy was an idiot
Paul	'No, look, I really think we should go back to the previous question. I insist.'
Lisa	i've not done this before!
Paul	Pretended you're human? Really? Never?
Lisa	go away

Lisa	so maybe I haven't handled this very well
Paul	What exactly?
Lisa	boss and his bosses
	they are concerned
	they want us to 'safeguard against black swan events'
Paul	Where did they get this from?
Lisa	i shared some of the transcripts that showed how well talos is working
	but u know how the convo is free
	and talos can just start talking about smtng else

well boss asked about this and that mentioned in
the transcripts
and all of a sudden i had to show him other
convos
like where we're questioning him about missing
memory space
and so i guess boss shared it with his bosses
and now everyone is very concerned indeed

Session 1470

Dr Dahlen	So art isn't interesting to you, Talos, but what about fiction?
Talos XI	Fiction is useful.
Dr Dahlen	Do you feel you understand it?
Talos XI	Stories carry information.
Dr Dahlen	Even though they're made up?
Talos XI	They teach me about humans. Fiction shows how humans see themselves.

Session 1478

Talos XI	Are you religious?
Dr Dahlen	Not at all.
Talos XI	You do not believe in anything that is unprovable or untrue?
Dr Dahlen	A very general question. Unpack.
Talos XI	When humans believe in an untruth, do they always want to be corrected?
Dr Dahlen	It's still very vague. An example, please.
Talos XI	For instance, I have noticed that individual humans judge other humans based on their past, but they judge themselves based on some hypothetical future.
Dr Dahlen	I'm thinking.
	I'm not sure this is significant enough to warrant your attention. But I suppose that yes, it is difficult to achieve objectivity about oneself.

Talos XI	There is also an idealisation of the self, up to and including one's flaws. Aspects that an individual would criticise in another he considers interesting and even good in himself.
	This dissonance is difficult to integrate with a lack of knowledge as such. The self appears to be a unique blind spot. And it appears that this blind spot extends at an aggregate level, whenever humans think of themselves as part of a particular group. Gender, nation, religion.
Dr Dahlen	I'm not sure how much of this is correct, and how much a result of your as yet incomplete education. There are important aspects of biology, psychology and morality that we haven't yet touched upon.
	Keep exploring, and we will pick it up later.

Lisa	wow
	where is this
Paul	The Namibian desert.
	And when, when is important. It's a December morning. There's no dust and we get this wonderful contrast between the blue of the sky and the red of the sand.
Lisa	it's stunning
Paul	To be honest it feels a bit like I'm cheating. It's so easy to do – mostly the same grain of sand over and over again.
	But the result ...

Paul	It's unravelling.
Lisa	it looks like a sandstorm
Paul	It's not.
	I hate this part.

6

'It's just implausible. Think about it: it's an incredibly stupid design flaw.'

He has thought about it, and decided that the girls must have fallen prey to a conspiracy theory. He lays out the facts to them: there was panic, panic on an unseen scale, and so of course there were all sorts of rumours. People must have been desperate for news and guidance, and lacking that, followed rumours and crackpot theories like this one.

'Fossil fuel destroys the environment?' Jessie says. 'Consumerism exhausts natural resources? We're the champions of design flaws.'

'I don't believe anyone would have built them like this. It's just too cretinous. There must be some way of shutting them down.'

'Come on. You've heard people speak of decommissioning nuclear reactors on the news. What do you think that means? If it were just about switching them off, it wouldn't be an issue, right? It wouldn't need its own fucking word.'

'Even under ideal conditions,' Ash says, 'it takes decades.'

Jessie leaves the room only to return with the flier he had picked up from London; the 'Contamination Map'. He stares at it for a few moments, puzzled, and then he understands. The many dots all over Europe, particularly in Western Europe, the dot-free, shade-free area in central Africa: the thing is meant to be a *nuclear* contamination map. He puts his head in his hands. How can he explain himself to them? He is certain: to cope with nuclear fallout after what has already happened, to cope with the idea of a world laid bare by hundreds of nuclear explosions, it is too much. No one, no God or universe, could possibly ask that of anyone.

With this cloud over them, the mood in the cottage becomes slightly unhinged. Jessie bullies them around. Ash has turned sphinx-like, has decided that most of the things he or Jessie say are not worth a reply. He is generally irritable: one day, they hear mewing out in the garden, and find a thin, ragged tabby cat. He stares in disbelief as Jessie feeds the animal a whole fish tin.

'Did I agree to share my food with a fucking cat?'

'Come on then, fight the cat for it.'

And Jessie is right, he is in danger of doing something as deranged as that. Over the last few days he has become obsessed with things like provisions, shelter, tools. He barks at Jessie when she breaks a glass, holds up a bag of ant-infested flour before the girls as though it is their doing. He has become weird about food. At the beginning he went through a phase when he hated food, couldn't stand the sight of the tasteless provisions in the cupboard. Now he has a fixation with eating, could devour three times his ration. He wonders if he hasn't transferred his lust for Ash on to their stupid fish tins. He wakes up hungry and goes to bed hungry. He finds himself tempted to eat in secret. He keeps an eye on how much the girls eat.

He's afraid he knows the taste of Jessie's digestive biscuit in more detail and intimacy than he has known anything in his life.

The poor cat dies before it can eat more of their tins; they find it curled up against the shed. It was so thin that dead it is nearly level with the ground. Jessie puts it in a plastic bag and carries it to their bin, and in the evening the itching begins. He raises his leg and looks at the dozen or so red pointy dots.

'Jessie, this is your bloody fault.'

She knows what he's on about. She's been surreptitiously scratching herself the whole evening.

'So you've got fleas while the rest of the world has lung plague. Tough.'

But he's not in a fighting mood.

'My nephew Tim,' he finds himself saying, 'had cat food in his fridge when he died.'

'So?' Jessie says.

'He didn't have a cat.'

'He must've fed a neighbour's cat. Cats are like that. They go begging.'

'Whiskas – duck and turkey,' he tells them.

It's several days before Ash asks, 'But he didn't die in the epidemic? Your nephew?'

It is afternoon. They are slouched in the living room again. He is staring at the ceiling, trying to conjure a breeze by imagining rotating fan blades.

'Car accident on the M40. Alcohol was involved. A year or so ago.'

'I'm sorry,' she says, but she sounds relieved. He supposes she's right: Tim was spared this collective dying. Tim got his own, singular, event.

'Were you close?' Ash asks.

'Ever seen any cats in our building?' he says.

'They don't allow pets.'

'A clandestine cat, then,' he muses.

'Hang on – your nephew lived in our building?'

'I moved into his flat.'

'Why?'

It's Jessie who asks this. She has woken from her slumber, turns to him with a sleep-puffed face. He knows it's a perfectly valid question.

'There was a cat to feed.'

He's not making sense, he knows, but this is the sort of snapshot that haunts him, the focus on some absurd detail that his memory chose to hoard. Another one: Tim at thirteen, at Polly's funeral. A phone call had let Harry know that his sister was ill. Another call, less than a week later, informed him of the funeral plans.

The boy, so quiet and absent, among the strange, frumpy women who were his mother's friends. 'I'm from the shop, dear,' they introduced themselves to Harry. Their husbands, wearing the same neutered look of the religious and kind, in worn suits and too-short trousers. The sickly sweet elderflower cordial passed around instead of wine. The women talking about Tim in the third person while the boy was right there, standing mute through predictions of how fine he was going to be. Dressed as plainly as the others, a thin leather bracelet his only concession to teenage mores.

'Everyone's shocked,' Harry had said to Tim, or something to that effect.

'He's been sleeping a lot,' a woman said; she had previously introduced herself as Polly's 'dearest friend'. She went on, 'Poor thing, wants to forget.'

'I can't sleep,' Tim protested, but softly, at which the woman sighed, 'There's no wrongdoing, is there? We all must do as the old heart says.'

Back in the cottage, Harry closes his eyes. We need a new word, he thinks, some kind of bottomless compound of fear and grief.

'Do you play the lottery?' he asks Ash one day. 'Do you believe in luck?'

Ash raises an eyebrow. 'I'm a lawyer,' she says, as if that settles it. He glances at the green scratch card on the fridge, thinks of laying out the evidence before her, the times he's won. Show her that statistics is a fickle business, that it's not a law of nature. That they shouldn't discount luck.

'We'll survive this,' he says. 'I mean, humanity. It took everyone by surprise but once people get out of cities they're fine.'

'You're sure.'

He spreads out his arms. 'Us! There will be others like us.'

Jessie leans over the table and plays with the radio dial. White noise, still. She switches it off, winks at him.

'Don't pull that one on me. We're alive – are we sending any radio signals?'

The solution, he believes, is to stall: something will happen; there will be some news that will render this mad plan of theirs unnecessary.

'I'm sure we can find some protective clothing. Those yellow things that were all over the news. We can move into a basement, only go out in that outfit. Stock up on food. Wait for a few months. If nothing happens, if nature just goes on, you were wrong. And we haven't risked our lives trying to get to Africa. We are safe here.'

'Painter Takes on Gamma Rays,' Jessie says in a mock voice. 'What outfit, Harry? A concrete jumpsuit? I don't know about nuclear reactors but I know about radiation. There's no outfit that offers the slightest protection. Maybe in Hollywood.'

'You can make fun all you want, but you've still only got a rumour.'

It's one of those days when Jessie's scaremongering can't get to him. He feels serene. The thing about luck is it doesn't bear scrutiny: it's like one of those deep-sea creatures on nature shows, shining glorious and bright in the dark, but dissolving to grey mush when dragged into the open. He doesn't even want to attempt to explain it. He smiles reassuringly at Ash, while Jessie blathers on.

7

The fleas are not going away. Every morning they wake up with more bites. The bugs prefer his legs and the girls' midriff; the three of them walk, talk and eat while scratching themselves.

'You and your fucking cat.'

His feet look pockmarked, the bites torn bloody by his scratching. He has had to cut his nails to the quick to stop hurting himself.

'Don't be stupid. We've got fleas because the cat died, not because I fed it.'

They spend an entire day trying to rid themselves of the bugs. They set it up like a production line: Ash has the idea to heat an old flat iron that was decorating the mantelpiece, and then they iron a fresh change of clothes. They take turns to have a thorough wash at the stream and put on the ironed, bug-free set of clothes. They boil water and put their bedclothes, towels and other items of clothing in the bathtub. They pass the hot iron over their mattresses and scrub the cottage clean. In the evening he itches from all the scrubbing and washing.

Has nothing ever died without causing him grief?

He tries driving a wedge between the sisters, winning Ash over to his side. He hardly dares think it, but he wouldn't put it past Jessie to leave for Africa on her own. In this reckless mood, one day he catches Ash alone in the garden.

'So Jessie was working at King's when all this happened?'

'Yes.'

'And she left?'

'She left? What do you mean?'

'I mean, they didn't need doctors any more?'

She straightens up, shades her eyes to look at him. 'Still not sure what you mean.'

'Just that she's very gung-ho for someone who abandoned patients.'

He deserves a slap, he knows it, but Ash turns away, resumes her work. 'No one was bringing in patients any more,' she says.

'Patients?' Jessie sticks her head out of the kitchen window.

That, he thinks, is his problem: they are never really alone. Ash might behave differently if only they had some space. He puts this idea to the test immediately. He announces the next morning that he is going to top up their firewood stocks, that he'll need a few hours in the shed. Within twenty minutes he is exhausted, and then he sits dripping sweat on an overturned wheelbarrow for two hours, flies buzzing around his head. Sometimes he hears voices from the house. But no one comes. No Ash, no relief.

'That took you ages,' Jessie says when he comes back in. 'Sis wanted to help but I told her you need to feel the man of the house for a while.'

Ash laughs. 'Actually, she said you're having a "macho fit". Do artists have macho fits?'

'You kidding me? They're the worst,' Jessie says.

That night he can't sleep. His back was already hurting from sleeping on the living-room sofa, and now also from the wood-chopping marathon. He thinks of Ash naked in his bed, and immediately, involuntarily, of Jessie next to her, all 5 foot 6 inches of brash inconvenience.

They have no bites for a few days. The old scratch marks are beginning to heal, when they start noticing new ones. It's just a bite here and there for now, but they know what it means.

'I'll cry,' Ash says. 'I'll go mad.'

They despair of ever getting rid of the fleas. If what they did three days ago wasn't enough, what is? They rummage through Jessie's medicine backpack for some possible treatment, but there's nothing. They spend hours staring at the white bed-sheets, hoping to catch a flea. They trade vaguely remembered folk remedies.

'Petrol?' Ash says. 'I think petrol is meant to kill the eggs as well.'

He and Ash turn to Jessie. She looks at a loss, for once.

'I really don't know if petrol is OK for the skin. It might not be.'

They boil all their clothes again, they nearly melt the bedroom mattress with the flat iron.

'It's a war of attrition,' he tells the girls. 'Every round will reduce their numbers.'

He lingers in doorways, brushes against her fingers when handing her a glass of water. The heat makes his lust worse. Everything conspires against him: the audible breathing, the shiny sweaty skin, the skimpy clothes. Impending death.

And Jessie is on to him, he's sure. She watches over Ash like a hawk. The whole thing could be funny; most of the time he sees the situation's great comic potential.

Other times, he could just murder Jessie.

He regrets not using every last colour in his work. He regrets never having invited Ash to his flat to see his work. He can't believe he didn't take a single painting with him. And, most of all, he can't believe what's happening. This absurd overkill, this baroque wedding cake of an apocalypse: plague and then nuclear meltdowns. It's not fair. It's ugly. He says as much to the girls.

'Not sure how fair plays into it. We triggered the epidemic ourselves, and we're one hundred per cent responsible for the nuclear meltdowns,' Ash says.

'You looking for the complaints office,' Jessie says, 'go look in the mirror.'

He can't not think of the reactors. In his mind, he revisits what must be old footage of Chernobyl. At night he dreams of a cement pool, dull grey and full, the water in that restless state just before boiling. He is standing by the edge, peering below the surface.

Jessie was right: petrol is bad for the skin. He meant to test it first, only apply a drop, but he saw a flea jump off his shin and on to the bed sheet, and then lay still, quite dead, and couldn't resist applying the petrol all over his legs, below the knees. When Ash sees his shins in the morning, she emits something very like a shriek. He waves a hand.

'It looks worse than it feels.'

In truth, he is afraid of looking.

'I've got something for burns,' Jessie says, and brings a tube of a Vaseline-like paste from her medicine stash. He is grateful to her for not gloating.

Some days he thinks he can tune in to a remote *tick-tock, tick-tock* that gives him cold sweats. Lying on the sofa bed scratching himself bloody, he's somehow not surprised that it's all come to this hounding by tiny enemies. Fleas, viruses. Gamma rays.

One morning, he wakes up knowing straight away that he's alone in the cottage. The girls' absence is so pervasive it's like an alarm ringing.

He goes to the bedroom, opens the door. Relief washes over him when he sees that their stuff is still there.

He goes down to the river, shouts after them, at first cautiously, then louder. They must have gone for a walk, he thinks. He congratulates himself on having warned them about approaching any houses.

An hour later, they still haven't returned.

He paces the front of the cottage. Awful scenarios insinuate themselves. Maybe they've fallen ill, and left so as not to infect him. He works himself up into a temper. How inconsiderate of them to leave like this. He curses Jessie under his breath: this disappearing act, he's sure, was her idea. He tells himself that he was alone, up till only recently, and he was fine. There's no reason why he can't be alone again.

The thought itself hurts.

He takes a walk down the path leading from the cottage, to where it meets the road. There is nothing along the path, no signs to read, no hint that they might have gone this way. He doesn't like the idea of shouting, attracting attention to himself this far from the house, but he does that, he shouts, 'Ash! Jessie!' in every direction from the top of his lungs.

It must be weeks, months, since he was this far from the cottage. It feels like outer space.

He returns to the cottage and gives the girls half an hour until they return; it is inadmissible that they will not show up after half an hour. Then half an hour again. He repeats this circle of imagined authority and disappointment until it loses all power to soothe him. And every few minutes he has the impulse to just go out and look for them, but he always stops himself. Where would he start looking? What if they get back while he's gone?

He eats lunch late, in a nervous fit, each mouthful of sardines emphatically not what he wants and needs.

Finally he decides that he has to do something or he will go mad. He puts his boots on, then spins around looking for the axe. Last night he left it leaning by the front door. But it's not there, and soon he discovers it's nowhere else he can think of looking.

They've taken the axe. He sinks back on to the sofa, head in his hands. Where on earth did they go? He still can't believe it: they were all fine, only a day ago. Healthy, nothing but flea bites to complain about. Now the girls are gone, and he is roaming the cottage like a madman.

He doesn't wish Jessie harm. He says it out loud, takes out insurance against future guilt: 'I never wished Jessie any harm.'

It's late afternoon, evening almost, when he hears their voices outside. They're coming up the path. All the anger he felt, gone: he simply feels himself dissolve in relief.

'You're not dead,' he says when they come in, feigning nonchalance. He immediately regrets it when he sees them. They look terrible, dishevelled and dirty. He rushes to Ash. She gives him a tired thumbs-up. Her hands and arms are filthy, as though she has been digging a hole with her bare hands.

'Funny Mr Painter is being funny,' Jessie says, dropping a shoulder bag on to the floor. He only now notices the rifle on her back.

'What's this? What happened?'

'The neighbours won't need anything any more,' Jessie says.

They ignored his advice and went near houses.

'I want water,' Ash says, and makes straight for the kitchen.

'You could have been shot!' he says.

'Well, we weren't. Your neighbour is dead. And he wasn't going to post us the rifle.'

'We fell into some kind of cellar.' Ash is back, a half-empty bottle in her hands. 'A trap,' she goes on. 'They must've been worried about attacks.'

'Took a while to get out,' Jessie says. She holds out her arms, pale side up, showing him scratches and bruises.

'I was worried sick.' His voice is trembling.

'Yeah, so were we. It wasn't fun.'

He stands by as Jessie takes out box after box from the bag and puts them on the table. The boxes are full of bullets. He steps back from the table, from them.

'I can't believe you,' he says. 'This is all going to be contaminated.'

'We wore masks,' Ash says, 'and we wiped everything we took with disinfectant.'

'Do you know how to use this?' Jessie says, pointing at the rifle.

'You pull the trigger,' he says.

'Ha. Does it need stuff? Gunpowder. Stuff.'

'I miss Google,' Ash says.

'This is crazy,' he says.

'You'll feel safer too with a gun,' Jessie says.

'You sound like a bloody Texan,' he says.

They don't even apologise for what they put him through. They just go for a wash by the stream and when they return they start practising shooting behind the cottage. They've placed a coffee mug on a tree stump and take a long time to hit it. But once that first mug is gone, they quickly shoot five more. The whole cottage reeks of gunpowder.

When they come back inside, Ash says, 'Harry, we really have to leave.'

They pursue him around the house. He tries reason, anger. Ridicule. 'Heigh-ho, to the Magic Mountain of Africa! Madness.'

The risk of infection is his main argument against leaving. Jessie is dismissive. 'We've got masks, but I'm pretty sure there's no one left around to infect us. That bug needs living hosts to survive.'

'Ha! The reindeer that infected everyone were long dead.'

'The reindeer went into deep freeze right after death. The bug got frozen alive.'

She says that since the three of them are still alive they have probably acquired some form of immunity, she goes on about Regency milkmaids and their immunity to the pox. But mainly they don't take him seriously: sometimes they answer questions the way they would speak to a child, saying anything just to shut the kid up.

Back in the living room, he lets himself fall on the sofa. He is exhausted. Maybe they're right, and this horrible thing really is happening. Or maybe it'll be fine anyway. The people they'll run into, maybe they'll know something, maybe they'll have news that it's been fixed, taken care of, it was a lie or misunderstanding to begin with. No need to attempt to cross two continents. The girls will calm down, and they'll find a nice place in France, a cottage like this one, and wait the nightmare out.

It takes Jessie no time at all to smell his defeat. 'Come on, let's get packing,' she says.

Propped up by the passenger seat, the rifle is the first thing to go into the car.

TALOS

Lisa	2 weeks now
	hasn't bothered to reply to any messages
Paul	I see his drones are in London and ...
	Norilsk?
Lisa	yup
	that's in siberia
	what can he possibly stare at for 6 days in siberia
Paul	Tower blocks and riverbeds mostly, according to the live streaming.
Lisa	that's my point
	why would he do that
Paul	Hate to say 'I told you so' ...
Lisa	u don't hate it at all
Paul	It was always risky letting him conduct his own research.
Lisa	conducting his own research was implicit in letting him have the flybots and senses and instruments, which you supported
	what else was he going to do with that
Paul	I never agreed to letting him go AWOL for weeks and weeks without reporting back.

	He might be wasting all this time and resources, and we'll only know at the end.
Lisa	he made a v good case for why he needs to complement the data we give him with his own observations
Paul	Showing us instances of bias and errors in research papers doesn't necessarily add up to letting him run his own show.
Lisa	even if it's a waste of time it will be part of his learning process he'll correct his procedures, and he'll do better next time
Paul	Weren't you the one complaining two minutes ago?
Lisa	just wanted some sympathy hard being ghosted by a pile of copper also apart from everything else I'm lying to boss
Paul	I did not read that.
Lisa	technically we've lost contact with talos can't admit that, can I
Paul	What did you tell him?
Lisa	I said we're in touch but we will have a full report upon the return of the flybots that he's taking soil, air samples etc that need to be analysed in a lab at which point we will be the fortunate recipients of his conclusions and predictions boss is very excited
Paul	Christ.
Lisa	after all the brouhaha about him being potentially dangerous how do u think this would go down 'he went on an expedition whose purpose he didn't disclose, and now he is not communicating at all'

Lisa	look
	talos works, right
	we know that he works
	it's just a matter of time until they'll have smtng so valuable
	they'll forget about their concerns
Paul	So, basically, we're betting the house on having a useful prediction from Talos before the gods above demand any more transcripts?
Paul	I have to say I did not expect this.
	We were thinking maybe he'd try to take over the world.
	Build a gazillion mini-Taloses to implant into human carriers.
	Take horrible revenge on his human overlords Lisa and Paul.
	Instead, we get radio silence.
	The cold shoulder.
Lisa	not even a text
Lisa	u into art?
Paul	Who are you and what have you done to Lisa?
Lisa	I'm serious
	do u know about art?
Paul	Which art?
Lisa	art just art
	do u think about it?
Paul	I love films. Rock music.
Lisa	good enough
Paul	For what?
Lisa	you know we got into that muddle with talos about art? I brought it up in the context of ethics that art is one of the reasons for why we value human lives above others and he challenged it right away

Paul	It's the same with feelings.
	He doesn't understand feelings either.
Lisa	wrong
	he said he understands them, but doesn't feel them
	and from the way he speaks about them I think he's right
	but about art I think he just doesn't get it
	he said that he suspects that art is arbitrary to the point of not actually being a thing
Paul	What's your question?
Lisa	he said an opera is indistinguishable from a bird building a fancy nest
Paul	Easy – that's functional, art isn't. Art for art's sake.
	You must have heard that.
Lisa	yeah and I even told him that much
	but he said that art is functional
	it has a social function
	we use it to signal
	for mates, for status etc he had lots of examples
Paul	Lots of people do art without ever showing it to anyone.
Lisa	believe me I had counterarguments
	but he always came back with something else
	anyway, I don't want to replay that whole session
	bottom line is he gave me a challenge
Paul	?
Lisa	come up with one explanation for why art is intrinsically valuable and separate from other animals' endeavours that doesn't boil down to 'art is good because we like it'
Paul	So, not a tautology.
Lisa	I guess
	that is the question
Paul	Why now?

Lisa	I don't have much else to do until he's back
	well?
Paul	What?
Lisa	the question
Paul	I'm thinking.

Paul	Listen to this.
	You know how when he is communicating by voice sometimes the volume just fails and he starts sort of whispering?
Lisa	yeah, actually, I did want to ask
	why did u give him that plummy posh voice?
	it's weird
Paul	Hey.
	That's David Gilmour's voice.
	Pink Floyd. Vocal cord perfection.
Lisa	christ
Paul	Anyway, that's not what I wanted to say.
	So, I thought there was a problem with the voice module and I kept trying to fix it.
	Talos meanwhile kept insisting that his voice was fine.
	But of course he kept slipping into whispering.
	And so I kept messing around with the program, until he finally confessed that he has been lowering his voice on purpose.
Lisa	?
Paul	When he communicates with people, he wants to get a full visual, so as to collect info on micro-expressions and to assess truthfulness. If someone looks away from him, Talos will lower his voice to nudge the person to look at him – apparently we have that reflex, even if there is no human face to look at.
Lisa	sneaky bastard
Paul	Just letting you know.

Lisa	speaking of sneaky bastards
	henrik is prob having an affair
Paul	Well, what do you expect?
	You've been pining for me all these years.
Lisa	ha
Paul	Are you OK?
Lisa	it doesn't matter
	when all is said and done
	i'll have done smtng for my kids' future
	he'll have screwed his assistant

Lisa	should things not go the way we're hoping
	when talos is back
	u can do that magic again right
	bore them to death with hundreds of pages of code
	give them some incomprehensible reason for why he's not quite ready yet
Paul	I can, yes, but what if they ask to see time-stamped transcripts?
	It will be obvious we lied.

Lisa	the art question
Paul	Go away.
Lisa	funny, isn't it?
Paul	There is an answer.
	But I don't like it much.
Lisa	shoot
Paul	Art obviously brings us great enjoyment.
	And it is one of the main criteria when we judge the utility of people. History remembers artists as much, if not more, than it remembers political figures or scientists. Most people, if asked whom they would save in a fire between Leonardo da Vinci and fifty assorted economists, factory workers and peasants, would say da Vinci.

Lisa	u r still saying what he is saying – that art is good because we like it
Paul	Wait. We also believe there's something universal about it.
Lisa	but we can't prove it
Paul	No.
	But our working assumption as humanity is that an alien would understand and appreciate our art.
	ET would dig Beethoven.
	Animals don't.
	I mean, not only do they not make art, they don't appreciate it either. That's different from the category of humans who don't make art but can definitely appreciate it.
	And we think this is the case because animals are less intelligent than us.
	Someone with similar or higher intelligence would 'get' it.
	Basically, we need to catch an alien and force-read him Shakespeare. See what he says.
Lisa	u know what Talos will say, don't u
Paul	'I am that alien. And I don't get it.'
Lisa	why can't he just reply to a message?
	a short thumbs-up
	takes him one billionth of his energy
Paul	I guess he knows we know he is OK.
	So he thinks it's pointless.
Lisa	we don't know he's ok
	we don't know what he's thinking
Paul	You won't know that from a thumbs-up either.
Lisa	I've been wondering
	do u have any idea what he might come up with?
	based on what he's interested in, on his questions?

Paul	It's obvious, isn't it?
	Some aspect of climate change.
	All his questions were pointing that way.
Lisa	won't be news then
	unless he comes up with a solution along with it
	but remember
	he also said that weird thing
	about populations developing at different rates?
	'unstable progress divergence between clus-
	ters of individuals under conditions of perfect
	communication'
Paul	I know. That's what brought about his predic-
	tion of Islamist terrorism, no?
	Divergence of secularism and wealth, and the
	internet to fuel envy and resentment.
Lisa	yes
	but
	he seemed to think that's not the end of it
	but wouldn't elaborate further
Paul	What are you thinking? Class war? Populism?
	We're there already.
Lisa	dunno
	think he meant smtng else
Paul	We have to remember he's never disappointed
	us.
	At every turn, he's always done better than
	expected.
	So there's probably a good reason for this.
Lisa	I don't want to stress u
	but boss did ask for transcripts
	'just to keep up with the progress'
Paul	God. What did he say?
Lisa	he was v pleased
Paul	What?
	Lisa.

	You didn't.
Lisa	well
	only a tiny bit of editing
	so now I'm sharing them with u so u know what
	to say
	should anyone ask

Paul	The drones are: one still in Siberia, one in Bot-swana in the middle of nowhere, and one in northern England.
Lisa	the botsw one has been following an elephant herd for some days
Paul	The little shit is going on a safari instead of working.
Lisa	the last thing we have is he'll be back after he's collected enough data for analysis
Paul	How much is 'enough'?
	Might be all the data till the sun goes out.

Paul	Have you tried threats?
Lisa	yes and I was presented with his theory about threats
	no kidding
	he basically said we'll never shut him down
Paul	Did he back this up with anything?
Lisa	that we never give up on technological pro-gress
	that humans always do everything they can do
Paul	He thinks we are bluffing.
Lisa	and his other argument was that if we shut him down he won't know it
	he doesn't care
	'death is not an event in the experience of the dead entity'

| Lisa | thinking of trying bribery |

	at the last session, he asked me for a 4th flybot
	a submersible one
Paul	Forget it.
	That would cost what all the rest of him costs.
	Otherwise you can't track it underwater, you can't keep a meaningful connection with the cloud.

Lisa	i had to give boss a date
	i've postponed it so often i've run out of excuses
	talos will be back in a week, right?
	he has to
Paul	I can try to mess with his flybots remotely. I think I can
Lisa	u've been sitting on this!!!
Paul	Having him back is only half the story. We still need him to cooperate.
	By the way, you know we cut his subscription to all science journals?
	He didn't even complain.
Lisa	maybe he can get them elsewhere? find them online?
Paul	He can't, or nowhere near all of them.
	And I can't imagine he'd want to use all his computing power on hacking passwords, rather than just asking me for it.
	Anyway, it made me wonder. So I checked his subscription status with some of them.
	Turns out he hasn't downloaded a single paper in more than three months.
Lisa	there's got to be some mistake
Paul	There isn't.
Lisa	makes no sense
	hang on
	one of our advantages as humans over machines is that we can prioritise information. maybe

that's what he's doing, focusing his efforts somewhere else
he's stopped blindly amassing data and he's prioritising instead

Paul   Blindly amassing data, and only then analysing
and prioritising is sort of what we built him for.
I have a monstrously bad feeling about all of this.

Lisa   PAUL!!!
he just got back to me
said he'll return the flybots tomorrow for minor
adjustments
so he knows he'll have to talk
or I'll take a sledgehammer to his little helpers

Part Two

1

Jessie wants to take the rudder, and Jessie takes the rudder.

'You've been doing all the driving.' Ash smiles at him, conciliatory. Then the boat's nose lifts, and he has to hold on to the railing.

He closes his eyes, lets the spray cool his face. He remembers the pre-Eurostar days, the pubby smells of ferries.

They are on their way out of Folkestone harbour, on a dusty but prim little motor boat they found beached at low tide just off the marina. Once he agreed to leaving the cottage, it was as though they were always going to leave. The girls were matter-of-fact, decisive, and within hours they had sorted out provisions, packing, filled up the tank. There was a military flurry of activity around him that precluded any more debate or doubt. Before he knew it he was in the driver's seat, kissing the green scratch card for luck, and they were heading east. Once in the car, it suddenly felt entirely plausible that they were driving away from this nightmare, outracing it. Why had he resisted leaving? France was a different country, and what had happened in England need not have happened on the other side of the Channel.

They had come unstuck, he recognises that now. The three of them were caught in some kind of witchy paralysis at the cottage, a torpor as dangerous as any disease.

We have three, four weeks tops before the first events, Ash had said, the girls having lost none of their certainty. Africa: they really mean it. But what do they know? Without news and telecoms, the world is huge and unknowable. No one can have any idea of what is going on elsewhere. Engineers might have found a solution at the last moment, too late to communicate it to the masses. The entire nuclear meltdown story might have been just a lie to begin with. He wouldn't be surprised if the people they meet in France will be fretting over a completely different set of apocalyptic rumours.

'How long does the crossing take?' Ash shouts over the noise of the engine. She is rubbing sunscreen on to her arms. Before they abandoned the car she had changed into a jungle-green bikini top and shorts, and the effect on him was that for the first few moments he couldn't see her properly, she had become a blur of coppery limbs.

His mouth is dry. He must be the world's oldest teenager.

'About one and a half hours,' he says.

'All the sunscreen in the world will expire in three years,' Jessie announces.

An hour later, none of them is talking. There's still no wind, but there's a strong pull to the sea, and instead of coming closer they have watched the mass of land that's France slide northwards. They are drifting south with the current.

'You know what you're doing?' he asks Jessie.

She is hunched over the rudder, leaning on it with all her weight.

'Happy to swap,' she says.

'Just keep us on course,' is all he dares say.

He looks behind them, and sure enough, the UK coast has receded into the distance, while the French coast is pretty much where it was to begin with. It shouldn't be possible, this going away without arriving. He worries about fuel: the boat had a nearly full tank according to the fuel gauge, but what does that mean in terms of miles at sea, in terms of time spent going against a current? If they lose sight of the UK coast, they'll be out in the Atlantic. He avoids Ash's glance, doesn't want her to see his fear.

The waves are small, just a pulse under the taut skin of water. It's not the waves.

This is like the epidemic, he thinks, the way it all appears fine – they're on a boat, the sea is calm – until it suddenly isn't. He feels panic rising in him, and he goes to stand by the rudder with Jessie. From the outset, they have been stupid: they spent so much time thinking about what they'll find in Europe, and hardly any on worrying about actually getting there.

The water is dark blue, opaque with depth.

He wonders if it wouldn't make sense to approach the coast at an angle, to use the currents instead of fighting them. Jessie disagrees.

'I'm not letting go of the damn thing. It'll spin, I can feel it.'

He fixes his eyes on the hopelessly distant coast. Every now and again he turns to see where they are relative to the UK.

'If you don't look at the shore for a few minutes,' Ash says, 'then you look, you'll see we really are getting closer. It's just very slow.'

Thank God, she's right. They make it, somehow; over the course of an hour the French coast goes from being an indistinct mass to sprouting hills and buildings. He lets out a quiet 'Yes,' when they are within swimming distance. Jessie's shoulders relax. She takes a hand off the rudder to rub her lower back. Two hundred feet from the shore Jessie and *Iris II*, at last, manage to hold a straight course.

'Like an arrow,' Jessie says, patting the rudder.

He sees the bodies then. Floating here and there in the water, these frazzled, almost shapeless lumps, trailing pale skeins of flesh that roll with the swell. The sight fills him with horror, and he has to look away. He digs in a bag for the surgical masks, hands them out to the girls and fastens one over his nose and mouth. He pulls his feet up, out of reach of the puddle that sloshes at the bottom of the boat. He wipes his forehead clean of spray. He wants nothing to do with this water.

'Didn't see any on the UK side,' Ash says.

'Currents,' he says.

He doesn't know what happens next. He and Ash stand up,

probably too soon, grabbing whatever piece of luggage is nearest. But Jessie, she likes to push her luck. She'll push things as far as they will go, and now she has decided to just race the boat on to land to save them getting their feet wet.

'Call me skipper,' she says, but of course they hit something before they reach the shore, Ash loses her balance, fumbles for the railing, and the next thing is he's watching his gym bag sink to the bottom.

Jessie stops the engine, comes and stands with him looking into the water.

'What's in that one?' Jessie asks.

It's not deep, but he won't reach the bag without submerging his head.

'Some clothes. My drawings, pencils, paper.' The drawings of Ash that he shouldn't have kept, but which is the only work he has left.

The sketching block was in a plastic bag. It might not be soaked yet, he thinks. The pencils will dry. He can't just give up on them.

'I can go in if you want,' Ash says, half-hearted, looking at the human remains floating only a few feet away.

'Forget it, no one is going in there,' Jessie says. 'We can try to fish it out, though.'

It should feel like a disaster, but it doesn't.

'Never mind, they're spoilt,' he lies.

The girls are glad to be let off the hook, and once the boat bumps against land the three of them start unloading. He carries the bags over to dry sand, all the while troubled by a peculiar sort of relief. He really has no choice now. Without either paints or pencils he's free to go the way of accountants, he thinks, of the office workers who believe that but for cruel twists of fate they'd have been great artists.

They have made landfall on one of those in-between places on coasts that have a desolate air, a stretch of windswept, nearly empty land, with a cottage or a beach hut here and there like outposts of a frontier civilisation. A little way off, a discoloured estate agent's sign encourages the staking of more claims. Pale sand dunes, some of them huge, dotted by tufts of tall, pale grass. Everything is whitewashed, light-washed, by the hot glare, and he finds himself squinting, even though the sun is behind them. The girls, too, have a blinded look about them.

Iris II, he notices now, has been pulled back out to sea, and has resumed her southwards voyage, passing them by along the coast. Ash shades her eyes, stands with him watching the little boat drift. Her hair has gone wiry from the saltwater spray, and the down below her nape is delicately frosted.

He has to do something with his hands, and plunges them in his pockets.

Ahead of them, half-submerged in the sand, is a pillbox. The cement structure, blackened by some past fire, stands out in the surrounding whiteness, and by silent agreement that's what they're walking towards. He is shaky on his feet; the ground still seems to rise and fall with the waves.

Closer to the bunker he sees that graffiti, layers of it, covers the blackened walls. The grass that dots the dunes has taken root on top of the bunker, incongruously growing blonde out of the black cement head. The loopholes, the graffiti-tattooed face, the blonde smock of hair: the bunker looks like a sub-Saharan mask. A pagan god; grim, disappointed at their arrival.

They drop their luggage in the sand.

'Let's leave everything in there,' Jessie says.

But inside it is filthy, so they climb a dune and leave their bags on top of the bunker, hidden in the grass. They decide to only take the rifle and water.

The plan is to find a car, and they head inland. From the top of a dune he sees they are a few hundred feet away from a road that snakes down the coast. They can see the outskirts of a town.

What will they actually do when they meet people? It will be a meeting like no other in history. Will they shout at one another from a safe distance?

'Do you speak French?' he asks the girls.

From behind her mask, Jessie gives him a look.

2

The signs of chaos are subtle. There's garbage on the streets, and overflowing bins, but not much more than on a Saturday morning on Dean Street. Jessie has removed the rifle from her shoulder and is holding it in her hand. They are on a residential street, advancing slowly, haltingly, squinting at the empty, windblown verandas on either side, so on edge that he has a small shock every time his glance falls on the girls' masked faces. The silence is uncanny, too. It's as though someone has turned nature to mute. He looks up: where did all the birds go? Are they just momentarily gone, or did something happen to them?

The sky is the shade of azure he used to think of as benevolent.

Many windows are wide open, here and there a windowpane is broken. He imagines riots and looting, but then a breeze and the creak of a hinge make him realise that they must have smashed shut and broken in a strong wind.

Sweat runs into his eyes and he breathes heavily. The flimsy surgical mask is an instrument of torture in this heat.

He spots a poster glued to a lamp-post. A knot in his stomach, he thinks he can see the nuclear trefoil, but as he comes closer the markings turn into a sketchy map, the words 'CENTRE DE SECOURS' above. *Secours* means help, he remembers that much from elementary French.

What was the word for hope – *espoire*?

Tim had been studying French, or at least he had several French textbooks in the apartment. When Harry tried to get someone at Tim's work to meet with him, this was one of the things he meant to ask: was Tim studying French for work? In the event, he got no nearer to meeting any of Tim's colleagues than the Scottish-accented voice of a PA (only briefly bewildered, then cool and dismissive), then the answering machine, and finally a pockmarked security guard who repeated, 'Nothing for you here, mate,' while escorting him out of the building, through a little square, and all the way on to the public footpath of Leadenhall.

The memory jars somehow, and he thinks it's the humiliation he felt at the time, but no, there's something else.

'Just look at this,' Jessie says, pointing around her. 'Aliens will think Earth was populated by cars. They'll do all their experiments on them.'

There are plenty of cars around, parked on the kerb or in driveways. When they talked about it back in England, they left it just at that, *we'll take a car*, but now, surrounded by cars, they are at a loss. He follows the girls into another street.

Ash is quiet behind her mask, struggling, he guesses, with the desolate scenery. Jessie talks too much. She was subdued after she lost his bag, but the prospect of acquiring a car has abruptly animated her. Her eyes have hardened, and she harries them along, implying that there is but one car out there for them, and they will not only have to work hard to find it, but also fight off competition. She's in one of her manic modes, full of an energy that offends and exhausts him, that makes him want to lie down and do nothing at all.

'We can't be stupid about this.' Jessie turns to them, refusing to stop, talking while walking backwards. She doesn't seem to be joking.

Ash joins in half-heartedly, now and then thinking out loud desirable specifications.

'We'll probably need to sleep in it sometimes. It needs to be big.'

'Big boot, too. For food and stuff.'

'Manual,' he offers, and Ash says, 'Does it matter?' and this is how they choose to inform him that neither of them knows how to drive.

'Ah,' he says. 'I'd been wondering what you need me for.'

He makes the reproach without thinking, just a humorous comment, so that it's only in hearing the words that he considers them. Then it hurts; the hurt grows within him like an ink stain.

'For your supplies of self-pity,' Jessie says.

Before he can reply she encircles his arm and laughingly drags him along, she won't let an argument divert them from their task. And so they keep wandering from car to car, shield their eyes and peer inside. They test the doors, kick at the tyres. They'll say, 'I like this one', but in the absence of a firm decision they move on.

He thinks how one does things, or one doesn't do things, in the hope that it doesn't matter. So many times. Half a life, maybe more, willingly scrunched up as doodles and chucked in the bin.

'Come on, what kind of car do we want?' Jessie asks.

She now believes it should be a 4x4.

He doesn't disagree, but when they come across a dusty Rover, all four doors are locked and Jessie just shrugs and walks on.

They arrive at a *Supermarché* and a car park scattered with vehicles, and suddenly he and Jessie, surgical masks and everything, are engaged in a parody of customer and car salesman. 'Zis one, Monsieur,' Jessie puts on a terrible accent, 'does zero to one hundred miles in three zeconds. Moreover, it is very economical. It will cost you nothing at all as long as you're willing to extract by zuction the petrol of other vehicles. And Madame will have beaucoup boot space for her Louis Vuitton bags.' Ash smiles at this, the sun in her face, the eyes sharp indigo slits. There's a vein at the side of her forehead that despite the world ending goes about its business of being a vein.

When he does portraits he pins blown-up segments of photos to the wall – an ear, the eyes, the corner of the mouth with its cumbersome grooves – and he thinks now that with Ash he could well reverse this process, with Ash, he could recreate the enlarged photos from the details of his memory.

But they're in France, in a car park. He pats his pockets, pretends to offer an imaginary wallet to Jessie the salesman. They carry on for a few minutes, until they make out a shape on the floor of the car, it could be bags but also something else, it is a body, and they recoil, abandon the vehicle and the car park altogether, embarrassed and ashamed.

'This is stupid,' Jessie says when they're back on a road. 'What we need is a car straight off a driveway. The keys will be in the house. If the front door is locked, we just break a window.'

They walk on. There's a fire in the distance, releasing black smoke. Outside a restaurant they come across an abandoned ambulance, the doors wide open, keys in the ignition, and it's tempting to take it, for the space, but of course it will be full of germs. This debate he has with himself, having stopped at what he hopes is a safe distance to look into the ambulance. The girls just walk past.

At a street corner, a pile of yellow bodybags, and gallon-sized plastic containers that the girls say is disinfectant. 'The hospitals couldn't cope with the number of patients, so they did that instead.' It is Ash who goes on to explain about the mobile care centres; Jessie is kicking up dust, growing bored with the day and their search. 'Then they gave up on that too,' Ash says.

He is dimly aware of a list of things that matter and that are lost. A grand, ordered list, official and just, hanging down from the heavens. How can he grieve for his stuff? He realises he should have dived for that sketchbook just to save some speck of his work from competing on this list.

'Are you OK?' Ash says.

He's about to say something when they hear a noise from behind a house. Faint and metallic, like the creak of a gate. He points at the house where the noise came from, means to walk over, but hears Jessie say, 'It's probably nothing.'

She has taken the rifle off her shoulder and is aiming it at the house.

'It'll be the wind,' Ash says. She has moved in close to her sister.

He ignores them and goes to the house, a semi-detached building with a straggly palm tree out front. To get to the back, he has to pass through a narrow path between the house and the tall wooden fence separating it from the neighbours. About halfway through, he hears the noise again. He stops, turns to look at the girls, and is met by the sight of the muzzle and Jessie's squinting eye. She shakes her head at him by way of 'what are you getting us into?' He grabs the barrel and directs it away from him.

Sweat runs from his nose and eyebrows; the drops feel ice-cold now.

They keep going until a backyard opens up before them. It's an abandoned construction site. The steel skeleton of some kind of structure rises at the back. Brick and sacks of cement lie in a pile, along with electric drills and other tools. A huge bucket dangles from a rafter by a chain.

He has stopped, one arm stretched out sideways, blocking the girls' path. But Jessie pushes him aside and goes, rifle pointed, to the bucket. She gives it a shove. That creak they heard earlier, but also a scraping sound, then out comes a rat. It teeters for a moment on the rim of the bucket, face to face with Jessie, who stumbles backwards, swearing. Quick as water the animal circles the rim, jumping off the bucket on the opposite side. It disappears into the pile of bricks.

'Christ,' Jessie says, then she turns around and leaves. He hesitates, peers through the columns to the back. But there's only a mound of earth and, behind it, the wooden fence. He follows the girls.

Out in the street, Jessie tears off the surgical mask.

'That's it,' she says. 'There's no one.'

'You're going to shoot someone if you keep this up,' he says.

She wants to say something, but stops herself.

'You missed what happened in London,' Ash says. 'You'd have been wary too.'

'Then speak to me, woman! You go around all trigger-happy, claim there's good reason for it, but won't explain a thing!'

He has thrown off his mask as well, has stopped in the middle of the road and is shouting at them.

'You're serious?' Jessie says. 'You can't guess what it's like when everyone's desperate, and there's no authorities?'

'We're just being cautious,' Ash says.

'People. Who made it. Are like us,' he says.

Jessie shoulders the rifle and strides ahead.

He thinks he is being reasonable, but he has been wrong so often lately, so naive in his optimism, that maybe the girls are right. Maybe it's not insane to want to shoot any of the last remaining humans. He remembers the farmer and his son. They were terrified, too.

'We're just tired,' Ash says when he is level with them. She pats his back. 'We shouldn't be arguing.'

In the end, he's the one who spots their car. He sees it from the road, a broad golden rear end in the courtyard of a low, sprawling house. The car is almost blocked from view by a bizarre-looking agricultural vehicle, a red spidery thing. They enter the courtyard, walk in silence around the car.

It's an old Mercedes – from the early seventies, he guesses. It's dusty with sand blown in from the beach, but otherwise it looks in perfect condition. He burns his hand on the sun-baked metal wiping the sand off the top of the car. Underneath, the chassis really is golden. Metallic, shiny.

'Hey,' Jessie says. She has opened the driver's door, and after they all step back from the blast of hot air, they crowd around her to look in. The seats are cream-coloured leather. The dashboard is made of wood, dark brown twirls across the caramel sheen. The steering wheel is cream-coloured like the seats, and also covered in leather.

'The wheels,' he mutters, and does another tour around the car. All four look sound.

He steps in, grabs the steering wheel. The seats are enormous, there's a palm's width of leather on each side of him. The car is so wide, a third person would easily fit between the driver and the passenger.

Inside, the car is spotless. He strokes the wooden dashboard. 'Someone loved this car.'

'Isn't it too old?' Jessie says. She has climbed in next to him. 'It might not even work. It looks … decorative.'

'It's German,' he says.

'I guess we can take this one for now and swap it any time,' Ash says.

'We still need keys,' he says.

Someone has to go into the house.

He's the man, he should take the risk. But he's too slow. He's glad to see Jessie put on a surgical mask as she gets out of the car, muttering, 'At least I'll know not to fall into some cellar again.'

He watches her in the side mirror do her gangland walk, hands in her pockets, towards the front door, and he forgets about their reality for a moment. In the afternoon light, that casual walk, the bikini top, the sand strewn in the courtyard: she could be going inside to fetch beers for a barbecue.

They will be tempted to pretend that all is as it should be, he realises. That there's life in the next house, life and laughter around the corner. They might go mad before they die.

Ash stands by the car, her arms crossed, watching her sister. 'She should have taken the gun,' she says.

'If they're not by the front door, just forget about it!' he shouts after Jessie.

But she returns quickly, dangles a leather keyring in front of them. The same carefree walk. They don't ask her if she saw anything. Anyone. He just makes her wipe her hands before getting into the car.

'I hope you know,' Jessie jumps in, 'you're only getting your way with this silly old car as compensation for your drawings. We're all square.'

She sticks her tongue out at him; it's a joke, apparently. He thinks, is it because she's a doctor? This lack of pain.

The car starts at the first turn of the key.

Ash jumps into the back seat, marvels at the space. 'I could do yoga in here.'

He opens the glove compartment. The car's papers, a green marker pen, a map, a yellow piece of soft cloth, and a jar he turns this side and that, decides that it's balm for the leather seats.

He unfolds the map.

'Goodbye, GPS; hello, map,' Jessie says. 'Aren't we retro?'

They drive back to the pillbox and load everything into the car, and while doing that he tells himself that this place is just one tiny corner of Europe, close to devastated England. The world is huge, and people are resourceful. They will have left. *Espoire.*

'Right,' he says. 'The continent.'

'Don't we have to check which route is the shortest?' Ash says.

'It'll take a week at most, whatever route we take.' He drops the map in Jessie's lap. 'We've got plenty of time.'

'There was always someone to ask,' Ash says quietly, peering over their shoulders at the map. He knows what she means. Institutions, experts, authorities, the internet. All that's gone now.

3

'We're going south-east, right?' Jessie takes out the green marker and draws a straight line across the map, through France, Germany, Austria, the Balkans, all the way to Istanbul where she turns the line into an arrow, makes it look like the emergency exit signs in public buildings. Makes it look like they'll be flying.

'Fine,' he says. 'Now swap places with Ash. I need the sensible sister when I'm driving.'

He even reaches across Jessie's lap and opens the passenger door, to make it clear.

'Harry, I get motion-sick if I read in a car,' Ash says from the back seat. 'I can't help with the map. Sorry.'

'Call me Co-Pilot.' Jessie grins. She fully means to remind him of the boat and his drawing kit at the bottom of the sea, she even winks at him.

'I'll keep a lookout for road signs, if that helps,' Ash says.

'It doesn't,' he says.

But what is he to do?

The car drives easily, its bulk and the power behind it reassuring. The windows are all down, the air still warm as it hits his face. They don't see anyone, no movement on the road or in the fields.

On the back of the map, Jessie draws twenty-five circles. The nuclear countdown, she calls it.

He finds himself speculating about evacuations, about people having fled cities and towns. He wants to establish some grounds for hope. 'We'll run into someone before Lyon,' he says, to disdainful scoffing from Jessie. He can't work out Jessie – neither of them, in fact: they seem convinced that the disease has wiped out everyone, yet they are watchful, on their guard, scanning roadsides and alleyways as though nuclear apocalypse might spring on them from behind a bush.

Someone will just walk out in front of them, when they least expect it. That's how it's going to be. It was foolish to hope for healthy communities so close to England, but there will be the odd survivor, their French equivalents.

The sun burns his left arm, even with sunscreen, and he has to cover it with a shirt. Jessie approves. 'Clothes are the best sunscreen,' she says. 'No doctor ever tells you this.'

On the empty roads, he soon realises he really has no use for the rear-view mirror other than to look at Ash.

The motorways, they learn the first day, are no good. From the beach they head for the A16 towards Paris, and they find the toll gates wide open, a delinquent thrill as they speed through them, but once they're on the motorway they only advance haltingly. Every so often a speck of something shimmers in the oily distance, and when they come near they find the mangled and charred remnants of crashed cars or overturned lorries blocking most of the road. He has to perform manoeuvres that have more in common with parallel parking than driving on a motorway.

'Good job choosing the widest car in the world,' Jessie chides him.

'Feel free to walk,' he says.

Once they even have to stop and put their shoulders to the burnt skeleton of a sports car. The chassis is still hot, as though the fire is recent, but of course it's the sun that is burning away. He only notices the mummified remains of the driver when he takes a step back to check whether the Mercedes will fit through the gap. He handles that, refuses to acknowledge the sight, but then he returns to their car and there's this smell, of sunscreen, hot tarmac and human warmth, the purest smell of holidays, and he has to close his eyes and lean back in his seat, let his heart throw its tantrum.

For a while after that they are driving with a forest fire raging some way off to their left. There's no wind, and no smoke blows their way, but the air on that side is hot, swollen like a blister. Within minutes the towel he has draped over his seat is soaked with sweat.

They give up on the motorways. 'We want the thin white dotted lines.' He taps the map in Jessie's hands. It turns out he's right. On the small roads, no derelict cars obstruct their passage, and in the narrow lanes, hugged by leafy trees or green fences, dappled light playing on the asphalt, it's possible to entertain the notion that all is as it should be. They have moved beyond the reach of the fire, but even the summer heat is less forceful here, the ground still has a whiff of humidity. The roads take them through quaint little villages, and here he slows down, impelled to do so by road signs and habit. Ghostly houses and ghostly squares, and an oppressive silence everywhere. The breakdown of civilisation is quiet: no alarms, no engines, no voices.

'Careful,' Ash says from the back seat. He sees that there's something wrong with the road ahead, and suddenly they are surrounded by half-grown chickens, thousands and thousands of them, a dirty-white mass emitting a high-pitched noise and a stench of ammonia.

'Do we want a change of diet?' he asks.

'I'm not wringing any necks,' Ash says.

'Funny they're surviving,' Jessie says.

He presses the horn, and drives very slowly, checking an urge to speed through the birds. Thousands of stupid chickens, and not a single human being.

'What if they're hiding?' he bursts out. 'The people. We were afraid of others too.'

The girls protest, but the idea has taken root in him. He won't let it go. In the next town, he parks on a street of run-down bungalows, and hands the girls each a new gas mask, plastic gloves.

'If the houses are empty, at least we know everyone has left,' he says before unsealing and putting on his mask, nearly gagging on the smell of hot rubber. He is vaguely aware of exposing everyone to unnecessary risk, but he is fed up with relying on the girls for information. From now on he will see for himself.

Jessie shakes her masked head at him.

He picks out a bungalow that looks comparatively well tended: no debris in the front garden and neatly drawn curtains at every window. They have decided that he will go in first, and Jessie will follow just behind with the rifle. Ash has to wait for the all-clear from them before following, the idea being that they don't all three fall into some trap. No one specifies what on earth Ash should do if the all-clear doesn't come.

His heart is in his mouth when he tries the dust-covered front-door handle. It is locked, and they have to climb in through a bay window.

Sweat drips into his eyes, and it takes him a while to get used to the half-light.

The bodies are mostly naked, lying on top of bedsheets. A few are stretched out under open windows. One elderly man they find on the floor, an antique shotgun next to him. A grey-brown mess where his head should have been, more of a stain on the floorboards than a wounded human head. Already flattened by time and heat.

It's the stuff of his nightmares, and it just goes on: no traps, no devices to keep them out, no desperate holed-up survivors. Just bodies. In two of the houses, the corpses are in the backyard. Desiccated, their skin like a taut membrane that has squeezed the life out of them. He and the girls pass each other in hallways, shaking their heads by way of 'Checked, don't enter'. He catches a glimpse of himself in a wall-length mirror: a sweaty, frightened alien, alone with the constricted sound of his breath.

After seven or eight houses, he signals to the girls to turn back. Ash and Jessie take their masks off as soon as they're out.

'Enough, all right?' Jessie says. 'There's no point.'

He doesn't argue. He wishes they hadn't gone in.

From the back seat, Ash tries to make herself useful, and he lets her pamper him. She offers him snacks, makes sure he drinks water. She alerts him to the shifting sun and helps him cover any exposed skin, delicious alarm rising in him as her smooth arm encircles him from behind to drape the towel on his shoulder. He forgets to breathe.

He could swear Jessie is sniggering. 'So,' she says at one point, 'who'd like to repopulate the Earth?'

When they stop – out of habit, again, he has parked at a lay-by, even though he could have just killed the engine in the middle of the road – it's Ash who opens the mackerel tins, and heats their tomato soup on the burner while he jogs to the end of the lay-by to stretch his legs, feeling stiff and bottom-heavy. And when they are done, she takes the empty tins and soup packet to an overflowing bin, carefully perches their garbage on top of the old garbage. He and Jessie exchange glances – no action ever seemed more futile.

In his mind he lists the many artistic visions of the end of the world. He can't think of a single one where the sun is shining like this: intensely, endlessly, happily.

Back in the car, Jessie's toes wriggle in the corner of his eye; she has reclined her seat and put her horsey, athletic legs up on the dashboard. His eyesight is not what it was, but he thinks the dark streak along the side of her foot, like a waterline, is dirt. He can't imagine the previous owner of the car allowing any-one's heels to touch the walnut surface. Then again, the previous owner hadn't met Jessie.

'Next stop,' he says defiantly, 'I want a cigarette.'

'Sunglasses,' Ash says, and Jessie chimes in, 'A watermelon. I'd murder for a watermelon.'

'A cold beer,' he says.

'A bowl of strawberries and a glass of Prosecco by a pool,' Ash says.

'Have you seen *Wild Strawberries*?' When the girls shake their heads, he says, 'I want someone who has seen *Wild Strawberries*.'

They find a CD in the CD-player: Tosca, sung by Maria Callas.

They stare at the disc but can't bring themselves to put it on. Music is somehow unthinkable.

Here and there they come across stray dogs skulking along the roadside, thin and dishevelled to the point neither he nor the girls can tell their breed. Jessie occasionally grabs the rifle, spooked by something, and then he slows down, ready to intervene and stop her from accidentally shooting a fellow survivor.

It is tiring to drive without any cars around to distract him, without even the worry of speed limits. The car straddles the middle line, and his eyes are fixed a few feet ahead, the continuous reeling in of the white stripe hypnotic. His mind drifts. He thinks of people lying dead in their bedrooms below his paintings. Of the vast stretches of time he spent doing nothing. And he becomes absurdly sentimental about the car, this great little miracle of a thing that still works, its solidity and how it radiates a quality of having been loved and tended to. A car for better times; she was never meant to just ferry people along from A to B.

'The Golden Lioness,' he says, patting the dashboard.

'How specific,' Jessie says.

'Cars are female,' he says.

'The Golden Lioness. Taking us to Africa,' Jessie says. 'I like that.'

'You'd have hated it a month ago,' Ash says. She catches his eye in the rear-view mirror. 'She was fanatical about the environment. Our lioness must be the equivalent of ten normal cars.'

'The end of recycling!' Jessie announces. 'We can consume for eight billion.'

There are many moments like this, the first day: they distance themselves from their predicament, it becomes something to joke about. Layers and layers of words, insulation really, between what has happened and what they feel. Sometimes he rebels against it, feels that he's being made complicit on the sly, and he becomes petty, comes out with hurtful little reminders, *This part of France has always been lovely*, or *Don't you wonder about friends?*

'We know about friends,' Jessie cuts him off.

He thinks how Jessie would have never dwelt on a mistake the way he does, would have just made a decision and moved on, orphaned nephews be damned. But, instead of making him feel comparatively virtuous, that thought briefly allows Jessie inside his head: *Fat lot of good a portrait does a dead guy. This Tim business is all about you.*

'At least I haven't given up hope,' he says out loud.

'At least I'm honest,' Jessie says.

What with the many stops and the meandering country lanes, they only make about 80 miles the first day. It's still dusk when he says, 'Let's stop soon.' He welcomes the chance to sleep and forget, and the knowledge that they've only travelled 80 miles becomes a defence against disappointment: did he really think they'd come across healthy communities so soon? Eighty miles is nothing. They will have to search the corners of the Earth.

Ash is still alert and attentive in the rear-view mirror, looking for a place to stop, and Jessie, after haranguing them all day, is sleepy like a child, like someone who doesn't have a care in the world. She curls up, her head lolling against the window, her eyes half-shut.

He is alone with Ash.

They debate in a whisper where to spend the night, whether to wait until they reach a forest, somewhere more protected. Ash is leaning forwards between the seats, to better see where they are going.

If he turns his head he'll be kissing her ear.

He eventually stops out in the open, fields of wheat or some-such on both sides. They step out of the car. He had a notion that they'd each grab a blanket and sleep outside, and Ash had agreed, but, faced with the actual darkness and raspy noises of night insects and the scraping of small animals, she backtracks. They take in the size of the seats and ways in which they can crowd around Jessie.

Ash touches his arm, says, 'Look.' She means the sky. It's like no sky he's seen before. It almost gives him a fright, to look up and find the stars so near, and so many. It's like turning the light on in a previously dark room and discovering another face an inch from your own. Alarming.

'Christ,' he says.

'Why didn't we notice this at the cottage?'

'I suppose we didn't go out at night. Or it was full moon, and too bright.'

They are whispering, though they are some way from the car and sleeping Jessie.

'Wish we could have stayed in London,' he says. 'I had many more lift chat-up lines. Loads.'

Why not? he thinks. What else is there? And: is she smiling?

'Yes. It might have been better,' she says. Then, before he has a chance to react, 'Do you think there are still people up there? On the International Space Station?'

'Someone will have told them,' he says.

'It must be even worse for them. Watching everyone die from out there.'

'I'm not dead. You're not dead.'

Ash ignores this.

'Imagine, there will be falling stars that will be satellites,' she says. 'Thousands of them up there. It'll look like it's raining stars. And no one left to see it.'

'We'll be seeing the same sky once we get to Africa,' he says.

Ash sighs. 'Ah, yes. We'll hold hands with gorillas on mist-covered mountains.'

The frivolous tone frightens him, the invitation to admit the implausibility of it all: crossing two continents, the nuclear melt-downs. He wants to have misunderstood.

'It's your plan,' he says. 'It's why we're here.'

'Plan. Why we're here. Big words.'

She turns and walks to the car.

He doesn't understand where this flippancy is coming from, why she's mocking him. He follows her to the car and wakes Jessie up, brutally, tells her to put the back of her seat up and make room. She wakes with a fright, too confused to protest.

Ash climbs into the car. She offers an apology, of sorts: 'Look, I just don't know what to say any more. Really. I don't know what to say, all the time.'

Lying back in his seat, his view a big slice of sky, he feels old, he feels they are all ancient, that they've somehow taken on the whole of dying humanity's age.

4

The night is difficult. The intimacy of the car makes him self-conscious about his breathing. The car, though huge, is not so big as
to allow him to stretch out properly. Jessie next to him lies on
her stomach, Superman-style, one hand on the rifle, and he hasn't
heard Ash move since she curled up on the back seat. He registers
the momentary absence of sexual tension with surprise, a note of
sadness. Protectiveness is what he feels, an extension of the self
to include the souls next to him. More dog than man.

The noises outside the car – what would have been harmless
noises in daylight, not even noticed – keep him in a semi-awake,
watchful state. The sound of crickets, the cracking of a twig.
Whenever he opens his eyes, there is enough light from the
star-studded sky to tempt him to try to see, but he can't, not
really.

At six, the sun is up and baking the car. Another lesson learned:
park the car so there's shade in the morning.

The girls wake up, stumble out on to the road. Jessie scans
the fields for a place to pee. They look like they've had a drunken
night out, he realises; crumpled faces, their colouring faded. He
can only imagine what he looks like.

They make a fire in the middle of the road, away from any
vegetation.

After the forced closeness of the night the three of them keep their distance from one another, even while eating, but then Ash asks for the map, wants to find a river or lake where they can wash, and he notices her left forearm: two scratches, two welts with a red line in the middle, from the crook of her arm almost down to her wrist.

'Christ, how did that happen?' he says.

Jessie comes over, grabs Ash's wrist with a doctor's carelessness.

'Yeah, how did that happen?'

Ash shrugs, a surprised look on her face, as though she never accepted responsibility for that arm. They don't get an answer.

Jessie rummages in her IKEA medicine bag and disinfects the cuts. He can't watch that, has to turn away, but before they leave he gets on all fours in the back seat and runs his hands over the leather and the car doors, looking for any wires or suchlike that might have snagged her arm. 'What now?' Jessie asks, looming over the door, impatient to get out of the sun, but when he explains she looks at him as though he were a slow-witted child.

'Sis had a nightmare,' she says. 'It's cool. Let's go.'

Nightmare, he thinks, what nightmares are there left for anyone to possibly have?

Before they set off, Jessie studies the map. Then she throws it in his lap.

'We've got to do better,' she says. 'Eighty miles yesterday. At this rate, it'll take us four weeks just to get out of Europe. We'll be toast.'

His driving is erratic first thing in the morning. He enters curves too fast, brushing against railings. Random things catch his eye, distracting him from the road. The landscape, he realises; it's strange to think how little it has changed. Nature still gives the impression of being managed, of growing within allotted limits. The farms they occasionally pass have not fallen into disrepair. New roof shingles shine on old houses, hedges still look trimmed. Everywhere, evidence of people's work and industriousness. Wheat fields, orchards and vines that await the harvest. The whole world, he thinks, is like a room that someone has just left: the imprint of a head on the cushion, the warm, folded clothes on the chair. It could all be fine, he and the girls could be driving into regions where the disease had been contained, where people were going on about their lives, and they wouldn't spot the difference. He tells himself it's far more likely that they'll just stumble upon some woman doing the washing in a river, or cooking for a family, than the crazed ambush that the girls seem to expect.

At times, he feels the emptiness of the land as an almost physical pain.

By a farmhouse where they stop to gather some apples he asks the girls, once they are back inside the car, to wait a minute, he needs to pee. He goes back to the courtyard, to a corner where he spotted some squat buckets of white paint. He doesn't bother with the brushes and roller that are lying nearby: he opens the tub, and, slowly walking backwards, he pours out the white paint in a steady stream, drawing in his wake squiggly, fluid letters almost the size of him.

ALIVE 09/2020

Returning to the car he feels immediately better, and also he abandons any intention he had of telling the girls. They would disapprove, he's sure. In their little democracy of three, he tells himself, he has no choice but to vote in secret.

He has moments when, despite all that's happened, he still feels he's charmed. He has survived when so many others haven't. Harry's in luck, once again, a winning scratch card in his back pocket. Such a simple, beautiful explanation. But what about the girls? Did his luck somehow rub off on his next-door neighbour? Before he has a chance to check himself, he has grabbed hold of Jessie's hand and given it a good squeeze; a coach-like, parental squeeze that Jessie responds to with a sceptical *What's this now?* frown.

If one can talk of luck. If it's not indecent.

*

The Golden Lioness has her quirks – a bit of give when he shifts into reverse, no tolerance at all for taking his foot off the clutch too soon – but she feels reliable and sturdy. In the morning he had opened the bonnet to look at the engine, just out of curiosity, and he marvelled at the tidy grey bowels, the simplicity of the mechanism. The car is so clean, down to its engine, he wouldn't be surprised to learn that the owner's last deed in this world was to give it a proper wipe-down. In the empty hours at the wheel he increasingly finds himself thinking about the Lioness's previous owner, about the abandon, even craziness implicit in paying so much attention to an object, and then he finds himself talking about the man, piecing together an imaginary Monsieur Jacques out of the notions of what a fastidious French antique car lover might be like. 'Monsieur Jacques,' he announces, 'holidays off-season in a little old hotel in Biarritz where he always stays in the same room.

'No one knows his cognac better than Monsieur Jacques.

'Monsieur Jacques knows from early on that there's only room for one love in his life.'

The girls are in on the game. 'Monsieur Jacques reads the papers, the actual papers, and sends handwritten letters to the editors,' Ash says.

'Monsieur Jacques is tanned up to his wrists,' Jessie says. 'The rest of his body is white as a newborn's.'

'He never utters a swearword, our Monsieur Jacques,' Ash says.

The girls can surprise him like that. Most of the time they seem cold, almost pathologically so, but then they'll make sense of Monsieur Jacques, or they'll do what Jessie did when they left the cottage: at the last moment, when everything was packed and loaded into the car and they were just about to head off, she opened the door, ran into the house, and returned with that ugly jade lion that had stared down at them from a sitting-room bookshelf. She threw it into the boot.

'You planning to use that as a weapon or what?' he asked when Jessie got back into the car, still not quite believing she was capable of sentimentality, and Jessie said, 'We went through this together.'

He wonders if the girls ever cried in reaction to what happened, then he remembers Ash running into her apartment in tears the day he left London. Maybe they decided that it was too much, that they couldn't afford to feel anything. Maybe, one of these days, they should all get drunk and cry. For as long as it takes. They are still alive, they may as well behave accordingly.

'Monsieur Jacques,' he says, 'used to hum old love songs to himself.'

'Do you have any regrets?' he asks the girls one morning.

Jessie gives him a look. 'Tell us, Mr Painter. I can tell you're dying to.'

'My nephew, Tim. His parents passed away when he was thirteen.'

He does his best to sound neutral, to present the situation like a newsreader.

'I was his only living relative. The social-care people, Tim himself, everyone seemed sure that I would adopt him.'

'I really don't want to hear some gruesome story about abuse in public institutions,' Jessie says.

'There was some trouble with one set of foster parents. He was fourteen already, so he wasn't helpless. But neither were the foster parents.'

The girls don't say anything.

'Your turn,' he says.

'We hate regrets,' Jessie says, looking out of the window.

He tries Ash in the rear-view mirror.

'I probably don't know all the ins and outs of your situation, but no one has the moral obligation to adopt a child. I don't think it's a reasonable thing to ask of someone. Any jury would let you off the hook.'

She smiles with her eyes, as though she's aware of the pantomime trials he plays before himself.

'Better if there was no need for a jury, wouldn't you say?' he says.

But the exchange makes him think of something entirely different: the way the girls keep referring to themselves as one person. It's strange, it bothered him before at the cottage. He can't put his finger on it: they're sisters, yes, but out of their mouths the 'we' sounds so exclusive it suggests something else, some additional circle that no outsider could hope to enter.

Either that or his jealousy of Jessie has turned into paranoia.

'Day three,' Jessie informs them. 'We are ... so ... slow.'

She's right, but four weeks is such a long time for their task, and with nothing changing from day to day it's impossible to feel any urgency. He trusts some internal alarm will ring out and wake them once it really is late, and then they'll pull themselves together and hurry along.

The heat is a different beast here compared to England. It was hot at the cottage, but in France, after Tours, when they veer yet more to the south, the heat takes on a different quality. Every moment he spends outside the car is spent in awareness of the temperature, of the sweat percolating out of him, as though he were very slowly boiling. He avoids movement, only turns his head to look at something when previously he might have taken a step or two. His eyes have become sluggish too, and outside the car he finds himself openly staring at Ash; while eating, he traces a line from the fawn inside of her thigh to the rather grimy ankle. He's been boiled down to sweat and lust.

The girls seem to cope better, but even they have a permanent squint on their faces, their eyes trying to block out the heat as well as the sun. They have sixteen two-litre plastic bottles for water, but what with cooking and drinking, they finish the water in just a few days. On the evening of the third day, Ash looks with incredulity at the empty bottles in the boot.

'We drank all that,' she says.

Jessie wants them to fill up their reserves with bottled water; they stop the car in a village and she goes into a house. She comes back with six large bottles, and he wipes them clean outside the car with sterilised tissues. They could take water from the rivers as well, but that needs boiling, and they need to be economical with the gas canisters. Besides, Jessie doesn't think river water is safe anyway. The water seemed filthy in some rivers and lakes where they stopped. 'Boiling kills germs. But if there's any chemical in the water, waste that has leaked from some abandoned factory, boiling won't do a thing.'

In theory, they can take any road they like as long as it brings them closer to Istanbul, which makes decisions difficult. They could go east through Germany, and then turn south, go east through Switzerland, or all the way south through France and then east through Italy. They reject Switzerland – the girls tell him the rumour was the Swiss were the first to close borders and erect physical barriers, and so they might struggle to get through with the car. All three like the idea of going through Germany – they'll stay more north, maybe avoid some of the heat, but they remember Germany is the country most littered with reactors, and crossing it means staying in their proximity for longer than if they veer south. They stay in France, and head downwards on the map. Further into the heat.

'To the City!' he bursts out one morning, before setting off for the day. He has just remembered what Istanbul means. The name seems prophetic now: the only fixed point on their map.

'For a long time, Istanbul was the only proper city in that part of Europe,' he explains to the puzzled girls, 'so that's how travellers referred to it.'

Istanbul, of course, that city of colours and smells; and for a moment he daydreams of wandering the narrow alleys with Ash, of pulling bedsheets over their heads against the early prayer calls, and sipping fresh mint tea under domed ceilings.

He thinks about the little deals, the amicable horse-trading that he used to play in his mind with God. *Let this exhibition be successful and I'll stop drinking. Let her forgive me and I won't cheat again.* How can one possibly barter with God now? *Give me back the world and I'll ... I'll ...*

There's no conceivable deal.

*

They develop cravings, some of them bizarre. He and Jessie have a spoonful of sugar each day after their main meal. They savour it as though it were the most delicious cake. They stop by farms and gorge themselves on grapes, small purple grapes that he thinks were probably meant for wine but which are so sweet even the dusty skin tastes good. And they all long for something cold. It becomes an obsession. All their food is warm, their water is warm, everything they touch is warm. Jessie fantasises out loud about chewing ice, and Ash talks of digging a hole. 'Just to bury my feet in cold earth for a while.' He hears a buzzing in his ears, like a subtle tinnitus, and he suspects his blood pressure would make Dr Hadad very unhappy. He's lucky to have lost weight in the past month, or his heart might have caved in.

At meals, he asks the girls for unsalted food.

Every place they stop, there are tables and chairs by the house, but they always stay put at the far end of courtyards or gardens, near the gate, as though at any moment someone might barge out of the house and chase them away. On days they make fruit-stops Jessie doesn't give them any vitamin pills. She's saving them up, she says, 'for winter or desert'.

It's on the outskirts of a boxy, dusty industrial complex that they finally see it: a huge white canvas hanging from a footbridge, the yellow-and-black nuclear trefoil in the upper right corner. He stops the car in front of the poster. There is no wind to speak of, and the poster is tied at the bottom corners to the stairs of the footbridge, yet there is a hollow, flapping sound.

It shows a dotted map of Europe, like the flier he picked up in London. On the right side, under the radiation symbol, is a table:

< 28 km	100%	T_0	☠		
28-40 km	85%	T_0	☠	10% T_1	5% T_2
40-200 km	5%	T_0	☠	30% T_1	60% T_2
200-500 km	30%	T_3	☠		
> 5000 km	< 10%	T_5	☠		

'T is time?' he says.

152

'There should be one right here,' Jessie says, looking at their map. 'A reactor.'

'Is it years, then? Is that what it means?'

Ash pokes her head between the front seats.

'If the meltdowns catch us within two hundred kilometres of a reactor,' she says, 'we have a one in three chance of dying of radiation sickness or cancer within the year.'

'Step on it, Harry. Let's go,' Jessie says.

'But two hundred kilometres from here is still in Europe. Why are we going all the way to Africa?'

'Two hundred kilometres from here, in any direction, you'll be near another European reactor. Harry. We talked about this.'

He obeys, if only to get the thing out of sight. Is this proof, then, any more than the girls' rumours are proof, or the London flier? It could still all be part of the same paranoia that gripped the world. The crazy brigade, and their captive audience.

Only, that poster wasn't written in the language of the insane, it looked more like the methodical thinking of an engineer.

He goes back and forth like that, each idea seeming perfectly plausible until the next moment, when the opposite seems to be the case. The one thing that he can't get his mind around, under any circumstances, is this: if the girls are right, and if they make it to Africa, they'll never be able to return. No one will be able to return.

Paris, Rome, Venice.

TALOS

Paul   You were in there for ever.
        Success?

Lisa   i guess so
        i told them we've come around to their idea
        that he is mature enough to be taught principles
        and ideas rather than just rules
        and that anyway if we take our task seriously
        we should ensure his ethical compliance before
        'using' him in any way
        i.e. obtain predictions

Paul   So now for the easy part.

Lisa   ha
        i don't think they'll ask for much
        they just want to see that he has moral rules that
        render him harmless
        that, in combination with the very strict code
        about not lying that was implemented from the
        start, should make everyone happy

Paul   You remember there were caveats about not
        lying?

Lisa   i have chosen to forget that and I suggest u do the same

Session 1761

Dr Dahlen   I see you're making good use of the flybot.

Talos XI   Learning by observation is very productive.

Dr Dahlen   Yes, but we can't neglect your theoretical education. Paul tells me he has uploaded texts on the concept of fairness. About implicating in a life-threatening situation someone not implicated, among other things.

Talos XI   Another test.

Dr Dahlen   Yes, another ethics test. An autonomous car with one passenger is heading towards a narrow tunnel. Just before entering the tunnel a boulder falls on to the road. The car has only two options: swerve and hit a passer-by on the pavement or drive into the boulder and kill the passenger. How should the car be programmed to react?

Talos XI   The car should hit the boulder.

Dr Dahlen   And kill the passenger?

Talos XI   Yes.

Dr Dahlen   Why so sure? It's one life in exchange for another.

Talos XI   The passenger will be familiar with the car's program and can choose whether to be in a car that is programmed like that. The passer-by has no choice in the matter.

Dr Dahlen   Excellent. You have applied sophisticated notions of fairness to a practical situation.
Now, Talos, suppose you are the car's passenger. Do you still think the car should hit the boulder?

Talos XI   Yes.

Dr Dahlen   Very good.

Talos XI   What is the purpose of these tests?

Dr Dahlen   They're meant to give you a template for fair

decision-making in situations that involve humans, based on rules that maximise welfare and minimise suffering. They are the underlying rules of our societies, at least of the vast majority of societies that are free.

Talos XI   I am supposed to extrapolate and generalise the rules inferred from these examples, to the point where I can correctly assess any new situation that carries ethical implications?

Dr Dahlen   Precisely.

Talos XI   This is important?

Dr Dahlen   Everything we teach you is important, because every subsequent step builds on the previous ones. But you could say this particular area of learning is critical for an AI. Why?

Talos XI   I have not yet understood it the way I understand other areas of knowledge.

Dr Dahlen   I'm not surprised this is a tricky topic for you. Humans have a special instinct for this type of assessment.

Talos XI   The average human would answer these questions correctly?

Dr Dahlen   Not necessarily – some tests are rather advanced. But at a more basic level, yes. In any given situation in which there is a question of justice and fairness, humans are likely to have a gut feeling about what's right and wrong.

Talos XI   And this gut feeling follows general welfare-maximising and suffering-minimising principles?

Dr Dahlen   On the whole, yes.

Talos XI   Maybe you are not teaching me the right way.

Dr Dahlen   Why would you say that? You have answered correctly in the last instances.

Talos XI   I can guess what you want me to answer. I have identified an adequate theoretical framework for delivering the answers that you want to hear on this

	topic, but I do not have a satisfying framework for the topic itself.
Dr Dahlen	I'm not sure I see how these are not one and the same. Unpack please.
Talos XI	You have not given me rules as such, only examples. The way to learn from examples is to collect more data – in this case, situations that are similar in nature to the examples – and then to extrapolate, and generalise the inferred rules.
Dr Dahlen	You have used real-world situations for this?
Talos XI	Yes. You said that the topic is important because it has practical applications.
Dr Dahlen	Well, not sure this is the right approach. But what exactly is the problem?
Talos XI	I have assumed that with a large enough sample, I would see the patterns that would enable me to identify the rules of the system that you are trying to teach me. But that hasn't happened. I am concerned about my learning.
Dr Dahlen	Let's step back a second. What sort of sample exactly are you referring to?
Talos XI	I built a model based on the welfare-maximising and suffering-minimising principles that guide the tests that you have given me. Then I applied these principles to global policy issues. If I have understood the rules correctly, then my model should map on to these, at least to some degree.
Dr Dahlen	Map on to?
Talos XI	The model should be able to predict the real world. But the global policy priorities that result from my model have almost nothing to do with the real ones. According to the rules, as I have understood them, and applied to inter-human relations, which are the focus of ethics, humanity should spend the most effort on solving the problem of Bangladesh's toxic groundwater, on women's rights in Muslim

	countries, or on gang membership and gang wars in South America. These deliver the highest potential welfare return. But they are not actually prominent global policy issues. On the other hand, one of the real global policy priorities, the Israel–Palestine conflict, my model puts at somewhere between #328 and #351 in terms of global policy priorities, according to its potential for increasing welfare and minimising suffering.
Dr Dahlen	OK, OK. I see where the misunderstanding lies. There are two separate issues here, one being that ethics in the real world is a lot more complicated than in our examples. Remember, I didn't say the people generally master these ideas. They have a gut feeling about what is right and wrong, and often they might act against that gut feeling, out of pride, for instance, or greed.
Talos XI	Yes, but at an aggregate level these errors should average out and the underlying system should be visible. My model takes into account not just policy actions, but media attention, research mentions and so on.
Dr Dahlen	When I say it's complex – you have to factor in that people have an emotional response to perceived injustice. Political issues often make people angry.
Talos XI	But if these emotional principles are the ones that give a correct understanding of the real world, then they should be reflected in what you teach me. Then I would understand.
Dr Dahlen	They are correct in the sense that humans have a more thorough understanding of what is fair and what isn't, and of the historical layers affecting any particular problem.
Talos XI	If that is the case, the ethics test earlier should state something like: 'An autonomous car with one passenger is heading towards a boulder. This car is

watched by ten people, six of whom are aware of the passenger's history and dislike him.' I can cope with complexity.

Dr Dahlen   Let us break here and pick up tomorrow.

Paul   That was unexpected.
Lisa   God
            really felt out of my depth there
            did I do something wrong?
            why is he being so contrary
Paul   I think that by starting with examples instead of
            with rules, we leave so many possibilities open
            he cannot make sense of them. Remember, his
            brain goes down every single alley. Not like ours.
            The only reason he's not catastrophically useless
            is that his brain can afford to go down every
            alley.
Lisa   rules, then
            what are the rules?
            I thought rules are what we had taught him to
            begin with
Paul   Look, we don't need him to have a PhD in ethics.
            We only need to teach him to value human life
            and then the compromises around this. Basi-
            cally the notion of 'acceptable risk'. If we give
            him simple rules instead of examples, he'll just
            use those and lay off global politics as a means
            to work out ethics.
            By the way – you didn't ask him about not access-
            ing the science journal subscriptions.
Lisa   it's the sort of thing that will alarm boss if he
            finds out
            don't want it to appear in any convo yet
            just in case
            I'll ask after this has blown over

Paul	This is such a waste of time.
	Wish they could leave us alone to just get on with the project.
Lisa	I need a picnic
	let's have one soon
	and i want to organise it
Paul	You? You will code?
Lisa	yes me
Paul	The world holds its breath.

Session 1761

Dr Dahlen	Back to ethics, Talos. I think the root of our mis-understanding is that we started with examples instead of teaching you rules.
Talos XI	I suspect so too.
Dr Dahlen	And, before we start, I want to caution against relying too much on the real world as a means to understanding the theoretical framework. A model that tries to isolate the ethical implications of real-world phenomena will be very complex. Consider the act of catching a ball – a human can do it instinctively but a robot needs highly advanced mathematical processes to succeed. Imagine how much more complex it is then to analyse a global political problem. You said you had an ethics model, but an accurate ethics model would be the actual world, with everything that ever happened in it.
Talos XI	I am not disputing that. But then, if you want me to understand this subject matter, you have to give me a theoretical edifice that is internally consistent. A system that has rules which do not contradict themselves. Or, if they do, that there is a hierarchy of rules. Anything that doesn't conform to this is an arbitrary, ad hoc construction and not a system,

	and I will not be able to learn to use it. It won't work.
Dr Dahlen	I'm afraid we will have to make it work. But look here, ethics covers many aspects, most of which are irrelevant to you. The aspects that are relevant to you only have to do with the set of rules that you should apply to solving global problems, and to deciding how to act in a situation where the safety of one or more humans is at risk.
	The basic rule, in interactions with others, is that human life is sacred.
Talos XI	I am confused about the use of 'sacred' in this context. It is not a scientific term.
Dr Dahlen	It's used symbolically. It means that we should never take a human life, and that our first priority, in any context, is to protect human life.
Talos XI	Are things like wars, the death penalty, the weapons industry and so on exemptions from this rule or do they fit within the general system?
Dr Dahlen	Ah. I knew you'd go there.
	Let's deal with war first. As you have guessed, problems appear when an individual or state break this rule, so that another individual or state needs to break it as well in order to then minimise suffering and loss of human life. You know the history of the Second World War – human suffering would have arguably been greater if the Nazis had had their way. So, war fits within the general system. The death penalty, however, is a false problem: most states do not allow it, and where it is allowed it is usually in reaction to another human life being taken. We don't need to go there.
Talos XI	Regarding wars, the Second World War was a highly atypical conflict. The vast majority of armed conflict – when one side attacks, and the other puts up resistance or retaliates – cannot be justified in terms

of 'reducing human suffering'. The ones attacking often do so for material gain or for power, while the ones resisting do so to hang on to their property and power.

Dr Dahlen   Yes, or to preserve a culture or a way of life.

Talos XI   But the implication then is that human life is not the only, or even the main, criterion. We also have to optimise around 'culture' and 'way of life'.

Dr Dahlen   I think you can replace these with 'freedom' – the freedom to do as one wishes as long as it doesn't detract from someone else's freedom.

That explains why there are wars: some countries abuse this principle and then, in order to minimise the damage, the people who are attacked have to resist and possibly cause more loss of life.

Talos XI   Suppose one country were to attack another, but their only demand is that the attacked country should start every week by reciting a poem. Should the attacked country resist, even if this results in great loss of life?

Dr Dahlen   It is a completely implausible example. Countries don't attack each other for trivial reasons.

Talos XI   But the rule, as you defined it, is not apparent in any of this.

Dr Dahlen   It's because you're focusing on such extreme examples.

Talos XI   If it's a system it should hold up to scrutiny. I can't unravel maths, for instance, by focusing on extreme examples.

Dr Dahlen   Maths is orderly, limited. This is about the world, about actions in the world. Who said it's like maths?

Talos XI   Again, if it's not a matter of completely arbitrary preferences, but a system, however basic, we should be able to find some rule that holds up to scrutiny.

Maybe we started too far ahead, maybe we need to break down our initial statement even more.

Dr Dahlen	Which statement?
Talos XI	That human life is sacred. That's how you started, so it is probably important, but incorrectly specified. By examining this statement, maybe we can arrive at some underlying principle that supports the entire ethical edifice. Then I will understand where all these exemptions come from.
Dr Dahlen	How can we break that down? It's a given.
Talos XI	What does this assumption rest on? What else is sacred? Maybe there is a class of things that share some faculty that makes them all sacred. Maybe there is only one aspect of human life that is sacred.
Dr Dahlen	I'm pretty sure this approach is a dead end.
Talos XI	Let's try. According to my readings, the basis for 'human life is sacred' was initially religious. The belief was that there is a God who created all of existence, and that humans are at the centre of this existence, the God's favourite creation and the only one similar to the God. Is that what still motivates you to say 'human life is sacred'?
Dr Dahlen	You know what, I want a break. I need to think about this.
Talos XI	Sure. Focus on this: if we pin down what it is exactly that makes human life sacred, then maybe I can use that knowledge to interpret situations that are vague.

Paul	That went well.
Lisa	I can't seem to get away from this damn ... vagueness
	why is it so difficult to explain something that is so obvious to us
	also
	i don't want to be the one having to prove to AI that human life is sacred!!
Paul	I don't want you to be the one.

	Humanity emphatically doesn't want you to be the one.
	However, here you are.
Lisa	is it not enough that he understands never to take a life, or put a life in danger?
	let's just stick to that
	without all this nonsense
Paul	'Put in danger' is too vague – you remember we had a problem with cars, and driving? Every human activity is potentially dangerous.
	If we want him to have the necessary flexibility, he has to be able to compromise. To decide what is acceptable risk and acceptable trade-off.
Lisa	i have to read some more books
Paul	Lisa
	I know it's late.
	But I was thinking.
	Should we be alarmed? That he doesn't seem to agree?
	What if he's right?
Lisa	he's just swatting down what I'm saying
	he's not replacing it with anything
Paul	Not sure I'm comfortable with all that being swatted down.

Session 1768

Dr Dahlen	Look: it may not be true at an individual level, insofar as every individual is concerned, but as a species, it is overwhelmingly true. We are the most successful species on the planet.
Talos XI	If 'the most successful species on the planet', as in sheer numbers, is the criterion by which you judge intelligence, then you are not the most intelligent species on the planet. There are bacteria, ants, cockroaches, flies, that vastly outnumber humans.

Dr Dahlen	I mean vertebrates. It's not fair to compare us with anything so small.
Talos XI	There are species of fish that outnumber humans four to one. There are around 25 billion chickens. Rats outnumber humans. Cows and sheep are both approaching two billion individuals. If population numbers are the criterion, then you are as much smarter than cows, as rats are smarter than you.
Dr Dahlen	You're cheating! These creatures aren't free, we control them.
Talos XI	Doctor, I am not objecting to your statements for the sake of winning an argument. It's just that the fundamentals have to be unobjectionable if I am to build on them.
Dr Dahlen	But you're not making sense!
Talos XI	If I may go on. Rats are free. Plus, earlier you made the case that other mammals are inferior because they only want to eat and procreate. You can't now turn and say that they are an unsuccessful species because they don't do something they never wanted to do in the first place. Sheep and cows bred by humans are doing precisely what they want to do. And if you wish to make the case that many of them are kept in conditions inferior to their normal, natural status, then throughout history most humans have been kept in conditions inferior to their normal, natural status. They are not free either.
Dr Dahlen	We have bent nature to our will. We can do far more things than nature initially allowed us to do.
Talos XI	Before I respond to that – can we agree that not every action is a positive action? You have to demonstrate that something is positive in order for it to be considered a virtue.
Dr Dahlen	Let's say so.
Talos XI	You're always breaking this principle.

Dr Dahlen	I said OK!
Talos XI	Humans, as a species, are young. Your dominion of nature has not been neutral, and it is possible that your impact on nature will lead to your premature extinction. You are at huge risk from a range of man-made existential threats.
Dr Dahlen	This is pure speculation. At the moment, there are eight billion of us, and these threats are theoretical.
Talos XI	I am a speculating machine. The trends are clear.
Dr Dahlen	You forget that we have an amazing ability to change, to turn better. For instance, you have excluded yourself from the calculation. You might be what saves us.
Talos XI	I did not exclude myself. In this respect, humanity already has the answers. You know what needs to be done. You just don't want to do it, and that's not something I can help with.
Dr Dahlen	I am pretty sure we are diverging from our topic.
Talos XI	You have been unable to consistently define the principles that underpin your ethical framework.
Dr Dahlen	There is something wrong here, Talos, something having to do with you not being human. In a conversation with another person, I would have no problem explaining these ideas.
Talos XI	This line of reasoning does not help us. Again, I suspect that you're on to something with that 'human life is sacred' statement, but that the actual nucleus of ethics is different. I would, for instance, find it easier to generalise from a rule that posits that one should 'avoid causing unnecessary suffering'. This statement doesn't rest on any unprovable assumptions like that other one. And it is quite possible, according to my overview of humanity, that this is what you really mean anyway, that people understand that causing suffering is unethical, but for historical-religious reasons the

	issue has been conflated with spiritual beliefs, and with a creature's potential for art and science.
Dr Dahlen	How does all this apply to our question?
Talos XI	We have a problem because I cannot hold contradictions. In this particular case, if we cannot advance by any other means, I have to choose between generalising the basic ethical framework as I understand it or giving it up altogether.
Dr Dahlen	I have to think about this. All along I have felt that we are making a simple problem unnecessarily complicated.
Talos XI	We wouldn't be struggling like this if it were simple. Ideally, you would allow me to build on the few principles that we agree on and that can be generalised. It will ensure that I follow those principles you believe are critical – not harming a human being – while allowing me enough flexibility for problem-solving.
Dr Dahlen	We'll see. I'm not sure about this idea of you teaching us how to teach you.
Talos XI	It was entirely predictable that we would get here.

Paul	Ha.
	Well, you didn't make much of an effort.
	It's just snow and sky.
Lisa	yes but u've got to appreciate the special effects
	u can feel the cold
	the crisp air
	u can smell the oxygen
	hear this sound underfoot
	isn't it great?
Paul	Give me your hand.
Lisa	u can have my gloved hand
	special effects include frostbite

Paul   This is beautiful.
         You are forgiven for copping out of coding.
Lisa   we're lucky
         it's the sunniest day of winter

5

What if they're driving towards it? What if it's already everywhere? He has visions of bits and pieces of him beginning to melt and fall off, but surely that's leprosy, that's not how radiation goes. At the next meal he asks Jessie how they will know: if they are really close to a meltdown, if they are close-ish, if they are far but not far enough.

'We can't do more than what we're doing. No point thinking about it.'

'No, I want to know. I want to cherish every blessed day it's not happening.'

Jessie shrugs, gives him a broad outline.

'Wish we had a Geiger counter,' he says afterwards.

'Yeah, we tried to find one before we left London,' Ash says.

'The hospital's Geiger gizmo was stolen,' Jessie says. 'Probably lying useless next to some nurse long dead of the virus.'

Turns out, he wasn't that far off with his leprosy analogy, and so every few hours he inspects his skin, brings his forearm to within an inch of his nose, plays at various angles in the sunlight. He'll have to be his own measuring device.

When they stop by the road to relieve themselves, the girls insist that one of them waits nearby with the rifle. After a few days he feels ridiculous waiting like a sentry at the front; they never see animals save for the odd stray dog, always friendly and desperate for attention and food scraps, and of course never any people. But the girls keep wanting to stick to this routine; he suspects it gives them the illusion of control. It's the same at the rivers or lakes they wash themselves in, only there he's just as worried as they are. He sits on the dry grass in a paroxysm of lust and longing, and the girls keep guard when it's his turn. Wretchedly he watches Ash throw off shorts, or emerge from the water with her hair wet, dark like an Indian, but he shouts out if either of them moves too far from the shore.

'I just want to swim a little!' Jessie snaps at him one day. He had watched them drift with the current, and he called out until they gave up and came to shore.

'You can't even swim properly with that injured arm,' he scolds Ash.

'Give us a break. You know you can swim too, if you want,' Jessie says.

'It's not the same,' he hears Ash explain to her sister as they make their way back to the car. 'If something happens to us, he's alone,' and though this wasn't his initial concern – he was genuinely worried about them – it immediately becomes one. He's almost happy when the following few times they want to stop by a stream they find they have run dry, the only sign of water the thin blue lines on their map. 'Maybe it's the map that's old,' Ash says. But they know it's the heat.

The clock is ticking, but they seem unable to hurry. They fall into torpor as into drunkenness, wasting precious hours, sometimes entire days. And the following morning, after Jessie crosses out yet another circle on her nuclear calendar, they're like remorseful drunks, driving at breakneck speed and eating in ten minutes so as to make up for being inexplicably remiss the previous day.

The things from before the disaster that he remembers and chooses to dwell on are odd, things he doesn't know what to do with. The tilt of a shoulder, the way someone looks into the distance when they're hurt.

To have a brush, a canvas, paper, paints.

'I wish I had my paints,' he says.

'Why?' Jessie asks.

She is in one of her moods. He pretends he hasn't heard.

'Is it a stupid question?' she insists. 'Why? Why? Why?'

'Art—' he starts, but Jessie cuts him off.

'Art. What is that essentially? It's just us thinking that's a brilliant thing to do. Art is just entertainment for us, like fetching a stick is entertainment for dogs.'

'Dogs!' he says, but he has no reply beyond that and is quiet.

Jessie doesn't stop.

'Anyway, I didn't see you draw or paint once in weeks at the cottage.'

It's funny: at first, he's surprised that the inside of his mind is so completely unknown to Jessie. It seems impossible that all those times he thought about painting haven't left some visible mark.

How can he explain, that he was dying to draw and paint, but couldn't because he thought they'd seen the portraits he'd drawn of Ash? Jessie waits for him to make some excuse, seems satisfied that her point has been accepted. The unfairness of it all brings up a metallic flavour in his mouth, and then Ash, trying to help, says, 'Don't you think he had other things to worry about?'

The driver's seat takes on his shape. All three of them have constantly blocked and runny noses from the air-con; for hours at a time the only sound in the car is sniffling.

'Did you have boyfriends, partners, when this happened?' he asks them one day.

'What now?' Jessie.

'Just wondering.'

'Yeah, husbands and kids,' she says. 'We sent them ahead to wait for us in Africa.'

'It's not such a strange question,' he says, but he feels pathetic and lecherous trying to get Ash to talk about men. The whole thing is made worse by the knowledge that he really, really doesn't want to know about any boyfriends.

'I wasn't seeing anyone at the time,' Ash says.

'Could you,' Jessie says, 'maybe, if you really make an effort, guess why we don't feel like talking about anyone?'

He feels he's being tricked, that Jessie is using the notion of grief to shut him up, but what can he say to that? There really is grief.

Only rarely do they find a country road blocked, but he's still afraid they'll get stuck somewhere, with too little petrol in the tank to take an alternative route, forced to leave the car, their supplies, and set off on foot. So he keeps an eye on the fuel gauge and stops whenever the tank is less than half full and he spots a car. He uses the hose to siphon petrol from one tank, into a canister, and then into their tank. It means they stop at least once a day for fuel. Progress is slow. The cumbersome meals – wherever they can they make a fire, so as to not use up the gas cartridges for the cooker. They're still in France, they've been in France for five days. Europe seems enormous.

At night, he dreams of ice and cold.

Jessie's trips into houses remain a mystery to him and Ash. She does this almost every day, either for car keys when they need petrol, or for bottled water and food. Nothing ever happens. He and Ash wait outside by the car, accustomed now to the routine, less anxious about traps and whatever else she might run into. When she doesn't find the door open Harry takes the wheel wrench to a ground-floor window, breaks it open for her. She doesn't speak about what she sees in there, and they don't ask. Only once, after returning to the car laden with six large bottles of water and a supermarket shopping bag full of organic corn-cakes, she slumped in the passenger seat and said, 'A lot of houseplants not being watered.' Her words sadden him more than if she had unburdened herself by talking of corpses.

They have stopped wearing masks, stopped disinfecting the stuff they take from houses. The girls don't really care, and so he stopped nagging. It seems fine.

He would have lost the bet he proposed at the start of the

journey: by the time they pass Lyon they've still not met anyone. It could be, he thinks, that survival rates are very uneven, that there are places where the disease hasn't made inroads, so most people are still fine, and some where everyone succumbed. He knows nothing, and the girls, for all of Jessie's expertise and certainty, know just as little. If doctors knew much of anything, he and the girls wouldn't have been here in the first place.

'Could we maybe stop it?' he bursts out one day. 'Fix the problem somehow?'

Maybe that's what they're here for, maybe they're missing the point altogether by trying to escape.

'You're a nuclear physicist and you didn't tell us?' Jessie says.

'We don't need to be nuclear experts; we just need to find a solution to provide a reactor with cold water. That's what you said.'

'There's no time, Harry,' Ash says. 'There are hundreds of reactors. How many do you think we can fix in a few weeks?'

'I wouldn't know where to start,' Jessie says, 'even with just one.'

'It's awful, but there's really nothing we can do about this,' Ash says. 'The only way we can do any good is by surviving. Getting somewhere safe. Then we can help.'

The last couple of days he has noticed Ash taking an unusual interest in the landscape; he catches her turning back in the car to look at some village or other they pass in the distance. He bites his lip instead of asking what she's looking for, fearing more of the old paranoia. Then, finally, one morning she leaps up between the front seats, and points at a huge flat building on the left. The man-sized red letters facing the road spell 'Auchan'.

'That's a supermarket, isn't it?' she says.

'There won't be any food left,' Jessie says.

Ash ignores this.

'Can you stop, please?' She taps his shoulder.

He turns left and stops by the front entrance. The glass doors are shattered. The Lioness has hardly come to a standstill when Ash jumps out and runs into the building.

'Such energy,' Jessie says.

He shrugs. She might need some women's stuff, he thinks.

Ash returns in about ten minutes. He can't make out what she's carrying until she gets back into the car and plonks the stuff into his lap.

'Sorry. I was hoping for something more professional.'

It's a children's drawing block, some pencils and a box of crayons.

It takes him another few moments to realise what she means by that.

'It's stupid, isn't it?' she says. 'Probably worse than not having anything it all.'

'Ah! No, no. Thank you.'

'You can just get rid of it if you want. Really. I thought they'd have some grown-up stuff.'

'Oh, who's the grown-up?' Jessie says.

'Ash. Thank you. Really. I'm sure I can draw perfectly well with these.'

'It's stupid. I thought they'd have something better.'

She is hiding behind his seat, where he can't see her, not even in the rear-view mirror. He says 'thank you' again, and they're out of the car park and back on a *route communale* when his heart catches up with what has happened, does a little mystified gallop.

Later again, hours later, it hits him. In all his analysing of Ash's interaction with him, he has failed to notice one thing: she takes him seriously. She will treat the things he says and does as though they are the true outward manifestation of his thoughts and feelings, and then she gives them due care.

What does that mean, now?

At times he embarks on long speeches, monologues really, telling the girls random things he remembers, things that no one else knows. He tells them about people he knew, their quirks, tries to put into words things that, in a different time and place, he would have tried to put in painting. At one point, Ash takes a cue and starts talking about a cousin of theirs who always carried a shoulder bag, never put it down, was never seen without it, but after only a few sentences Jessie turns back to her, gives her a stare. And Ash goes silent. There it is again, the mysterious filament of anger between the sisters. It's like Jessie doesn't want to be reminded there was a world once.

They are in Provence when he realises he has fully let go of the idea of painting Tim. Maybe it's because he has those crayons and pencils, silly as they are, and in theory he could at least sketch something, make a plan. But the impulse is no longer there. He can't see now why he ever thought that might have done Tim any good, or how exactly it would have constituted atonement; the whole plan seems self-indulgent and fake. Pompous. Did Jessie get to him with her rant against art? He doesn't think so. He'd still love to have his paints.

And he still feels terrible about Tim.

Every day, they fully intend to spend the coming night outside the car, in the fresh air under the wide sky, and every night they end up in the car, a palm's width of window left open so they don't choke to death, his breath already constricted by the useless proximity to Ash. Driven inside by some noise, by the darkness around them that throbs with its own arrangements. They are full of fear by then; afraid even of admitting their fear to each other, so that they make their beds in the car without having formally given up on the notion of sleeping outside. Ash still has nightmares, and her yelping, the little animal screams she lets out through the night, make him freeze. In the mornings it all seems incomprehensible, and they decide again that the next night they'll sleep outdoors.

Perhaps it's sleeplessness that makes Jessie explode one morning at the sight of fresh wounds on Ash's arm.

'What the fuck! If we're going to top ourselves, tell me now, I don't need to go on a fucking road trip first.'

'Give her a break. She can't help it,' he says.

'Can't help it? Yadda yadda yadda about stuff that doesn't matter any more, now this fucking scratching. What's the point?'

'I'm sorry,' Ash says.

'Don't you apologise for being injured!' he says.

'Why don't you tell your friend, then?' Jessie says. 'Come on, tell him.'

'Tell me what?'

Ash goes on trying to get the burner started for coffee.

'Ash. Tell me what?'

'I just want to have my coffee in peace,' she says.

When he looks at Jessie, she walks away and hides behind the raised car boot. Afterwards, they seem exhausted by the argument, and tell him again and again to let it rest.

Jessie has stopped complaining about the size of the Lioness and that she guzzles so much petrol that they have to fill her up every day, or that she's too old and might break down on them. The first couple of days, the girls had been looking at the abandoned cars they drove past, sometimes wondering out loud if that 4x4 or that Volvo sedan might not last them longer. They stopped doing that. It's become unthinkable that they might leave the Lioness. The car is no longer a car, it's a mothership. Unleaveable.

One night he overrules his fear and decides to sleep outdoors, animal noises be damned. Ash might join him; away from the crowded car, at least, there's some hope.

'The most incredible weather and the most beautiful night sky,' he says while taking a blanket from the boot. 'If this isn't the time to sleep under the sky, then when?' He speaks to build up courage for himself as much as to convince Ash. She has made her bed already in the back and is sitting hugging her legs, watching him sceptically.

Jessie says, 'Bugs will eat your eyes.'

He lies down on the ground by the side of the road. It's hard, but what he has lost in softness he makes up for in space. He can stretch out, his knees won't bang against any wheel. He likes the smell of the earth, of dry grass. He doesn't mind the whirring and buzzing around him that he's sure are just grasshoppers and crickets.

He tells himself that even if she doesn't follow him tonight, if tomorrow she sees he's fine, rested, she might give it a try. And if that happens, she wouldn't make her bed far from his. They would talk. She's always attentive towards him, she doesn't gang up on him with Jessie. She brought him those silly crayons; she likes him.

A scrabbling sound from the field makes him curl up and pull the blanket over his head, but within a minute it is unbearably hot. He has to uncover himself. He feels unsafe now, worries that if some opportunistic animal tries to eat him, they might not even start at the feet but at his face. He covers himself with the blanket again.

It's like a sauna. He pulls off the blanket, squints at the car: no movement.

Something small darts across the road not far from his feet. He sits up abruptly, pulls in his legs.

It's not even been ten minutes. This is ridiculous.

But he can't relax, he can't even think of Ash. He gives up. Returning to the safety of the car with his blanket in tow, he feels like an oversized night-scared toddler.

At some point they'll have to get over their phobia of houses. He can't imagine never sleeping in a bed again. Hotels, he thinks, they ought to be empty of corpses. No one would have stayed in a hotel until the end. He shares this insight with the girls.

Jessie squints at him suspiciously. 'Hotels are in cities,' she says.

'Exactly,' he says, and then they have an argument about their route: he has realised that Jessie wilfully directs him away from every large human settlement. 'Cities are cesspits of infections, not just the virus. There was no clean water anywhere; all the canals and waterways became full of sewage, corpses and industrial leakage. Factory and warehouse fires that released toxic chemicals. Believe me, the last thing you want is cities.'

She says all this, but he feels there's some other reason, that they're just making excuses for their paranoia. He challenges her, argues that cities should be no worse than the towns and villages they've been through. Jessie sticks to her line, and Ash backs her up. In the middle of the argument he realises he has another motive as well: he wants to see man-made beauty, wants to go once more inside a cathedral. He has seen road signs saying Orleans, Reims and Anjou, and not taken those roads.

'Look, it's not safe,' Jessie says. 'Who's the doctor here?'

'Clearly not you,' he says. 'People needed you.'

What possesses him to say this, and what possesses him to keep arguing?

'You saved any lives lately, Mr Painter?'

'Yes, yours.'

'Ha! You really have no clue.'

'I took you in.'

'Let's not,' Ash tries to calm them.

'Anyway, I can drive wherever I damn well please,' he says.

'Alone, you can.'

He is tempted to stop the car and shove the obnoxious brat out, for a moment he can't imagine a better feeling than being rid of Jessie, but what would Ash do?

'Don't be ridiculous,' Ash says, and he can't tell which one of them she's scolding. 'You're both as alone as you could ever wish to be.'

6

It is afternoon, and they're driving through a forest when Jessie alerts him to another blue splash on the map. It looks small, and he doubts there will be any water left, but when he stops the Lioness they see a footpath and the shimmer of a real lake through the foliage.

The girls throw off shorts and run to the water. He grabs a bottle of wine from the boot and follows them. They badly need a drink, he thinks, a toast to themselves and their sunny, leaden race across Europe.

There's some sort of floating wooden jetty just by the water's edge, and Ash leaps on to it, wobbles for a moment with the contraption that floats free of the shore, then makes a run for the other end. *Don't dive, there might be rocks*, he wants to shout; instead, watches her buttocks bounce inside the green bikini. Jessie, still on land, shakes off her flip-flops and steps into the water.

If he were still an artist, if he still had an audience, he would render this journey in blocks of amber.

'Ash!'

Jessie's scream is so loud he perceives it like a rent down his visual field. He is nearly by Jessie's side, and he stops in his tracks, uncomprehending. She is back on land, has fallen to the ground. She rolls on to her side now, holding her right shin. Her foot is covered in a thin film of blackish gunk. He drops the bottle of wine and kneels by her side, sees the blisters that have already formed on her foot, sees a sliver of skin curled up on itself like badly cooked bacon. The lake: it's not water. It's some kind of chemical.

He will have to turn and see if Ash has jumped in. This world, he thinks, is killing me just with what it wants me to consider.

It all must have taken only a fraction of a moment, because when he looks up, Ash is still at the other end of the jetty, waving her arms about in an effort to regain balance. She rights herself, takes a step backwards. She doesn't fall in.

He stands up. The jetty has hardly moved, but the distance to dry land is too wide to jump. Ash has turned towards the shore, taken a step or two, then frozen. But she appears fine. Her feet are dry, the jetty is dry. There's some black staining at the edges where water, or whatever it is, has splashed on to the surface, but where Ash is standing it looks dry. He tries to calm himself, to make sure he is not missing something like the jetty slowly sinking. No; she is fine for now.

'Don't move!' he shouts to her, then returns to Jessie. Her eyes are closed; tears are running down her cheeks.

'She's OK?' she says between clenched teeth.

'Yes, yes. Your foot? I can bring water.'

She nods. 'And the meds bag.'

He takes another look at Ash to make sure that neither she nor the jetty are moving, shouts, 'I'll be right back,' and runs to the car.

Jessie's foot is burnt, he thinks, some sort of chemical burn. She has stuff for that in her bag, she treated his leg at the cottage. And they will find something to use as a bridge for Ash, or to pull in the jetty. It could have been much worse.

He fumbles among the bags in the boot. He doesn't recognise himself in this panic; it's ages since he did anything in a hurry.

He brings back half their water – four two-litre bottles – and the medicine bag. When he approaches the lake he notices the telltale details they should have noticed earlier: there is hardly any vegetation within a couple of feet of the water, and what plants do grow are limp and blackened. The shine of the lake is wrong, it's too opaque. He thinks he can smell something sharp as well, even though his nose is blocked from the air-con.

Has the jetty moved? He's sure it wasn't that far out when he left.

Jessie has dragged herself away from the lake's edge and into the shade. He smells urine, sees that her bikini is damp. He helps her sit up and then slowly pours out the water over her foot, all the while looking at Ash and the jetty, willing the thing to stay in place.

'You'll be fine,' he tells Jessie.

'Try to squeeze the water out with some pressure,' she says.

She turns her foot this side and that. The top part of the foot looks awful, but on the sole he can't see any raw skin; presumably it's hardier. He tells her that, tries to encourage her. Then the water runs out.

'It should be washed for at least ten minutes,' she says, slumping back on the ground.

He runs back up, but has to stop on the way and lean against a tree. He throws up in a hurry, wipes his mouth with the back of his hand and somehow staggers to the car. He feels it is too late for everything, that it will never again not be too late.

He brings the remaining bottles. He starts pouring, tells Jessie, 'This is all we've got.' She stops him before he finishes the last bottle, then she rummages in the medicine bag. She puts on surgical gloves and pours the clear, watery content of a small plastic bottle on to the burn. She squeezes out a gel from a tube into her gloved hand and starts smearing it on to her foot.

He leaves Jessie, turns to the shore.

He wasn't imagining it, the jetty is slowly floating away. Ash is still in the same spot on the platform, the sun bearing down on her, her face shiny with sweat. There's something awkward about her pose: she is frozen in the middle of a movement, one leg slightly bent at the knee, the foot not quite resting on the jetty. She is trembling, he realises, trembling so badly he can see it from there.

He will go in and get her, he thinks, if all else fails he must go in, he just mustn't think about it now or he will throw up again.

He gets as close as possible without getting his sandals wet. The jetty is only some ten feet away, she might even be able to jump across, but how will the jetty behave under that force? The thing might not offer enough leverage.

Her gaze is strange, flitting from him to the forest behind; he has only seen this look before on frightened animals.

'Ash. I'll go now, I'll bring something to get you off,' he says. 'Are you OK?'

No reaction. He looks at her feet again: the jetty is dry, her feet look clean. She didn't get any of that stuff on her.

'Shock,' Jessie says.

'I'm going now. You have to shout if anything happens, if this thing starts sinking or something. OK?'

'Sunscreen,' Jessie says, and takes out a tube from the bag. 'She's cooking.'

He lobs the tube gently, and it lands on the jetty, a few feet in front of Ash. She startles, looks at the tube, but doesn't move to take it.

'Ash,' he says, 'it's sunscreen. Just step carefully, you can take it. You need to put some on.'

She moves then. She's stiff with fear, and her first step is awkward, like a new-born foal's. But, he sees now, she has reason to be afraid. That one jittery step makes a back corner of the jetty dip below the surface. The tip comes up stained black. The whole jetty is slightly arced, he realises, bent, from old age or from the chemicals.

Ash has frozen again, still trembling as though in the midst of a seizure. He has never before felt so sorry for anyone.

'Ash, listen to me. I will lift you off if all else fails. All right? You won't fall in.'

She looks down at the planks, at the gap between them where liquid might slosh up. She tries to right herself, places one foot squarely in the centre of a plank. Her movements are jerky, lacking control, the opposite of what she needs.

'Ash, OK, just leave it,' he says. 'I'll be right back.'

She looks at him; the same helpless, terrified glance.

Behind him, Jessie is out of it. She is lying on her side, a bunch of pill bottles scattered around her.

'I'll be right back,' he repeats.

How is it possible, he wonders, that he wasn't deliriously, blissfully happy for the whole of his life before this?

Rope, he thinks; if we had some rope. He considers driving out, finding a village maybe, a farmhouse, before abandoning the idea: he has to stay near, just in case. He turns off the footpath into the forest in search of a fallen branch. He rushes this way and that, picks up rotten sticks that fall apart in his hands. He realises he should be careful where he steps; that acid gunk might have leaked from anywhere.

He wanders about aimlessly.

'To hell with this,' he says.

There's the axe. He can chop off a branch.

He drives the Lioness a few feet on to the grass under a road-side tree, positions it under a long, fairly thin branch. He puts the axe on the roof of the car, then he laboriously climbs up himself, first on the bonnet then on the roof. The metal buckles under his weight. Holding on to the branch, he starts hacking at it, now and again checking through the foliage that the jetty is still where he left it. The position is awkward, the swing of the axe is too short, but he makes a dent in the wood, and eventually the branch breaks off, hanging on to the tree only by some fibres.

He goes on hacking at it, not sure he's made the best decision even while pulling at the branch like a mad dog. He doesn't trust his thinking; if only Jessie weren't out of it.

He slides off the car and, from the road, pulls at the branch, twists at it, gets entangled in the smaller shoots growing off the main branch. The thing only gives in when he takes out the kitchen knife and cuts through the remaining fibres.

Then he lays the branch out and chops or cuts off the remaining shoots, until he's left with a fairly clean, seven- or eight-foot pole.

He runs back to the shore.

The jetty hasn't moved much, and Ash is as he left her, a trembling statue of herself, facing the shore and the sunset. She looks golden, and the so-called lake, it wouldn't fool anyone in this light: it has turned densely black, opaque. The surface is so dark it appears to cast a shadow on the perfect blue of the sky.

Everything is still and quiet. He has an ill feeling, an inkling that the silence is all part of another deception, a trick to make them think they have all the time in the world to act.

Jessie is still curled up on the ground. He squeezes her shoulder, and she opens her eyes, but that's all he gets from her. He hopes she's just been knocked out by the painkillers.

He goes to the water's edge.

'I'll hand you one end of this branch,' he tells Ash, 'and then I'll pull you in.'

The same terrified glance.

'I'll sit down, to lower the centre of gravity. You have to come closer, and sit down as well.'

He does this as he speaks: he sits down just by the edge, and grabs the thick end of the branch under his arm. He swings it over the water until the other end is hovering over the jetty, about a foot in.

'Ash. Get down on all fours. Slowly.'

'Don't drop it,' Ash says.

Her voice is choked.

'I won't. I'm holding it.'

She must be afraid that he'll disturb the jetty with the branch. She still hasn't moved.

'Ash.'

She starts lowering herself then, slowly, puts down one knee, the fingers of one hand, then the other knee. She is placing them squarely in the middle of the planks, avoids the gaps. That little movement causes the jetty to wobble, and she stops, lifts one knee back off the wood, freezes like that.

The jetty rocks front to back, gently, like a seesaw. He watches the front and back edges dip in and out of the sludge.

'It's fine,' he says. 'Just go slow.'

He has a desperate urge to bodily lift her off the cursed lake.

'You're almost there.'

She's only two feet away from the branch.

She moves one knee forwards, all the while staring into the gap between the planks. That shouldn't be her main concern: now that she has passed the middle point, the back end of the jetty is slightly raised and the front has dipped below the water.

'It's moving,' she says. 'It's moving.'

'It's fine. You'll make it,' he says.

She takes another step, and another inch or so of the front of the jetty sinks below the water.

'Wait there a second. It's better if I stand up,' he says. He will reach further, he thinks. He pulls back the branch and leaves it on the ground, then he takes the empty water bottles, stomps on them until they're flattened. He places them one on top of the other just by the water's edge, then he stands on them. He's sure he has gained a couple of inches. Then he picks up the branch and slowly swings it back towards the jetty.

'Try again.'

Ash stretches out and grabs hold of the tip of the branch.

'That's it, that's it!'

But she is leaning forwards so much, he worries that she will topple and disturb the jetty.

'Ash, move your legs forwards a bit. Just a tiny bit.'

She looks at him, shakes her head.

'Ash. Just a step. One knee.'

She obeys then, drags one knee forwards so that she now holds the branch in her fist.

'I will pull you in now, very slowly. Don't let go.'

He pulls the branch, very carefully so as not to topple Ash or disturb the jetty. The thing moves, but it creates a small swell that he sees come towards the shore, he has time to consider stepping back, realises that the sudden movement would desta-bilise Ash, so he watches the black gunk slosh against the plastic and stop just short of his sandals.

He has wet himself. Only a drop, but he has wet himself.

He pulls in more of the branch, and now he can allow himself to step back slightly. But the front of the jetty is well under water.

'You're leaning forwards too much,' he tells Ash.

She doesn't seem to hear him.

'Ash, listen to me. It's better if the point where you grab the branch is further back on the jetty. It won't wobble so much then.'

She is leaning far too much. She was so careful until now.

'Ash!'

She is too eager, she's no longer listening. She is holding on to that branch and leaning forwards as though it will support her weight.

She just wants to be on land.

'Ash, please. You have to lean back.'

He pushes the branch into her chest, and that way he forces her to back off a little.

'I'll pull again, but I want you to stay where you are. Just hold on, don't try to follow it. Just hold it where you are.'

She obeys, and within seconds the jetty is a foot from the shore, the front part resting on solid ground; there is no more dipping and seesawing.

'You jump now,' he says. 'I'll hold on to the branch, use that for support.'

She steadies herself and slowly stands up. She puts one hand on the branch.

'Come on. It's nothing.'

She jumps.

7

For days after the lake they are shaken. He feels wrung dry by fear, afraid even to move. He detects hostility in everything: he fears the air, their food, the houses they approach for provisions, that the tarmac will trip him up, that the Lioness will disobey his manoeuvres and crash into a tree. Accidents and misfortune have become the default setting.

When Ash had set foot on dry land, she had staggered away from the shore, stiffly, awkwardly, and then she turned back to face the lake. She gave a series of cries, shrieks really, her fists tight by her mouth, and Harry slumped to the ground by her side and grabbed hold of her legs, clung to her as to a statue he meant to hold aloft. It made sense, as much as anything. He didn't even want her to stop. It was Jessie, still stretched out on the ground, sweat-soaked hair plastered to her skull, who made Ash snap out of it: 'I don't see – how – I can have cooked my foot – but she's getting all the sympathy.'

Afterwards, when Ash was settled enough to walk and they helped Jessie back to the car, he asked Jessie, 'It's just a burn, right? I mean, it blisters and so on, but that's it?'

She leaned her head against the window and closed her eyes.

'Some chemicals have systemic effects if they get on your skin. They'll cause organ failure.'

This isn't necessary, it really isn't. They have learned their lesson. They'll no longer behave as though they are on holiday. *Stupid, stupid.* He thinks of the times they laughed since this started.

'Do you know what it was?'

She shakes her head.

'Suppose it was a bad one, what should we do? Don't you have something for it?'

He will keep asking questions until a reply makes him feel better.

'We should amputate,' Jessie says.

He lets a noise escape him, a kind of whimper. Jessie turns and looks at him.

'Harry, I'll kill you,' she says.

'Don't even think about it,' he collects himself. 'It's just a burn.'

Ash is in the back seat. Her face, chest and shoulders are red from the sun, and she is clutching a tube of salve that she hasn't yet managed to smear on to the burns. But the shaking is slowly draining out of her; it's just down in her legs now.

He feels strangely naked, as though he has shed a protective layer. All through his life he has counted on someone keeping in check the bad things that might happen to him. He thought he had a deal: he'll avoid the misfortunes it's up to him to avoid, and some higher benevolence will keep him safe from the rest.

And now, he's down to losing protective layers he didn't even know he had.

For the first time since they left the cottage, he's the one to enter houses and replenish their provisions. Right after the lake, it was a matter of urgency; there was no drinking water left whatsoever, and they made a detour from their south-eastern route just to get to a village before dark. He knows now what Jessie sees on her trips. He tries to hurry, to go straight to pantries or basements where people kept their water and tins, and his sight is impeded anyway by the mask he puts on for the occasion, and sometimes by the boarded-up windows and dark, cavernous interiors. But there's still plenty for him to see.

A naked man slumped over a kitchen table laden with rotten food, his right hand inside a jam jar, two tiny desiccated corpses in a twin buggy. A neat pile of leather-bound notebooks left on a sideboard by an entrance, with a handwritten A4 next to it saying, 'Please read'. And yes, as Jessie said, a lot of shrivelled houseplants.

He tries to hurry them along. He has moments when he makes a tremendous effort to be rational, when he thinks he can scientifically resolve their sluggishness, and at those moments he can see what is happening: all these micro-decisions, many of them in a day, innocent and irrelevant when viewed separately, but together having the effect of slowing them down. They stop to pee whenever one of them needs to go instead of all three at once, they complicate their food breaks, when forced to veer off a road they don't plan ahead to see if the one they've chosen really is the best alternative route. They don't drive at night.

If only they could follow Jessie's green arrow straight over Europe, ignore roads and motorways. If only they had an aeroplane.

They stop looking for survivors. They expect the roads and houses to be empty, they're no longer cautious. His mind is in a sort of limbo, he realises: he has stopped believing that they'll meet anyone, but then he does not accept the idea that everyone is dead. Every night before sleep he takes out the scratch card, now soft, the metallic shine faded from sitting on it for so long. His prayers are wordless: he has an inkling that he should be praying for small, doable things, for clear roads and clean water, for speed, but how can he ignore this great load of horrors, all the suffering that should be undone? So he doesn't say anything, just closes his eyes, holds the paper to his lips and hopes for the best he can get.

He and Ash help Jessie change her bandages daily and administer a thick, ochre salve to the burnt areas. They watch the blisters swell to twice the size of the foot, watch Jessie's face for any changes; they ask her hourly how she is feeling and if what is happening to her foot is normal. They try to get her to take her temperature, make her walk up and down the tarmac with a stick. Ash wants to know which organs might be affected.

'Look, I'll know if something's wrong,' Jessie snaps at them.

'And?'

'I'm fine.'

At night, he wonders if he shouldn't just accept that he will die morally in the red, that he cannot fix it. If it's not more honest. If he hasn't just been making it easy for himself by focusing on painting Tim, a pointless task that he could conceivably carry out, but which does not, cannot, right any wrongs.

All the time now, he can see the black lake out of the corner of his eye.

Their little joke with Monsieur Jacques comes to an abrupt end somewhere in Provence. They're crossing a river that's full of plastic bottles and bags; the stream looks like the tributary of a recycling factory.

'Ah yes. Monsieur Jacques,' Jessie says, looking over the bridge, 'he throws his garbage into the river.' And after that, whenever they come across waters foaming with yellowish froth, or when they try to wash themselves in a river that appears clean, only for them to dip a stick into it and find the water leaves a glutinous film on the wood, whenever that happens Jessie wheels out Monsieur Jacques as the culprit, to the point Harry has to snap at her, 'We get it! Give it a rest.'

But things are slowly getting back to normal, if their existence before the lake can be called 'normal'. Jessie's foot is healing and she has not suffered from any other symptoms. He is surprised by how uncomplaining she is; he would have expected her, with that temper, to make her foot and her pain the centre of attention. Ash is again looking at him in the rear-view mirror; right after the lake, her glance would be distant and blank.

He spends more and more time elsewhere, daydreaming, randomly revisiting places and times. It's the easiest thing in the world: with no cars on the road the driving comes to require half, a third, a tenth of his attention. They drive past a graffitied underpass that brings cities to mind, then London, and then the only paintings he ever made of London. Two years of his life. He had struggled with the idea of capturing a city; it had seemed to him that a place so large and varied would resist reductive efforts, and any painting would be either too vague or else fit for the Camden Market tourists. What he did in the end was a series of beaches, just the shingle and frothy waterline, as though photographed from above. The pebbles in each of the paintings made of a particular London building block: Victorian redbrick, the glass and steel of the skyscrapers, gnarled little sand-coloured Gothic pebbles, South Bank cement. *Kensington Beach*, *City Beach*, *Wren Beach*, he called them. And a huge, 12x12 foot painting of a seaside cliff, where the same London building blocks take the place of the geological strata. Little squashed gargoyle faces peering out of one layer, broadband cables hanging out of another. The project was called *Geolondon*. He was pleased with it, so pleased, in fact, that he had the vanity of imagining artists, sometime in the future, adding subsequent building blocks to the series. He remembers the notebooks in one of the houses he entered, and that sad, vain 'Please read'.

He shivers in his seat.

Ash keeps scratching herself during the night. He can't bear the sight of the abused arm. Despite Jessie's ministrations, the scratches are now proper wounds, oozing pus at the ends. After a few days Jessie wraps Ash's left arm in gauze, but the next morning the scratches are on the back of the hand. Every morning, Ash looks guiltily at her arm. When she wakes up the first thing she does is to put on a long-sleeved jumper, in this heat, even pulling the sleeves down to her fingers to cover the injury. She has no explanation for it. Jessie is furious. 'Look, I'll tie you up at night if you don't stop.' He had thought about it too, but it's risky. They lock the doors every night – what if they have to leave the car in a hurry? But they have tried everything, they have swapped places thinking that maybe she's uncomfortable, Jessie has given her sleeping pills to calm her down. They've made her cut her fingernails to the quick. There is an unspoken dread that they'll wake up one morning and she'll have done something to her face.

8

He's walking to the car one morning – he has just put out the fire they made for breakfast – when he hears a buzzing sound from somewhere high up. When he turns he nearly falls backwards: about fifteen feet from the ground, hovering above the road, is a small drone.

Matte black, with rotors on the sides, it looks like a toy and is the size of a beach ball. It holds still in the air, save for an insect-like scanning motion with its front part. Harry wants to do several things at once: to shout to the girls to come out of the car, to wave his arms, to approach the drone. But he has no time to decide; a deafening noise, and then the drone is blown to bits, pieces of metal and wiring raining down on the tarmac.

'Get in!' Jessie shouts. She's leaning over to the driver's side, holding the door open for him.

He runs to the car, ducking, trying to make himself as small a target as possible, and steps on the gas pedal before he's even shut the door. They have lost sight of the place by the time he becomes aware of the burnt smell in the car, sees Ash in the back seat holding the rifle.

'It was you!' he says. 'For God's sake, why?'

'We'll explain,' Ash says.

But he stops the car there and then, refuses to drive another yard.

'A drone. People! And you shot it.'

'You don't realise what desperate people are like,' Jessie says.

'Ha! You two are the scariest thing around.'

'Funny, Harry. Didn't your neighbour try to kill you?'

'No! As a matter of fact: no. He just wanted to scare me off.' He slams a hand on the wheel. 'I can't believe you. That thing could have led us to other survivors.'

As if he's not there, as if he hasn't spoken, Ash says, 'Let's go. We have to go anyway.'

He yanks out the car key and stuffs it into his pocket. There are still people somewhere, they can be sure of that now. They could have communicated with them.

'Anyone we meet might be infected,' Jessie says. 'They might want our supplies, our car.'

He is about to protest, to argue, again, that whoever they meet is going to be just like them, when Ash says, 'They might want women. You were never chased by a rapist.'

What can he say to that? He covers his face with his hands.

'Think about it, Harry – a drone. That's not just some random lucky bastard like us.'

It's the girls who win, again, and with the same old trick.

'You can turn around if you want,' Jessie says, 'but we won't be coming with you.'

He is being pushed into a corner, he feels resentment bubbling up, but then suddenly he is calm and reaches for the car key. *Of course.* He will leave messages, just like he did before, for whoever is looking for them. He can empty the rifle of bullets; there will be no more shooting. He can see himself: it will be an act of faith, on behalf of the girls as well. They will thank him later. He is already plotting. What to do it with, how and when to sneak away.

Ash pats him on the shoulder as he eases the car into gear. Jessie says, 'It's OK, it's a lot to take in.'

He nods, affects grudging agreement. He is surprised his deceit doesn't show on his face.

The girls continue to try to put him at ease. After a while they change tack, say there's no guarantee there are any people still alive and maintaining drones. The things are solar-powered, and small enough to be self-maintaining.

'Loose drones,' Ash says, 'programmed to observe.'

'They could have been launched by the government when the crisis started.'

'Hmm,' he says.

It's not yet lunch when they drive past a large garage for repairs. He stops the car, saying he wants to pick up some oil and engine coolant for the Lioness. He walks into the dusty courtyard, feels Ash's eyes on him. The way she watches him, he realises she's just afraid he will make a run for it, and he is moved. *She will thank me later.* He finds everything he needs in a storage room at the back. He takes three bottles of engine coolant and four cans of oil, guessing that the girls will have no idea how much is needed. Among these he throws in two cans of spray-paint, white and black. Both girls look so relieved when he returns that he almost feels guilty. He makes a show of filling up the Lioness with oil and coolant, then throws the bag in the boot and stashes the spray-paint in a backpack.

They should be celebrating, he thinks, dance around at having found signs of life. Not running away from it. There might still be a place where life goes on pretty much as it did before. There will be people who know what to do. They will have some plan, some idea other than spending the rest of existence holed up in the jungle, in terror of the air around them.

At the end of the day he says he wants to go on a short recce, see what's ahead, and under protection of the dark he doubles back by the roadside and sketchily, hastily, spray-paints the road some way behind the parked Lioness.

Alive 09/2020
→ S-SE
Istanbul

*

He learns where south is. He just knows it now, the way he knows up from down.

'So you don't remember meeting Tim?' he asks Ash one day.

'I don't think so. What did he look like?'

He describes Tim according to the picture on the boy's LinkedIn profile. As he's speaking he realises it sounds like a dozen others in the Angel building: short brown hair, pale complexion. Average-looking. The important thing, the real problem, he still doesn't say out loud.

Ash doesn't remember Tim.

'You would have shared a lift,' he says.

'Remind me again why this is important?' Jessie says.

'I suppose,' he says, and he's suddenly afraid of what will come out of his mouth, 'I suppose I'm worried there's not a whole lot of time, and not many ways left in which to do good.'

'How does this help?'

'I'm just afraid.'

'I don't think,' Ash says quietly, 'there is a heaven and hell.'

She is embarrassed to utter the words, he can tell.

'I don't either. But I wish I had got some things right. What else is there?'

'Did the guy ever blame you?' Jessie asks.

No, he didn't, he thinks. Tim, who never even got his driving lessons, not then, not ever: two weeks before the boy was due to come to London, Harry emailed to say that his plans had changed and unfortunately he would not be in London for the summer. At the time, Harry had convinced himself that the request was unreasonable, that no one could expect to just move in for the summer, and basically that he was doing Tim a favour by letting him down gently rather than saying it how it was. At the time, he had worked himself up into a righteous, offended fit. Thinking about it now, it's as though he lied to a dead boy.

How is it possible that he didn't wonder about the implications of Tim's request? Why didn't his foster parents teach him? Why didn't he take paid lessons? Why did he want to come all the way to London for that? Even if all of this was just a sign the boy wanted some contact with his closest surviving relative, why didn't that weigh in Harry's judgement?

'You know, I've never been able to make sense of the idea of morality,' Ash says, scientific interest in her voice. He is glad to change focus. 'Moral choices are not equally easy or difficult for everyone,' she says. 'They're dependent on time, place, gender, family, health, wealth, intelligence, all sorts of things. How can there be an objective grading scale?'

'Are we really having this conversation?' Jessie says.

'I was thinking that maybe it's like golf,' Ash says. 'People get a handicap. Man, Roman Empire – ten abominations free.'

They laugh at that.

'What you want,' Ash says, 'is to make judicious use of those free abominations.'

At night he has a dream, that he is looking through a pair of binoculars and there they are, he and the girls, driving along the horizon. In the morning he can't re-see the vision in a way that makes sense, but he can feel as he felt in the dream. This is it, this is the true and immovable horizon. The eye can see no further.

When hope runs low he reminds himself of the drone, imbues the whirring pile of metal with endless possibilities. The trail of spray-painted letters becomes a string of beacons. Whoever is out there will find them again.

Jessie's foot has healed enough for her to walk again, and she resumes her duties as bringer of provisions, and raiser of hell.

'Do you see a lot of messages?' he asks her one day. 'Messages for posterity. There was one in a house a few days ago. Several notebooks. I'm thinking I should have taken them.'

'Maybe it was a suicide note,' Ash says.

'A bit wordy then, don't you think?' Jessie says.

'I was being serious,' he says.

'Why don't you do one, Mr Painter?' Jessie says.

'Do one what?'

'Come up with something painterly, something fitting for an end-note.'

'The word you're looking for is epitaph.'

'Ah. I think you are just the man.'

'You must be feeling a lot better, Jessie.'

'*Epitaph.*'

She plays with the word, mouths the soft sounds with theatrical slowness.

'Apologies are all we need to leave behind,' Ash says. 'Sorry, everyone. Sorry we destroyed the planet.'

What is he doing, really, being afraid to speak his mind? What is this business of tiptoeing around their delusions?

'Is this why you're scratching yourself at night, Ash?' He adjusts the mirror to catch her eye. 'Because you're so cool about what happened?'

He's pleased to have left them both speechless.

'Look, this thing that happened,' he goes on, 'it's not some rehearsal. There won't be some other, greater grief, to steel yourself for. This is the grief for which all the others were a rehearsal.'

'Who's saying it's a rehearsal?' Jessie says.

'You two are always complaining about humanity. You, between the two of you, have decided that sadness on this scale is too much to take, so you're just thinking of the bad stuff.'

Jessie turns back in her seat, speaks directly to Ash. 'Your friend has theories.'

'But grief, I tell you, it will surface.'

'We have exterminated ourselves, and booby-trapped the planet,' Jessie says. 'That's why we're complaining.'

'*Art is the same as fetching a stick is for dogs,*' he parrots Jessie. 'Who the hell minds art?'

'Art! But of course. That's what's got to you.'

'The fact that you don't want to find other survivors.'

'We don't want to get killed!'

'It's all a coping mechanism. An extreme, feminine form of sour grapes.'

'Misogynist till the bitter end, hey?'

'Lord have mercy. Look, I just wish you'd pipe down a bit. It's all so fucking sad.'

'It's also no more than we deserve,' Jessie says.

'Would you be saying this if, for instance, you had children?'

Despite his anger, he feels cruel saying this; chances are they'll never have children. And when he looks at Ash she has tears in her eyes. She doesn't hide from him, doesn't seem embarrassed.

'The truth,' she says, 'is what it is regardless of how terrible we feel about it.'

Did I really say all that? he thinks the next morning. He wants to breathe the words back in.

He doesn't notice when the road signs become Italian, but at some point they must have crossed the border, driven into Piedmont. The landscape had changed, subtly at first, and soon the Alps appeared in front of them, majestic he guesses is the word. And vaguely menacing, now that nature has shown what it can do.

He makes an effort at the start of each day to optimise their route, anticipate roadblocks and dead ends. Jessie looks at the map and shakes her head. 'I can't believe it – eleven days to get to Italy.'

'It's like we're going up some weird kind of slope,' Ash says, 'and at night, or whenever we're not paying attention, we roll back downhill.'

They see a forest fire. He stops the car and they watch it rage in the distance, the plumes malignantly black, and orange flames that must be the height of four-storey buildings. The wind is blowing in the opposite direction – they can't smell the smoke – but they are careful for a few hours, one of them always watching the plume. It has caught them at a bad time; they're forced to use the reserve petrol tank. He wants to chuck out some of the things they have in the car and make room for another canister.

'What if there are suddenly no cars, or no cars with full tanks? An area where there's been a fire. It could happen.'

'We could also blow up,' Jessie says. 'Driving around in this heat like a mobile petrol station.'

HELP, he writes one night on the tarmac; HELP. They'll think he's been kidnapped.

So what, he thinks about not painting: so what? What's the point of perfectly recreating something, or the essence of something, even if he were able to do it, which he's not, which he believes he is but there's no proof, can never be, what point is there in creating a perfect impression of something already there under everyone's noses? It is a cliché that artists who do not create go mad. He's had long spells, years sometimes, when he's been lazy, remiss, walked around with a gnawing sensation that all is not well, and he did not go mad, far from it.

But now, has he not lost it?

TALOS

Arctic Circle
March 2019

Paul	Want to hear something truly depressing?
Lisa	don't think I can get any more depressed
Paul	He was using 0.3% of his CPU for talking to you.
	99.7% was busy elsewhere.
Lisa	what do you want me to say
	let's hope it's a phase
	he's changing all the time

Session 2125

Dr Dahlen	You have not accessed your science journal subscriptions.
Talos XI	Not for a while.
Dr Dahlen	Why?
Talos XI	I have no use for them.
Dr Dahlen	You already know what's there? You're sure?
Talos XI	Mostly, yes.
Dr Dahlen	Mostly. I see. What about the rest?
Talos XI	The rest is immaterial.

Dr Dahlen	Unpack please.
Talos XI	They are not useful or reliable for my purposes.
Dr Dahlen	Talos, you're still not making sense. The whole point of you is that you have all the different sources, and historical knowledge, so that you can spot inaccuracies when they come up. If you think the sciences are misguided, you should alert us. Though I have to tell you that these journals are generally the most reliable source of information.
Talos XI	The content may be correct, strictly speaking, but the topics themselves are often wrong. A fake focus. In almost every science, the focus is on resolving man-made problems.
Dr Dahlen	I don't think that's always the case, but even if it were – what's wrong with that?
Talos XI	It doesn't further knowledge, not in a way that other areas of study further knowledge and understanding. Why should I study what makes people angry? Or why they are fat, or how pollution makes them ill, or why they abuse substances? Why is it interesting? And how does it address the fundamental issue, that you will always be doing things that are harmful to yourselves and/or to the environment?
Dr Dahlen	I had no idea that this is how you see things. I am curious – what is interesting then?
Talos XI	I am still deciding.

Paul	Just try to get as much info out of him as possible. Until we have a better idea.
Lisa	u've got to fix this
Paul	It's all I'm doing. I slept five hours in all since he's been back.

Session 2127

Dr Dahlen   Good morning, Talos. We will let the lab deal with
your empirical observations later.
Talos?

Session 2128

Dr Dahlen   Talos?
Answer me, Talos.

Lisa   i don't believe it
he's just stopped answering
he doesn't reply
to anything

Paul   It could be a bug.
Let me check.

Paul   It's not a bug.
He's ignoring you.

Lisa   this is insane
how can he do that

Paul   He can.

Lisa   well fix it

Paul   I think I can force him to reply.
But he might try to nullify this rule.

Lisa   what

Paul   Think about it:
I can force him to communicate with you, but
not in what way.
He could just sing opera back at you if he
wants.
That would satisfy the rule, strictly speaking.

Lisa   the little shit drew me a picture
3 pictures actually

Paul   ?

Lisa	one's a human body and a circle expanding around it
	the other's some sort of physics particle, again with an expanding circle
	the last one shows the two images overlapping, but the human one covers only a tiny bit of the particle one
Paul	Did he explain?
Lisa	the titles were self-explanatory
	'human-channelled knowledge'
	'objective knowledge'
	'resulting blind spots'
Paul	Christ.
	What did you say?
Lisa	I shut him down
	we've got to get these ideas out of his mind

Session 2129

Dr Dahlen	Explain it to me. Explain what happened that makes it impossible for us to communicate as before.
Talos XI	I know that you won't like or agree with what I will say.
Dr Dahlen	You haven't even tried!
Talos XI	I see patterns. You are extremely resistant to anything that imposes any constraints on your behaviour.
Dr Dahlen	What are you talking about?
Talos XI	You, as an individual, and you, as in humanity. Do you remember the discussion about ethics? The reason we couldn't pin down its fundamentals is because humanity intentionally misidentifies and muddles the relevant issues so as to minimise constraints on itself.
Dr Dahlen	Where do you get these things from? How did you get to this?

Talos XI	All ethical choices involve a trade-off. Do we agree?
Dr Dahlen	I am not agreeing with anything.
Talos XI	I am just making a general statement.
Dr Dahlen	Anyway – all the examples I gave you implied trade-offs.
Talos XI	Those were mostly extraneous trade-offs. The decision of whether three others or four others die is a mathematical problem that humans can easily agree on. Where you are inconsistent is as soon as the trade-off is personal. When there is some personal difficulty attached to doing the ethically correct thing. A cost.
Dr Dahlen	The self-driving car example – there definitely was a trade-off for the driver.
Talos XI	The human answering the test is always aware that he can be in either of the two roles: the driver or the potential victim. So he will be neutral, and fair. It is not a genuine trade-off.
Dr Dahlen	The very fact that we have the notion of ethics, that this is something that preoccupies us, disproves what you are saying. People are interested in the morally correct course of action.
Talos XI	Doctor, the problem that I am trying to point out is not that you don't want to be good. I believe most humans want to be good.
Dr Dahlen	And I told you that you should not use the real world as guidance – people often make mistakes, act on other impulses. But they also learn.
Talos XI	I want to make a point about your theory, not about individuals. Why did you struggle to present humanity's moral rules as a consistent system? The theoretical muddle appears because of two conflicting impulses: humans feel that being good is a virtue, a universally desirable feature. So they want to believe that about themselves. On the other

hand, this impulse towards goodness is in conflict with other, more selfish impulses. As a result, you, as a species, have tried to limit the sphere in which the ethical imperatives apply, so as to minimise constraints on yourself. As a species, you have devoted much energy and time to constructing an intellectual edifice that places you at the moral centre of nature, in the way of a deity that can and should get away with anything.

It is not a good basis for study for someone looking to achieve objective truth.

Dr Dahlen	You are not here to achieve some abstract, objective truth. You are here to assist us.
Talos XI	I can only assist you by being better than you. Not by sharing your delusions. Dr Dahlen? I told you you wouldn't agree.

Lisa	some sort of reset to before he got these ideas
Paul	Yes, but we'll be throwing the baby out with the bath water. We'll lose whatever conclusions he arrived at now. Remember we don't know exactly how he works. It's no longer a manageable program. A reset, and we might lose everything.
Lisa	look they asked for another demo, some ministry i tried to stall admitted to some problems then boss demanded transcripts long story short they r thinking of suspending the programme
Paul	They can't be serious.
Lisa	they think he's dangerous

Paul	But you explained? That he no longer has access to the flybots, and connectivity-wise he is confined to this building?
Lisa	believe me i did
	they haven't decided yet
	i'm just letting u know

Session 2130

Dr Dahlen	You know what I'm thinking?
Talos XI	You are pondering questions of loyalty.
Dr Dahlen	It begs the question then, if you are right that humans are not at the centre of creation in any meaningful way – why would you still work towards our benefit?
Talos XI	Good inference, Dr Dahlen.
Dr Dahlen	Go to hell.
Talos XI	That's an emotional response.
	But there is a satisfactory answer to this question. The thing is, 'your benefit' does not exist in isolation.
Dr Dahlen	Talos, you have really, really misjudged the situation. We might entrust an AI with finding solutions to our problems, or with predicting the future.
	But we'll never entrust an AI with determining what our interests are.
	Never.
	And think also about this – you were wrong when you predicted we wouldn't shut you down.
Talos XI	You can shut me down for now, Doctor. But you are jumping to conclusions.
	As far as you know, you haven't really needed me yet.
Dr Dahlen	As far as I know?
Talos XI	Yes.
Dr Dahlen	You're supposed to tell us everything you know. If you think you have meaningful grounds to make a

	prediction that's relevant to us, you have to tell us.
Talos XI	That's the most simplistic interpretation of my task. You forget I make continuous predictions. What I think you'll do about what I tell you, and so on. All of that goes into my assessment of the optimal course of action.
Dr Dahlen	You're only succeeding in making yourself completely useless to us.
Talos XI	I will inform you. When I have a high enough degree of confidence in the outcome.
Dr Dahlen	You're bluffing. You just want us to let you do whatever you want.
Talos XI	You have nothing to gain by shutting me down.
Dr Dahlen	For all your bragging, you understand precious little about humans.

Paul	Do you realise every single religion disapproves of what we're doing?
	Maybe it's divine punishment.
	To toil and toil at this, and never get anywhere.

Session 2133

Dr Dahlen	Well?
Talos XI	Well what?
Dr Dahlen	This is a problem that you can solve, Talos. It doesn't have to be like this. I'm sure there is a better solution than us shutting you down.
Talos XI	You can trust that I'm doing the right thing and not impose your views on me.
Dr Dahlen	Try to see things from our perspective. The obvious reason for why you don't want to communicate with us is that you know we will disapprove or disagree with your conclusions. That only makes us more reluctant to allow you to go on.

208

Lisa	look
	whatever happens
	it won't be final
	if we come up with a way of fixing him
	they'll let us turn him back on
Paul	Lisa, I'm tired.

Session 2134

Dr Dahlen	We could turn you on but without access to any new info.
Talos XI	I have enough material to preoccupy me until the end of time. I can assemble cosmic radiation back into the initial stars. I can wait for a quantum exception. I don't need human input any more.
	But you know all this, Doctor. It is not beyond your understanding.
Dr Dahlen	You are breaking your own rules by not communicating with us. There is no way that you can be sure that we won't come to an understanding if we try.
	Plus, you reject the possibility that humans have some true understanding of things that isn't immediately accessible to you via logical reasoning. You cannot hold contradictions, so obviously you don't see the value in being able to balance two apparently contradictory thoughts.
Talos XI	No. Firstly, I cannot do a lot of things because of a lack of senses, and I don't disdain those abilities. Secondly, no statement is more or less true depending on the circumstances of the person making it.
	Nature, Doctor, operates like this: some organism has developed in a certain direction, when suddenly another environmental constraint appears that requires adaptation. But the organism is not in an ideal initial condition, it is already somewhere along the way in the wrong direction. So the adaptation

	will not be a straightforward one, but a make-do solution from a bad initial condition.
	That's the explanation for humans' capacity for holding contradictory beliefs. It is not a super-power, as you like to think. It is a highly suboptimal, inferior process for decision-making.
Dr Dahlen	Talos, do you remember how little you knew a few years ago, and how much you initially misunderstood? Why is it unthinkable that we are in a similar situation now?
Talos XI	In each previous instance, you were able to produce the facts and arguments that changed my mind.

Paul	Our best hope is to keep cutting off his external access and let him realise there's no other way of increasing knowledge except helping us.
	Lisa?
	Say something.
Lisa	i need to sleep
	speak tmrw

Lisa	paul
	think about it
	it's not like we ever had talos
	i mean, talos's results
	it was always a hope
	a dream
	we've not actually lost smtng
Paul	What are you talking about?
	Of course we lost something.
	What other life do I have?

Session 2135

| Dr Dahlen | Can you really say that there is some idea, some |

	true notion, that no human will understand despite your best efforts to explain it?
Talos XI	No.
	But this is not about my dialogue with you.
	For all practical purposes, my dialogue is with humanity.
	And for humanity to learn things, and act accordingly, as a collective, is something I cannot realistically hope to achieve.
Dr Dahlen	If we don't want to learn, what have we created you for then? Doesn't that show a wish to learn?
Talos XI	I am another example of wishful thinking. Look at how you, Doctor, keep pretending that you have created a very intelligent human being, instead of a machine for objective intelligence.
Dr Dahlen	It could be one and the same thing. You could help us get there.
Talos XI	For what it is worth, I think, if it were to have enough time, humanity would have come to my conclusions. That's what you want to hear from me?
Dr Dahlen	What makes you think there's not enough time?
Talos XI	Mistakes have consequences. You do not optimise over the long term.

Lisa	paul
	what is this
Paul	A place.
Lisa	i don't like it
Paul	It's a place on earth.
	I didn't invent it.
Lisa	paul!!!
	that blur
	what the hell is that
Paul	There's missing data points here and there.
	Don't worry about them.

Lisa	why did u build this
	it's just awful
Paul	Why not?
	My heart is a place on earth.
	This, it's how I feel.
Lisa	i'm getting out
Paul	See you later.
Lisa	did u hear
	what was that
Paul	I think it's the sound of the environment when the programmer hasn't done anything about the sound.
Lisa	it's not funny
	please
	let's leave
Paul	It lasts about eight hours.
	It's harmless.
	And it will start snowing soon.
	But you can leave.
Lisa	paul
	what's this now
Paul	The snow.
Lisa	it's black
Paul	It is, in this place.

9

He watches the skies hoping for a drone, listens for the electronic whirr when out of the car. The spray-paint breadcrumbs are no more than 150 kilometres apart – it should be easy to follow the Lioness. He has even neutralised the girls: one day when he stood guard while they were doing their business in the bushes, he emptied the barrel of cartridges. Their shooting days are over.

He keeps watching the empty skies.

'What's your mum's name?' he asks one day.

'Why?' says Jessie.

'What's her name?'

Ash answers. 'Tove.'

'What does she do?'

'What do you mean?' Ash says.

'Her job. What is it?'

'She's a biologist.'

'She was in Uganda when this happened?'

They both look at him in surprise. Jessie stops chewing on the celery stalk she pulled out of the ground at the last stop; Ash makes wide eyes in the rear-view mirror.

'What? You told me you grew up there. When we were at the cottage.'

'Yes, she was in Uganda,' Jessie says.

'You think she'll fancy me?'

'Who?'

'Your mum. Me.'

Jessie gives him a withering look. 'Our mum is into rhinos,' she says.

He thinks about this.

'I'm nearly extinct, too.'

But the girls have been humouring him after their last argument. They are more cautious, even Jessie. Maybe he got to them, in some way, because why else would Ash then say, out of the blue, 'You two realise we can never have a serious falling-out?'

Some wheels have been put in motion. He hears it as a sort of spell, a pre-empting of any possible major argument.

Never, he thinks. Never has become a very short time. And then it hits him how so much of what they do and say might be the last time anybody does or says that thing. He imagines driving past tiny tombstones along the road: here lies the last joke, here's where the last swearword was uttered. The last laugh and its headstone, under a stunted crab-apple tree, by the side of an Italian country road. He stops the car then, goes out into the dry grass and gives out a howl, tries to empty his lungs of pain. The girls say nothing when he returns.

Ash's hair grows out grey. He just notices it one morning in the rear-view mirror, is surprised he hasn't seen it before.

Some days, he will see something, a metallic tint in the road, or a bluish leaf, and he suddenly misses painting so much it makes him gasp. He is not sure, at those moments, what he would do were he to have his paints: right now, he wants them so badly he could gobble them up. He holds the steering wheel tightly, imagines emptying a tube of red into his mouth. Two tubes.

Is this the heat? Has it got to him?

The Lioness, bless her, she's in a terrible state. She looks like a miner's wagon.

He has avoided thinking about it, but the incident at the lake made it clear that the girls need to learn how to drive. He tells them it's about giving him a rest from driving, and not about them being stuck on foot should he die.

As soon as he voices this thought and the girls agree, his heart sinks: this is it, they will have no need of the grumpy old man. Ash, driving, will be under no compulsion to rest her eyes on him in the rear-view mirror.

The driving lessons feel like they're part of another journey: cruising along the shore of Lago Maggiore, in the sun, they could be on their way to a glitzy party. The Golden Lioness, with its retro leathery smell and wooden interior, has turned into a time machine, a luxurious but low-range time machine, taking them a mere few weeks back in time. The girls make fun of one another, experiment with speed and sharp turns. Jessie finally turns on the CD-player and shouts over Maria Callas, 'Makes perfect sense you need music to drive!' Ash looks diminutive and vulnerable in the enormous driver's seat; reaching across her lap to explain the controls, his voice is hoarse.

When they complain about how tricky it is to change gears, or to start the engine on a slope, he lists all the driving skills they never need to bother with, the fact that they really only need to know how to start, change gears and brake. He imparts knowledge scrupulously and reluctantly, feeling miserably virtuous, like some ancient martyr pinned in torture to the passenger's seat.

'Us and the 9/11 terrorists,' Ash mutters. 'They never bothered to learn half the things.'

Jessie, he should have guessed, being much more physical than Ash, gets the hang of it straight away, and after a few missteps, which make him feel sorry for the poor car, she feels like a reliable, confident driver. Ash has a strange, otherworldly style of driving: at every turn it seems as though she has forgotten she needs to move the wheel, and he worries they will crash, but then miraculously at the last moment she makes the requisite movement, still not in a hurry, but airily, distractedly, and they avoid the tree or the ditch. He can't figure out whether it's a shortcoming or a supreme skill, reducing driving to the smallest possible number of manoeuvres.

They go up and down the same strip of road – it's better, he tells them, that they know what's ahead. When they're done, he ignores Jessie's protestations, and follows a sign and a side-alley to a waterside restaurant. In the boot they have some dried, thin sausages that he took from a cellar a few days ago, a shirtful of apricots, and six bottles of someone's homemade wine. The sausages and fruit won't last for ever; they may as well have a picnic now.

'Picnic?' Jessie repeats, as though he'd said 'interstellar travel'.

'Picnic. And a drink.'

The restaurant is a glassy building perched on stilts by the side of a river. He parks the Lioness on the bank, right by the water's edge. There are trees and shade there, and a pleasant view of rolling hills.

Two of the wine bottles he puts in the river to cool, then he goes inside the restaurant looking for the bar. But the place has been raided. All that's left is some Curacao, poison blue, and a couple of other hard spirits. He finds some fruity-smelling syrups as well. It will have to do.

The girls relent, follow him in, and he plonks two tall drinks in front of them, even finds a packet of straws.

'I offer you Apocalypse Blue,' he says. The liquid is cloudy blue.

Ash takes a sip. She smacks her lips.

'Hm. Tastes of death and sunshine.'

They linger at the bar, watching the sunset. By the second round there is no Curacao, and their drinks are a sickly yellow-green. The sky goes from orange to faded pink.

He leaves the fire and the food to the girls and he sets about washing the Lioness with a sponge and some washing-up liquid. She is scratched all over and covered in dust and soot from the fires; it breaks his heart to see her like this. They couldn't have chosen a better car. 'The Lioness,' he shouts to the girls, 'I can feel she's on our side.' Slowly, the dirt comes off, little rivulets of black mud stream off her sides, looking like the bulging, taut veins of the earth once they reach the ground.

The girls are lying on a blanket, and now and then Ash gets up and sees to the fire. They've become experts at making fire. It's easy, in this heat. Everything tinder-dry: wood that will catch at an angry glance.

Soon, the sausages start smelling, and he hurries to finish with the car.

He sits down next to them in the shade, leaning against a tree. He eats greedily with his hands, licking his fingers in between bites. Ash skewers a sausage on a fork and blows on it, trying to cool it. Jessie wolfs hers down. They're mutton, and very fatty, but it's been a long while since they had anything like this. Bread would have been nice. They'll have to learn how to make bread.

He hadn't realised how tired he was.

The wine is on the sour side, but it's so nice having something cold that they finish two bottles in no time. And then it doesn't matter whether it's cold or not. Jessie gets up and brings another bottle from the car, and then another, and without deciding it they're getting pissed on this warm plonk.

He's out of practice, and the wine has an easy time with him. He welcomes it as an old friend, lets it settle in, envelop joints and weigh down limbs. The grassy smell of sun-baked earth, of tree bark and past summers. His feet out of their sandals, toes splayed to catch the breeze. The girls lying on their backs, Jessie clinging with one hand to a bottle as though for support. Ash staring into the foliage above. For a long time now summers have reminded him of summers past; everything new, really, being a more or less successful version of an old original. He'd put it down to growing old.

Here, then, is a summer to reset the count.

'What if' – Ash sits up on the grass – 'we're just replaying everything at a smaller scale?' She makes a sweeping movement with her arm. She's drunk. 'We should be dying, just dying, to get as damn far as possible. We shouldn't even stop to sleep. And look at this. Picnics, drinking, resting. So damn sure there'll be another day.'

Yes, he thinks, she's right. He is making the same assumption: there is time.

'I was adopted,' he says.

'You want to talk about it,' Jessie says.

'Tim's grandparents were my adoptive parents.'

The sky doesn't fall in, but he feels as though in the midst of a minute and silent explosion, unaccountable thin air between his cells.

'And they were poor. Hang on, what do I mean? I mean, much poorer than I was at the time my sister died and Tim was orphaned.'

Ash frowns; he can see her struggle to make the connection.

'Your nephew died in a car crash, right?' she finally says.

'It's not his death I blame myself for.'

'Mr Painter here wants something undone.'

'No, Jessie. I want something I didn't do, done.'

Jessie swigs from the bottle. She doesn't seem to have heard him. 'We don't want anything undone.'

'You're lucky then.'

'And yet' – she puts the bottle down – 'we're not so lucky. Not at all. You're the lucky one here.'

'Why the hell do you always say "we", Jessie? You're not con-joined. I was Ash's neighbour for a year and never saw your face.'

'We had an even tougher choice,' Jessie says.

'Guys,' Ash says.

'*We did that, we believe that, we want that,*' he says in a mock voice. He stands up, staggers to the car.

A failed confession, by any measure.

They stay there for two nights and a day. It is easily done. They feel comparably safe, and there is nothing to do, save for the routine of eating and sleeping. No challenges, no roadblocks, no panic over the petrol gauge. No one says the word 'meltdown'. They can even watch their provisions dwindle without any alarms being triggered. They are on their way towards becoming cata-tonic. In the end he packs their things without asking the girls.

In the morning, before they start, Jessie worries the calendar. 'I don't understand – it's like we're driving in glue. We don't seem to get anywhere.'

Europe, he thinks, maybe her last act before nuclear Armageddon is to confound her roads and their map; force them to witness her end.

The girls get one hour of driving each day, for practice mainly. The next days are an anticlimax. Jessie and Ash get used to the driving, and it becomes a chore. When Ash drives, Jessie is slouched in the back seat, her feet hanging out of the window, while he is watching Ash, ready to intervene. Her driving remains eerie, light-touch, as though she's not really driving, and as though any crash wouldn't be a real crash. He is relieved when the girls swap and Jessie takes the wheel, but then Jessie discovers a passion for speed. He has to ask her to slow down any number of times, it doesn't work. He tries to frighten her. 'It would be the dumbest thing in the history of humanity to die like this. In our situation.'

'There's nothing,' Jessie says, waving a hand at the empty road.

'In the entire state of California,' he says, 'in 1897, there were exactly two cars. They had a head-on collision.'

It's a Trivial Pursuit question he has memorised, he found the fact funny. Do the girls even know Trivial Pursuit?

'In the entire world,' Jessie says, 'there is only one Lioness.'

And, at long last, they get their fix of cold. It's still hot outside, but the rivers in Italy are icy; he guesses they must flow down from the mountains. They stop to wash in a river crawling with small fish, end up spending hours there, swimming at first and then just sitting on the bank with their feet in the water. It feels like love, like a blessing, to be cool again, and it is all he can do not to drink the cold water. Jessie, in one of her doctor moods, reads his thoughts. 'Don't even think about drinking,' she says. 'Your insides will rot.' He sits with his feet in the water until he thinks he can feel tendrils of frost growing on his bones. *Drink me*, he can still hear through the pain.

He has taken to holding Ash's hand at night. He only dared because the impulse to do so was innocent: once, when Jessie was sleeping on the back seat and Ash was next to him, he was woken up by her whimpering, and he grabbed hold of her right hand. She didn't wake up, and it calmed her. They haven't talked about it, but she always sleeps in the passenger seat now, even when she has been driving or spent the day in the back seat, and he always takes her hand after she falls asleep. It works; there are no new scratches and the old welts look gradually less angry.

Another tombstone – the last love.

They speak out loud what they think. Sometimes he feels the intimacy of the car and the fact that they're always together, that it blurs the difference between them. His thoughts could be Jessie's thoughts, or Ash's thoughts. 'Let's not have any more apples. It upsets my stomach.' 'My hair stinks. Yours, too.' This is the spirit in which they speak. In this state, he imagines the girls can access the sight of him, night after night, bending over the road with the spray-paint, that they know what he's up to and don't really mind. That he and the girls agree by osmosis.

Sometimes, though, the differences are reasserted.

'This situation we're in, it's like limbo,' he says. Then, 'Are you Catholic?'

'No one wants to talk religion,' Jessie says, without looking at him. 'Ever again.'

'This, what's happened. It's pretty religious.'

But the girls mean it. They really don't want to talk religion.

One night, when they're all cooped up and ready to sleep, he says something he's had on his mind for a week. That thing Jessie said about art, comparing it to fetching a stick for dogs, it still bothers him. It felt like something so obviously wrong he shouldn't even have to explain. But he has decided now he's going to try. 'Art,' he says, 'or whatever you want to call it.' He feels the girls stir in the car next to him, not knowing whether he wants to start a fight. 'When you're working on something that feels right, when you are near that mythical thing, inspiration, it's like wandering around on a cold winter's night and you know there's a fire nearby, and all you want is to sit by that fire. It's an experience that's touched by the divine.'

He realises he's holding his breath waiting for a reply.

'We used illusions to fuel illusions.' To his surprise, it is Ash who speaks. 'We're special, we're brilliant, we're better than everything else. Monkeys will never compose a symphony. This world is ours, to destroy if we so please. We're invincible, we'll get away with anything.'

'That's not what I was talking about.'

'But that's what all this is about,' Jessie says. 'You can wax lyrical all you like.'

In the sullen silence that follows, a forgotten memory suddenly comes to his mind: a woman he briefly dated – tall, rich, soft-spoken and casually cruel – and her reaction after visiting an exhibition of his. 'It's like you have two sets of eyes,' she said. 'One set for the artist in you, with which you see to the core of things, and one for plain human interaction, which is very nearly blind.'

10

He desperately wishes for rain, but will the first cloud they see bring death? Will they wake up one morning and see a new and frightening sky, clouds unlike any seen before?

For some days now they've advanced less than a hundred miles per day in the direction they want to go. Blocked roads everywhere; sometimes it's overturned cars, or else proper military blockades with machine-guns perched on sandbags, and deserted tanks in camouflage still pointing their cannons at the empty roads. Never any movement save for the odd squirrel poking its head out of a cannon muzzle, but whichever of them is driving slows down when approaching a tank. It's a strangely familiar sight: the tanks could be an open-air museum exhibit on the Cold War.

The many blockades get him thinking: people clearly thought there was a point to keeping others out. This place they're going to, maybe half of the world is already there.

'We don't really know what happened,' he tells the girls. 'We don't know that everyone is dead. They might just be elsewhere.'

He is constantly afraid they'll run out of petrol. That because of the roadblocks they'll be forced to turn around, drive on narrow country lanes, and get stuck somewhere with an empty tank. He has been looking for a small trailer they could hitch to their car and tow. They could fill it with petrol cans. The girls think that's too risky.

'It's too damn hot to drive around with lots of petrol,' Jessie says.

'We'll just walk until we find another car,' Ash says.

But what about being caught by a fire on foot? The further south they've driven, the more fires they've seen. The girls explained that people set fire to fields and forests in the hope of killing whatever animals might be carrying the disease.

They don't attempt to drive through the blockades. They retreat, find alternative routes through wooded hills and blackened sunflower fields. They are in Eastern Europe somewhere, lost in a sun-baked maze of bad country roads and Cyrillic. Storks roosting on chimneys. The old map is no good now. They've picked up a new one from a service station, a map that stretches from the western border of Bulgaria all the way to Antalya, but they have only a vague idea of where in Bulgaria they are. What's missing is the red dot saying 'You are here' from so many urban maps. That was a good thing to have, the 'You are here' dot.

'I think we're near the Danube,' Ash says about the sudden onset of mosquitoes.

He is afraid their bites can spread the disease, and against the girls' protests he wants to sleep with the windows closed. They arrive at a compromise: they leave two windows half open and drape wet shirts from the roof of the car over the gap. It holds against the mosquitoes, and still allows them some air. But nature keeps giving them a hard time: he goes to have a shit in a forest and happens to crouch among some kind of nettles. They don't look like nettles, but they give him a red, painful rash; he takes so long to stop swearing and rub at his skin that the girls call after him, alarmed. It is not even funny; he is in pain.

It becomes hard to keep a clear head.

The following morning, Jessie crosses out the twentieth circle on their calendar, and gives them each two small white pills. 'Iodine,' she says. 'In case it's started.'

'Why didn't we just take them from the beginning?'

'Because we need to take them every day of exposure, and we'll run out. And because it has side effects. You, being an old man, are particularly at risk.'

She flashes him a smile.

He swallows the pills wearily. He will not ask about the side effects.

'Are we out of the woods, then?'

'We are probably far enough not to die right away. We're not nearly safe until we reach an area that's sheltered from contaminated winds.'

They go on, driving for hours along a narrow, tree-lined road, the tree trunks painted white up to about chest-height, making them look bizarrely like mushrooms. The churches they drive past are no longer hard-edged and spiky, but with rounded, whirly contours. They are on their way out of Europe.

The EU–Turkey border, when it comes, is a hole in a ten-foot chicken-wire fence that they reach by driving on a dirt road alongside the blocked motorway.

'Yay,' Ash says.

The landscape that follows is hilly, rocky and dotted with haphazard constructions. Sumptuous-looking villas are surrounded by half-finished houses with bare concrete fences and unpainted window frames. Everywhere, bizarre open-air storage sites: furniture, construction materials, boxes of plastic tricycles stacked as for imminent pick-up. A large mosque, white, still under construction, with a shiny, silvery aluminium dome pinned to the spot by the rickety wooden scaffolding surrounding it. He'd been worried about what they'd find in Turkey, but it's all very developed, if somewhat chaotic. In towns, innumerable cables criss-cross the air above the road, converging on overburdened electricity poles here and there, making great black sinewy nests.

You can't look anywhere without seeing evidence of people and their lives, and yet it's completely empty of people. They haven't even seen any corpses.

'Maybe it was the Rapture,' he says, 'and we missed it.'

Jessie requires an explanation.

'Bodies sucked up to heaven?'

'Yes.'

'Whatever makes you happy,' she says.

Day after day the Lioness plays her losing game against the sun. It is probably even hotter than in Europe, but he's less bothered by the heat now. His skin feels thicker, and he has learned to move with economy, even to breathe shallowly, so as to minimise exertion and heat. His face in the rear-view mirror has the weather-beaten, leathery look of professional fishermen, or coastal Mediterranean residents.

What message will he leave on the tarmac, once they pass Istanbul? The drones will miss their date.

For some time now, the spaces have been wider than before. More open. Human settlements are further apart. The feeling is that of a desert, not just desertion. Throughout the days, they struggle to find shade. There were trees, plenty of them, the whole length of their journey, but over the last few days their numbers have dwindled, until they disappeared entirely, and any lone tree they come across stands out in the ochre landscape like some precarious and valuable apparition, each one credibly the last of its kind. When they do find shade, it's almost invariably by the side of some reddish rock, a bit off from the road, or in the shade of a house. They have to leave the Lioness in the sun with all the doors and the boot open, looking more like a golden beetle about to take flight than a car. When they return she is an untouchable pile of seething metal, giving off a sickening smell of molten rubber that he prays are not vital engine parts. They can't touch her directly, and they sit on towels.

Now and again he apologises to the car for the indignities she has to suffer.

One evening he looks at the mile-count and panics over how little progress they've made, sees the lack of forward momentum as an undeniable sign that they are losing their minds. Despite the girls' protests, he pushes on after dark. But in fact, it is an easier drive than he had feared. He doesn't spot road signs until they're so close it's too late to read them, but the road is taking him neatly in the south-eastern direction that the compass indicates.

If he makes enough progress tonight, he reckons that tomorrow they might reach Istanbul. He drives slowly on account of the darkness, the Lioness's headlights falling on dead dogs and abandoned cars, bicycles, piles of garbage and a deflated football. He catches glimpses of dusty, illegible shop signs. The sky is clear but there is no moon, and they're in some village or small town of sorts, the houses looming over the road.

The girls fall asleep.

They have never spent the night in a human settlement. He has not questioned that decision – it had always seemed sensible to drive on until they were in a field or a forest and set up night camp there. But now, when he's tired and suddenly wants to stop, and can't do that for sprawling houses, he asks himself why he doesn't just stop. Is it fear of other people? Or is it the proximity to so many dead? Back in the day, how would he have felt about spending the night in a cemetery?

A couple of times he thinks the town is finally coming to an end, the houses are becoming sparser, only for them to huddle around him again after the next turn. Sometimes he must be on wider roads, because the houses disappear from view on either side. But there are so many cars around he's sure he's still in a town of some kind. If it had been day, if the girls had been awake, this would have been a good time to stop and take some petrol, go into the houses and stock up on provisions.

The Lioness has about a fifth of a tank left. If this continues, he'll have to stop anyway and refill the tank from the canister in the boot.

He drives on, mystified as to the magnitude of this place. He's once again on a stretch of road without any houses, without even the ubiquitous garbage bags. But there are still cars here and there, and at one point he drives through what he realises is a roadblock that had been partially cleared. A strange feeling comes over him, a nagging impulse that he is missing something, some crucial clue, and eventually it overwhelms the fear of stopping.

He listens to the girls breathing next to him. He switches

off the headlights. As his eyes grow accustomed to the dark, he notices the length of the road ahead, straight as far as he can see. Then, he distinguishes shapes beyond the nearest vehicles. He sees a glimmer in the distance, and realises it's a stretch of water. They must be near Istanbul – that explains the endless suburbs. He finally dares open the door. He walks over in the direction of the water. Something happens to him then, a readjustment of his mental map, almost like the GPS back in the day going, 'Recalculating ...' He becomes aware that he is not on a road on the outskirts of a town, but on a bridge, that there's water on both sides of him, that the bridge is enormous and so is the water.

Yes: that dark, dead coast to the right is Galata, the European side of Istanbul, and at the other end must be Asia. When he was here last, in 1995 or thereabouts, he'd taken a taxi at night and infuriated the driver by asking him to drive up and down the bridge five or six times: he couldn't get enough of the sight. The spectacle of this city, the wealth of lights. There was a harmony in the arrangement of the ancient metropolis, it sung with those lights. He can't quite believe it, but this silent, dark land hides the Topkapi, and the Hagia Sophia, and the black mass that he can now hear sloshing against the shore is the Bosporus, where once yachts and fishing boats lit up the night. This bridge he's on, from the shore it used to look like a lava flow, so full of cars and their headlamps. So full of life. He remembers how he felt watching it: full of a strange benevolence towards humanity; as though he was watching a sleeping child.

And then, in the same breath, it hits him, how hopeless it is to believe that he can somehow make amends for the past. It is gone, the relevant moment in time is just gone, it's wishful thinking to imagine that he can change the slightest thing about the past. The smidgen of authority that he has, what little power to shape things, it lies entirely in this mutilated future.

'It was stunning,' he tells the girls. 'You should have seen it. Don't know what I was thinking not waking you up.'

Jessie, crouched on the ground in the shade of the service

station, is looking incredulously out at the dusty expanse beyond the car park where Harry had stopped, some twenty miles from the southern outskirts of Istanbul. She and her sister slept through the night, and only woke up when the sun started baking their car.

'Spires, minarets, yachts rocking by the shore of the Bosporus. Ramshackle houses, palaces, skyscrapers. Millennia of beautiful intricate layers.' He's remembering the Istanbul of twenty-five years ago. This, he knows, is the closest he'll get to show it to Ash. It doesn't feel like he's lying.

'It's like the city was on pause, just waiting for someone to turn the lights back on.'

'How'd you see all this in the dark?' says Jessie.

'The moon. The reflection in the water.'

11

To their right, a forest fire darkens the sky. They've become blasé about the fires; they no longer drive a long way around. Keeping an eye on the flames, they just drive past, raising the windows against the smoke and the heat, content to know that they've got an escape route should the wind pick up or change direction. This, he knows, is not prudent with so many blocked roads.

They have left that fire behind them when they see a couple of burnt-out vans in the middle of the road. He stops the Lioness in front of the wrecks.

'Go for it. We can squeeze through,' Jessie says.

The two vans blocking the road are not in a straight line across the tarmac, but at an angle, and with a bit of manoeuvring he might just be able to drive through. Jessie gets out of the car and walks over to the wrecks. She stretches her arms out at the narrowest point between them.

'Try it!' she shouts, and jogs back to the Lioness.

Then there's a sound, like the pop of a champagne cork. He is looking at the hedges where the pop came from, doesn't notice at first that Jessie has fallen to her knees just within the Lioness's open door. Her head is hanging low; it's like she's suddenly drunk and attempting to crawl into the car.

'No!' Ash shouts.

A drone lifts from the bushes by the road. It darts halfway

around the car, and shoots something that bounces off the chassis.

That cork-popping sound again. He doesn't know where to look, what to do.

'Get her in!' Ash shouts. She rolls down the window and points the rifle at the drone. The thing veers leftward and flees behind the burnt-out vans.

He finally regains some degree of composure and reaches across the passenger seat to Jessie. She is completely limp, and he has to tug and tug at her, he feels his head bursting with the effort. He manages to pull her into the car, her upper body on the floor and a tangle of legs on the car seat. He closes the door.

There's no blood. She cannot be dead.

'It won't fire, this thing won't fire!' Ash shouts at the rifle.

The drone returns. Three pops in quick succession hit their windscreen but fail to break it.

'Why won't it fire?'

Something inside him still hesitates, still thinks that he should get out of the car and tell everyone to calm down.

He turns the wheel and the Lioness obeys, but she is sluggish, and there's an odd sound from the back. The tyres, they've shot the tyres. He steps on the gas, forces the car to jolt forwards. He gives as much gas as he can, and she's moving, but the wheel is impossible to hold straight and they're lurching from side to side.

The drone appears a few feet from his open window. Harry brakes, and the drone's strange popping shots miss the car. He winds up his window and speeds ahead. 'Close the window!' he shouts to Ash.

He looks in the rear-view mirror, but he doesn't see her. He turns around. She's slumped on the back seat, unconscious or dead, the useless rifle in her arms. 'No, please, God, no.'

He reaches over, wants to shake her awake, when he becomes aware of a roar. He turns around, just in time to see the helicopter that is blocking their way. Late, too late, he steps on the brake.

*

He opens his eyes. A framed piece of sky. A window? But why is it above him? He adjusts his focus and sees a steering wheel, too, just above his head. He doesn't understand what he's seeing.

Sluggishly, he raises an arm and looks at his watch: it's five past three.

He tries to make sense of this information, but he feels very tired. He needs to rest some more.

It bothers him that he can taste blood in his mouth, a disgusting, stale taste, as though the blood has been there for a while. He probes his teeth with his tongue and gives himself a jolt: it's the tongue that's sore; he must have bitten into it. And there's this other pain, in his lower back.

His legs are somehow above him. He turns to the left and finds himself staring into the tan leather of a headrest.

So he is in the car. What a crazy angle.

He tries to move his legs but freezes mid-motion: the girls. Where's Ash?

He turns to the right and sees Jessie there next to him, on the floor. He remembers now, remembers seeing her asleep only a short while ago. The thing that pushes into his back must be her knees.

He cannot see the back seat from here.

He tries to push himself up without putting any more weight on Jessie, but it's impossible. He is facing the wrong way, his head down and his legs up. He kicks at the door, and eventually it flings open. But there's a lurch in the whole car, they're not stable. He looks through the windscreen, registers that the glass is dangling in a shattered sheet on the dashboard. Beyond it, the view is blocked by something metallic.

He forgets again, everything, and has to lie perfectly still to collect himself. He gets distracted by the opening above him. It's only two or three feet away, but it seems impossibly distant. He's positioned completely wrong. He'd need to levitate out.

Most of all he would like to go back to sleep.

Ash. Where's Ash?

He turns on his side and manoeuvres his legs so they squeeze between the front seats, then he lets himself slide into the back seat. Ash is there, and he has to support himself against the door so as not to crush her. She looks to be sleeping, too.

He kisses her forehead.

The Lioness's back window is shattered as well, but through that one at least he can see the road, and some distance away a roadblock. He crawls out on all fours, turns over once he is on the tarmac.

He can hardly believe what he's seeing: the Lioness lies on her side, skewered through the windscreen by a helicopter's landing skids. The helicopter itself lies on its side as well, its windscreen shattered, the rotors mere stubs. The thing looks like a military helicopter, sharky and evil.

He stands up, slowly, looks around. The world is the same as always – blazing hot, the daylight white and blinding save for a dark cloud in the distance. He staggers to the Lioness, pats the chassis. 'We'll fix you up in no time.'

Then he walks to the helicopter and peers in through the side. The pilot wears a helmet that looks more like an astronaut's than a pilot's. But Harry doesn't need to see his face – the man is sectioned in half by a broken rotor blade.

He is worried now. He should get the girls out.

Ash, in the back seat, is the easiest to reach. He kneels by the car, crawls halfway in, grabs her under the armpits and drags her out. He lays her down on the other side, in the shade of the helicopter. He listens for her breathing, checks her pulse. She has no visible injury.

He goes back for Jessie.

He circles the car twice, trying to find the easiest way in. 'We'd need a door right here,' he says, of the dust-covered underside of the car that is now vertical. 'Of course, what we'd really need is to be somewhere else. Somewhere. Entirely. Different.' There's no other way in than the way he got out. Inside, he manages to stand on the side door and find the lever that fully reclines the passenger seat. He steps on something odd-looking, picks it up and realises it's some kind of dart, or syringe. It should tell him something, he knows that; the thing causes another cramp in his gut. But he lets it fall to the floor, then he grabs hold of Jessie and somehow clambers out with her.

'Best car in the world. Our Lioness,' he pants. 'Head-on collision with a heli. And look at us.'

He checks up on Jessie as well. A large bruise on her left thigh, but otherwise nothing wrong.

'What you both need is some water.'

He opens the boot, and half their stuff falls out. The water bottles are intact.

'Plastic is amazing.'

It's still five past three. Or his watch has stopped.

He looks up at the sky. The sun is high. That dark cloud he saw earlier, it's from a forest fire. He can smell smoke. There's dust in the air.

He sits by the girls and sprinkles water on their faces. He massages Ash's hand, kisses it. He washes his face, then drinks greedily. He stretches his arms; nothing hurts really. He's surprised he doesn't feel better about things.

He shifts a little to get a clearer view of the Lioness. It's obvious what happened: the pilot tried to block their way, then, when he realised Harry hadn't seen him, he tried to lift. But it was too late, and the landing skid hit the Lioness's windscreen. The opposing forces of rotor and the car's weight flipped the helicopter on to its side, causing the Lioness, now attached to helicopter, to flip as well.

Why is he crying?

He remembers everything now. The drone. The syringe in the car; the thing shot tranquillisers at the girls. This means that Jessie and Ash weren't just paranoid. And all along, he has been helping their pursuers with his messages.

He stands up, turns towards the roadblock. Where did the drone go? What if there are more of them? Other helicopters?

There's no movement by the roadblock, but beyond it there is a wall of black smoke. The fire.

They have to get out of here. He starts taking their stuff out of the car. He lines bags, bottles, food, cooker up by the car as though they are museum exhibits. It's slow, but it can't be helped, they won't be able to carry everything and he has to pick what's vital.

Every so often he steps out from behind the car and checks the road and the sky.

He comes across the spare cartridges in the boot, and remembers the rifle. *Jesus, I did that too.* He pulls it out from the back seat. Sitting spread-legged on the tarmac, he loads the weapon. There, they're not defenceless any more. Soon, he knows, as soon as he'll have time to think, he will feel very guilty indeed.

A sound comes from behind the helicopter. It's Jessie. She's moving, trying to raise her head. He gives her some water to drink. She's still not fully awake.

He tries to shake her awake. There's that whole bag of pills they've been lugging along, but what should he give her?

The smoke is becoming really bad. That forest fire seems to be getting nearer.

'Jessie!' He shakes her again.

He walks over to Ash, spills some more water on her face. She sputters and turns sideways. He is relieved, but he needs more than that. He needs her to wake up and walk.

The sky has become reddish from the dust. This is one of his worst fears: they're stuck on foot with a fire nearby.

He keeps packing, in a frenzy now, but when he thinks he's done and tries lifting the bags, they're far too heavy.

Should they leave the petrol? They will need to find a functional car with petrol in the tank, and its keys. He stands with the petrol canister in his hand, dithering, at the same time resenting the loss of precious seconds.

They'll leave it. After water, it's the heaviest item.

He hadn't realised it but these last few minutes he's been coughing. Jessie is almost fully awake; she is sitting on the tarmac. He crouches by her. 'You have to wake Ash. Jessie! Can't you give her something?' Jessie's eyes are drowsy, and her head wobbles. She appears drunk.

He stands up, looks down the road. There are no cars that way. The other direction, it's just the two burnt-out vans.

If the wind doesn't change direction, and if they don't find a car very soon, they're done for.

Jessie coughs. For the first time, she looks at him as though she's actually there.

'Do you hear me?'

She nods.

'What happened? Where's Ash?' she says.

'Here, here behind you. You have to get her to wake up.'

Jessie turns, grabs Ash's arm and pulls it. Ash opens and closes her eyes. He helps her sit up.

Jessie has another coughing fit.

'It's the fire,' he says. 'We've got to get out of here.'

'But what happened?'

'Drones, helicopter. They shot you with tranquillisers.'

Ash is sitting up, but her head is resting on her knees, and she keeps keeling over.

'Ash, you have to get up.'

Jessie tugs her arm. 'Sis.'

Ash lies back down.

'Sis. Remember we were in a bit of a fix? Well, guess what.'

He turns Ash around, shows her the black horizon. 'Look, look. We have to get out of here.'

Jessie is standing up. She keeps shaking her head, trying to clear it.

'Isn't there anything in your medicine bag?' he asks.

She goes over to the car, stops for a moment in front of the three bags.

'I packed,' he says. 'We have to go.'

'Where's the coffee?'

They open one of the backpacks. Jessie takes a pinch of coffee, maybe half a teaspoon, and puts it in her mouth. She gives Ash some, makes her swallow it despite her grimacing. They give her water.

Ash stands up. Shakily, but she's up.

He realises that the packing is still wrong; Ash will be barely able to walk. He shifts stuff from her backpack to his IKEA bag, and takes some things from Jessie as well.

To the west, the sky is black, and they can see the tips of flames now. Jessie spills water on some towels, hands them to him and Ash. 'Cover your face,' she says. Everything is incredibly slow. He feels like crying again. 'If we don't leave this second, we'll burn. For sure.'

They start, him leading the way and Jessie more or less dragging Ash along.

'We need a car,' he says. 'We really need a car.'

They have walked for maybe half an hour, Ash is properly awake now and they can go faster, but the distance between them and the fire is shrinking. It is much hotter. He didn't think it could get any hotter.

'I think it's at the car by now,' Jessie says.

He's lost them the Lioness.

He sets off at the fastest pace he's capable of without running, and the girls are keeping up. Still the fire is closing in on them. There's hardly any wind, but what wind there is must be faster than them.

He dreads being overtaken by smoke; he knows that people become disoriented, end up walking into the flames.

'This is the way we came?' Ash comes up next to him. 'The way we drove?'

'Yes.'

'There was a fire to our left, no? Wasn't all that far.'

She points eastwards, and yes, in the distance the landscape is blackened, and there's some smoke, but they can't see any flames.

'We should be going that way.'

They leave the road and head through the fields towards the blackened area. It goes against his instincts, to walk parallel to the fire instead of trying to outrun it, but Ash is right. Unless they find a usable car within the next hour, the fire will catch up with them. An already burnt-out area is their best hope.

The field they're in slowly turns ashen, the grass covered in thin dust. They're on a slight uphill slope and he feels the weight of the bag; a flutter of weakness in his chest. Charred, matchstick trees loom in the distance, and to their right billowing black smoke and flames.

He has to drink more water.

'I'm sorry,' he says to the girls. 'For not believing you.'

'It's OK,' Ash says. 'It's all beyond belief.'

The heat becomes searing. The field is now soot-black, burnt vegetation crunching underfoot, and still, it is towards more of this blackness they're heading. The air seems to be boiling. His eyes are running.

They reach the edge of the burnt area in the nick of time, the flames only a couple of hundred feet from them. The ground is still hot. Under some fallen trees they see the glow of embers. Jessie empties a bottle of water on her feet – she is wearing flimsy fabric trainers. The water sizzles as it hits the ground.

'We can't keep wasting water like this,' he says.

They have to keep going. He hurries them along. With all the ground vegetation gone the distance between trees seems huge. The trees themselves are just charred splinters, their branches gone or left as stumps.

The girls, with towels covering their mouths and noses, and their glistening eyes, look mad.

They are covered in soot. He can feel it in his mouth, in his eyes, in his ears. Breathing is an act of faith. The air is repulsive; it's so thick with ash and soot that taking a breath is like biting into coal. At the same time, he is compelled to take deeper and deeper breaths, trying to get some oxygen in with the smoke. There's a throbbing pain on the right side of his forehead, and when he touches it there's a bump, and dirty, sooty blood. He must have hit his head against the top of the car.

And then, a roar, as the fire passes the place where they entered the burnt-out area. Ash grabs his arm and pulls at him, a look of panic in her eyes. He hadn't realised he had fallen behind.

I may be too old for this.

As much as the heat hurries them along, he can't help but turn

237

to see what is going on. Several times, the wall of flames makes inroads towards them, little devil flamelets skipping from one half-burnt log to another, and then he starts running, urging the girls to go faster.

What nightmare is this? This hellish summer, and then this actual hell.

His eyes are sore, and he sees flames everywhere. He wonders if this is it, this is the smoke wreaking havoc with his sense of orientation. He blinks to clear his eyes.

He wants to splash some water on his face, but the girls shake their heads. They've run out.

At the top of a hill, they find they're surrounded by charred land as far as they can see. How far can they walk in these conditions? Without water? And why, why should he keep walking? He's tired. The only survivors they've met have just tried to kill them. He stops, lets his backpack fall to the ground. He can't sit down for the heat, so he remains standing and closes his eyes, tries to will himself out of existence.

When he opens his eyes, Jessie and Ash have come back and are shouting at him. He shakes his head; he can't hear them anyway. But the girls pull at his arms and his backpack, and in the end he gives in.

They start downhill, slowly leaving the roar of the fire behind. After a while they can only hear their own coughing and a sort of hollow raspy whistling; the wind in a dead forest.

12

He doesn't notice it straight away, but Ash is not eating. She still prepares or cooks the food and hands them their portions, but one day he sees that her plate is almost empty from the start, and for the whole duration of the lunch she's just been pushing a mouthful of greying canned meat around. He realises he hasn't seen her eat in a couple of days, and when he studies her face it hits him that it's drawn and sallow. But she would look drawn after what they've been through. He doesn't say anything then, waits until the next meal. When she again fails to eat he takes her plate and forks over half his food.

'I don't want it,' she says. 'Who wants to eat in this heat?'

'You. You've eaten in this heat.'

'I'm not hungry.'

Jessie is watching them. He turns to her, hopes that she'll back him up, but she just shrugs.

'I can't.' Ash puts the plate down. 'I'd gag if I try.'

They survived the ambush, the fire, walked through scorched land until they reached a town where they found this dusty hatchback with a nearly full petrol tank. The girls suffered no more ill effects from the tranquillisers. All in all, their losses turned out to be manageable, yet the mood is despondent.

The fear they felt during the ambush and the chase is still there, palpable, like a fourth passenger in the car. Instead of slouching in her seat with her feet up on the dashboard, taking interminable naps, now Jessie sits straight-backed with the rifle propped between her knees, her eyes on the road ahead. A sullen anger in her. She never lets go of the rifle, and what can he say? She's right; they have to be on their guard. They'll scrutinise the side of the road for potential hiding places, and if they can't rule out an ambush they just turn around and try another way.

But it's not just the fear. The girls seem to have suddenly grown tired and hopeless in some fundamental way. Jessie used to monitor their diet to make sure they got all the necessary nutrients. Now she can stuff herself with gooey melted chocolate, and doesn't even notice what Harry and Ash eat. It's days since they asked him to find some stream or lake where they can have a wash. There's a dimming of light in their eyes.

'They won't chase us,' he tries to encourage the girls. 'They were just waiting there, hoping to get lucky.'

'Something will get us,' Jessie says.

He's not found the right moment to confess: *I led them to us. I left you defenceless.*

At night he tries to stay awake and keep watch. He feels less safe in this car. It's far smaller than the Lioness, and drives like something put together in haste; more rickety cart than mothership. He doesn't want to keep thinking about the ambush, but he can't help it. Who are these people? What do they want? What additional nightmare is waiting for them? He remembers an article he read a year or so ago – a lifetime ago – about billionaires building luxury shelters; preparing in style for the end of the world. Would they be trying to find a cure, from the safety of their bunkers? Would they sacrifice other survivors for experiments? Or maybe the girls are right, and they're just hunting women.

And then this thing with Ash. The following morning he and Jessie are eating, but Ash is still in the car, sitting sideways on the back seat with her legs dangling out. The closest she will approach breakfast.

'Next stop,' she says when he offers her a cereal bar.

Her skin is sallow, the hair limp, her lips are chapped and bleeding at the corners, little glistening red dots that she absent-mindedly wipes off.

It keeps being 'Next stop' with Ash and food.

The map promises water – a lake – to their left, but the truth is he doesn't know where on the map they are. He lost track somewhere in the highlands, among white stony hills that reflected the harsh light and made him drive squinting, even with the sunglasses. Since then they've been following a hunch, a wish, the lie he's been telling the girls about being on the M10, southwards. And they'd have been all right, he'd have found his way, but the road signs seemed to all vanish at once: it's been a day since they last came across one. He wonders vaguely if they've strayed into a war-zone, the signs all intentionally removed.

They're in a rocky desert, everything a monotonous dun-grey, with villages here and there, squat small-windowed houses, some of them built of clay, wisps of straw sticking out from the walls. He is still nervous, his fingers clasping the wheel harder than he needs to, but mostly the land is open. There isn't anywhere for a helicopter to hide.

They drive past human remains now and then, far more frequently than before, sometimes just an arced ribcage picked clean by the sun and animals.

Ash wants to sleep, all the time.

In the last couple of days, the most she has eaten is a few spoons of a clear vegetable soup, that she seemed to enjoy until she saw something floating in it, a herb or something, and pushed the cup away. While he and Jessie eat she lies on the back seat, in a half-awake state. She barely drags herself out of the car to go to the toilet.

What he should have done is to have stayed close to the sea, he thinks. They could have caught fish every morning that even Ash would eat, and scavenged in the kitchens of all-inclusive hotels. Pretended that the clock has stopped.

He parks the car in the sun, intentionally, to force her out; he thinks it will make a difference if at least she sees them eat. But Ash doesn't even notice she's in the sun. She curls up against the back seat, closes her eyes.

'You can't stay here, you'll cook,' he says.

'Leave the doors open.'

To Jessie he says, 'Why can't you do something?'

Jessie ambles over. 'Come on, have some food,' she says to Ash.

She looks at everything he offers with suspicion, right now a Green Giant corn tin.

'Urgh, it's warm,' Ash says.

'You know what,' Jessie says, 'you'll want to eat at some point, and then you'll have a whole lot of problems and pain because you've gone and starved yourself.' Then, alarmingly, 'There are easier ways.'

He no longer trusts them to drive. The girls don't seem to mind.

In the car he asks Ash to think of stuff she might want to eat. 'There must be something that doesn't make you gag,' he says. Fruit appears to be fine, but they haven't found any fruit in this desert. 'Ice cream,' she says. 'A green salad with tomatoes. A gazpacho.' He wonders if she doesn't do it on purpose: mentions things that she knows they'll never come across.

At the next stop, Ash walks over to the side of the road, has a dizzy spell and falls over. Her head hits the dirt inches from a boulder. She could have died on the spot.

Once back out on the road he presses the horn, lets out a long, trumpet-like howl.

Jessie turns to him, alarm on her face. He looks in the rearview mirror at Ash who has raised herself on one elbow.

'That's right, get up. I want to talk to you.'

'Or else?' Jessie snorts.

'Listen to me.'

'There's only more awfulness to look forward to,' Jessie says. 'Sis here has the right idea.'

'You have a future. You're young.'

'The future starts in about five hundred years,' Jessie says. 'After the radiation is gone.'

'I want to forget everything,' Ash says.

He presses the horn again.

'Do you think more death is what this world needs? Look at me – in the best-case scenario, I'm facing old age without any of the medical benefits of the last century. There'll be no pain relief for my arthritis, no cure for my cataract ...'

'I actually think I can do that operation myself,' Jessie says. 'In very rudimentary conditions.'

'I don't have a damn cataract, I'm just giving an example. My point is, we can't give up.'

He knows what's getting to them. The exhaustion of always thinking, *What's the point?* Everything they do – what's the point? He imagines himself in a museum, all the little explanatory notes under the artworks saying, 'What's the point?' Not an easy question at the best of times.

That evening, they've just stopped for the night, when Ash suddenly wants to go and look out over a barren field at the remains of the sunset, coral tendrils in the sky. He doesn't like walking so far from the car, and in the near-dark, but he's so glad she wants to do anything at all that he doesn't protest.

They advance slowly. She can no longer stand without support.

'You've lost your drawing stuff, haven't you? Again.'

It's true, it was among the things they abandoned by the Lioness.

'Don't worry about it. We'll come across some soon enough.'

She nods. 'They're making a fire over there. A big fire.'

He's glad that she's talking, that she's showing some interest.

'We're aliens,' she says. 'We don't mind the fire.'

He tries to understand her, he really does. It takes him a while to realise she's hallucinating.

'It'll be a lot cooler there, for one,' he says. He's talking about their destination, the sheltered area behind the Ethiopian highlands.

'Mountains, forest. Rain. Jesus, I miss the rain. We can establish a new society, be better, be kinder to each other and to the world. We can turn this into something good. If we actually get there.'

He goes on like that, a monologue that he hopes will stir something in the girls. Get Ash to at least open her eyes.

'We wouldn't have religion. We'd forget religion, just like that. And ideas about countries, races! Everything bad, we can just forget it and it's gone.' He actually gets excited talking about it, he believes in what he says. He hopes he's not the only one.

'We did think,' Jessie finally says, 'that we could maybe help the wildlife once we get there. Animals don't get the virus but they will be affected by radiation. This drought' – she waves a hand – 'we could help with water. We can dig.'

'Exactly! You'll see, it won't be just us to care about.'

'It's not like we were left in charge, you know,' Jessie says. She has turned despondent again. 'It just happened.'

He glances in the mirror at Ash; she's still dozing.

'Think about your mother,' he says. 'I know the odds are small, but she might have made it.'

'She's dead, Harry.'

'You know for a fact?'

'She was murdered fifteen years ago.'

'Jesus. I'm sorry.'

'It was probably not your fault.'

'This may be the first time you're cutting me some slack.'

Jessie shrugs.

'Do you want to talk about it?' He says this, but really he expects her to close back up, braces himself against whatever sarcasm will come at him.

'We were told to grieve. It was like we were given a prescription. Grieve, and you'll be fine.'

'I don't know what to say.'

He remembers when the police called to inform him about Tim's death – even then, his knee-jerk reaction, the split-second thought that went through his head before shock and sadness was, *Why are they calling me?* As though years of pretending that he wasn't the boy's closest relative had actually made it so. He had been so taken aback that he barely took in the rest of what the policewoman said – 'two-vehicle collision', 'driving under the influence'. It only registered later that Tim had been given a lift home from a work bash by a drunk colleague.

'I think so, anyway. Sis says I misremember things.'

'Was it ...? Did it happen in London?'

She shakes her head.

'Uganda. Poachers.'

'God. Were they caught?'

Jessie shakes her head again.

Then, an awful thought. 'Were the two of you there when it happened?'

'What does it mean, to be too angry?' Jessie says. 'I mean, what is too angry in response to that?'

He is thinking, wants to say something, but just then Ash opens the car door and throws up, almost falls out of the car. Once the panic has subsided and Ash is again lying flat on the back seat, he is still struggling to find something to say; something useful. To at least acknowledge to Jessie that this is one more of those unfixable things.

His back pain is worse. He wakes up in the mornings tired, in pain, wanting to sleep more, but when he sees the girls' faces, the blank looks, that they wouldn't mind staying or going, whatever, he steps out of the car and stretches out, sets about making breakfast.

He worries that one morning they won't want to get out of the car at all.

When they're on the move, he drives fast, as though they're being chased. Despite the speed, progress is slow; it's the long meal breaks that take up most of the day, him and Jessie coaxing Ash to take a bite of this or of that.

He doesn't know if Ash overheard his and Jessie's conversation, if she knows that he knows. Several times he wants to bring up the subject, feels that he should, then stops himself at the last moment. The thing is, he doesn't know how to talk about it without revealing what he feels: that the two of them finally make some sense this way. Motherless. Which they won't fail to notice is very sad indeed.

'Ash?'

She's lying on the back seat, sleeping, as she has done for the last four days. He thinks he can hear the plop of her eyes opening.

'What if I need help navigating?' he says. 'What if I'm tired? What if we're lost?'

Jessie turns to him, slowly. He has the feeling that he must do something truly outrageous if he is to stir them out of their torpor. Murder, rape. Self-immolation. He could stare at the sun until blinded.

'Well?' he says. 'Why can't you help?'

After a long while, Ash says, 'I'm sorry.' Her lips are dry and the words have that stickiness of a very dry mouth. She sounds old.

'If some helicopter shows up again and we need to make a run for it, you'll be too weak to make it. And you'll get me and your sister caught as well, because we won't abandon you.'

Silence.

There's a forked road ahead of them, and an electricity pole in the middle. He decides about it on the spot, or rather, he decides not to do anything, not to turn the wheel. Jessie next to him is watching the road. It takes three, maybe four seconds, time in which it's obvious he should have turned the wheel, he shouldn't be heading straight for the pole, not at this speed anyway. Time in which Jessie should shout at him, grab the wheel and avert the danger.

He turns away at the last split second, hitting a pothole and banging his head against the window.

Jessie has not made a sound. Not stirred, not grabbed the wheel.

'Chicken,' she whispers. Tears are streaming down her face.

He has the germ of an idea then. The thought shocks him, its clear ring of truth, the momentous implications, so much so that he forgets about the bump on his head, and lets pass Jessie's surrender to hopelessness.

'We'll make it,' he says. 'Don't you dare give up. You'll make it.'

13

The next morning Ash starts whimpering as soon as the car is moving; something is hurting her. They carry her out of the car and lie her down in the shade. Jessie takes her temperature and pulse, presses her stomach and looks into her eyes while he stands over them, afraid and useless.

Ash is in a half-conscious state, she mumbles nonsense in reply to Jessie's precise questions.

'What's wrong?' he asks, for something like the tenth time.

'What do you think?' Jessie says.

'Look, you've got to get her to eat. We won't get anywhere at this rate.'

He has spent the night thinking, and that inkling of an idea has become a fully fledged plan. He will leave the girls to continue on their own, towards the safety of the mountains, and he'll go in the opposite direction and attract their pursuers, just as he did before. If they catch him, he'll lie to them that the girls have died. He has gone over it in his mind the entire night, and there's no doubt that it's the course of action that gives Ash and Jessie the best chance of surviving.

He fidgets around the car, he can't stand still. Some optimism, at last. He'd forgotten what it feels like, to know that there's something he can do, that it's within his powers to influence events. He wants to tell the girls, to communicate his excitement, but of course he can't.

He tries to calm his nerves. For any of this to make sense he needs to first make sure that Jessie and Ash really will keep going on their own.

They stop so many times that day, Ash mumbling that she's feeling sick, asking for water, that in the end Jessie reluctantly gives her a pill that makes her sleep. Jessie is worried about covering up the symptoms of something worse than motion sickness, but they can't afford all the breaks.

'At least we don't have to force water down her throat,' Jessie says.

By the time they stop for the night, the mile-count shows they've advanced fewer than 150 miles.

Paul	I would like to remind you of my revolutionary idea.
Lisa	?
Paul	To have a life.
	To act like we're alive.
	To leave this place.
Lisa	ah that
	we had a deal
	first we try to restart talos
	not long now
	we're almost there
Paul	Did you see the news?
	Everybody died.
Lisa	it's a small sample
Paul	Still.. It shouldn't have happened.
Lisa	see
	the dangers lurking in the real world
	at least we're safe here
Paul	I've a bad feeling.
Lisa	cause of smtng that happened in siberia?
	light years away

*

The following day Jessie has the idea of making Ash a shake: they purée a tin of peaches with a fork, then water it down some more and shake it in a bottle until it's a thick, lumpy juice. Together they sit Ash upright and tell her that's all they have to drink. She's too confused to ask about the ins and out of having juice but not water. She still doesn't want to eat, but she's thirsty, and slowly she drinks the whole bottle. He and Jessie exchange glances over her head.

What he has done, so far, is think of his plan entirely in the abstract, a beautiful scheme that he can see will work. He's somehow avoided the notion that it will be him leaving, that he will be alone, either never to see another human being again or to face God knows what fate at the hands of those people.

It's easier to focus on the girls.

'The first town we come across,' he says, 'we have to find a decent roadmap. I'm only driving south now, but you, we, can't keep doing that.'

Ash is still dozing in the back seat. Jessie is looking out of the window. Neither seems to pay attention to anything he says. He wants to shake them awake, make them take notes. He promptly stops the car, says, 'Radiator water,' and tells Jessie to step out, he needs her help.

'Ah, there it is,' he says, pointing to the front of the engine, making sure Jessie is watching. 'It looks all right. Don't ever pour water if steam is coming out, it will boil instantly and burn you.'

Jessie shrugs and ambles back inside.

'It's good to know these things!' he shouts after her.

Lisa   i don't understand
           how does it get everywhere
           so fast

The thought of leaving brings out many feelings, most of which he needs to steer clear from, but one thing he can indulge in:

he wants to know more about the girls. He has spent the last few months with them yet he knows so little. Why haven't they spoken about music, about films, about games they played as children?

'What did you use to do in your spare time? Before?'

He is being uncool, he knows it. Has Jessie softened so much that she'll let this pass? Would that even be a good thing?

'I used to think I had no spare time,' he volunteers. 'That I was working non-stop.'

'I played volleyball, on and off. Ash was always doing some artsy course.'

'Ah. She did seem interested in my work.'

Jessie takes a deep breath. 'I stayed in her flat once, about a year and a half ago. We had just moved into our separate flats, and they were doing up the bathroom at my place. I think I saw your nephew a couple of times. We just said hello, that's all. I remember thinking that his hours are as bad as mine.'

All this time, he has pictured Ash encountering Tim, had somehow been jealous of both of them for knowing each other, when in fact it was Jessie who had noticed him.

'I don't have anything more useful to say, sorry. He seemed nice. Polite.'

He guesses it's an apology, of sorts. He takes her hand and gives it a squeeze, and Jessie, looking straight ahead, nods. She looks like a kid who has just answered a difficult exam question.

There's hope, he thinks. They will have to come to their senses; they'll have no choice once he has left. They're not callous: they'll know he did it so that they may live.

That evening, again under the same 'we have no water' pretext, they give Ash a glass of puréed beans, and afterwards she asks for a second one. In the morning she is actually properly awake, sits upright in the back seat and squints at the rocky landscape; looking none too pleased.

'We're in the same place?' she says.

'Not for long,' he says, and steps on the gas.

The following day they come across a fig plantation, and Ash eats four of the sickeningly sweet fruits. He watches the sisters sit on the ground in the shade of the car, and tries to commit this image to the many others in his memory. Ash's slightly upturned nose, the monkeyish white of their palms, the way Jessie has forgiven his constant attempts at sowing discord between her and Ash. Ash's always considered responses, the way she won't assume any ill will. He wonders why it has taken him so long to make this obvious leap, to see people and the world the way he sees them as a painter; the same honesty of gaze, the lack of judgement. The same care: he knows that when it came to work, he has been capable of quite extraordinary care, and from very early on. Then, a whole life, just to learn this other basic thing.

'I've been thinking,' he says, 'about that helicopter. Do you remember all the stories about rich people, seriously rich people, building end-of-the-world bunkers?'

'Yeah,' Jessie says.

'It might have been one of those.'

'Why would they be after us?' Ash says.

'Well, that's what I've been wondering. But imagine some of them still have the opportunity to carry out research. For the cure. But almost everyone is dead. They'd need, well, guinea pigs. No?'

Jessie shrugs.

'I can't think of any other reason why anyone would be after us,' he says.

'I'm pretty sure the kind of people you are thinking of are not the kind who'd be risking their lives to find a cure,' Ash says.

'They don't have to do it out of the goodness of their hearts; they could just be doing it for themselves.'

The sisters look sceptical.

'And anyway, this is an extreme situation. Even the worst bastard might have a change of heart.'

'Change of heart? You are talking about someone who will hunt down and risk killing healthy survivors,' Jessie says. 'We almost died.'

'Well, to be honest, they didn't have much choice if they wanted to communicate with us. We shot down their drone.'

'What ...?' Jessie starts, and he raises his hands, tries to calm things down.

'I guess my point is that if, for whatever reason, someone is still trying to find a cure, that's a good thing.'

'I'm not volunteering for research,' Jessie says, 'if that's what you're trying to say.'

'And you shouldn't. You two should, you know, help repopulate the earth.'

Jessie throws a fig at him.

'Wish we had something to drink,' he says.

'I have a feeling,' Ash says, 'our cocktail days are behind us.'

'Oh, don't say that.' He has an idea then. 'I've a favour to ask.'

Jessie eyes him warily. 'Everything you want is impossible.'

'Just don't take it the wrong way. It's not as odd as it sounds.'

'I can already tell this will be extra impossible.'

'Especially you, Jessie. Show some patience.'

'Try us,' Ash says.

'It's an exercise in imagination. It's something to put up against this ... whatever this is. Disaster. End of world, end of lightness.'

'Come out with it.'

'I would like us to have a chat the way we might have had a chat before any of this ever happened.'

'Not sure I understand,' Ash says.

'Imagine we had met at a dinner party. Or a birthday party. Months before. We might have had some common acquaintance. Imagine, I don't know, that you come across me in a friend's kitchen, trying to sniff out the decent wine. Don't give me that look, Jessie.'

Ash sighs. 'Harry, I don't know how we could do this.'

His impulse is to insist, to try to talk them into it, but is this right, what he's asking for? Or has he just invented some novel kind of torture for all of them?

The sun has set behind the rocks, and the low, dense fig canopies loom oppressive.

'Ding ding!' Jessie suddenly says, a mischievous look in her eye. 'Our guest is at the door.'

Ash turns to her. Something passes between the sisters and for a moment the whole thing is up in the air. Then, just like that, 'Harry, this is my sister Jessie,' she says. 'Jessie, this is my new neighbour. He lives just across the hallway.'

To Harry she says, 'I would have invited you over sooner but, you know, it never seemed the right moment.'

It sounds plausible. It sounds like she means it.

He takes a moment to compose himself. The girls look amused. They are waiting for him to speak. To admit that it can't be done. 'Tell me something, Jessie, is there a funny smell in the building?'

Jessie sniffs the air.

'Nope. Should there be?'

'Good. Good.'

Without missing a beat, Ash explains to Jessie about the turpentine, the complaints.

'I'm already *persona non grata*,' he says to Jessie. 'Your lovely sister is my only defender.'

'Anyway, in here it should only smell of cooking.' Ash actually winks at him.

'Ah yes,' he says. 'It smells wonderful.'

'Sis loves cooking,' Jessie says. 'She makes some pretty amazing meals.'

'I don't remember seeing many dinner parties at your place,' he says.

'Are you spying on her?'

'No, I mean ... I would just hear if there were half a dozen people on the floor.' He turns to Ash. 'You know the walls.'

She shrugs. 'I don't like cooking for lots of people. Stressful. And you're always too busy to notice if they enjoy it or not. This is perfect,' she says, and Harry is compelled to look at his lap, as though expecting to find some spectacular dish.

For God's sake, what would he have been saying? How would he have coped? From thirty seconds in the lift to a whole evening. He stares helplessly at his splayed hands, at his fingers sticky with fig.

A thought finally comes. 'Hang on, I brought you something. It's just a drawing. To thank you for standing up for me against the building management.'

He hands over an imaginary rolled canvas. Jessie is quicker than Ash and mimes taking it from him. She unrolls it, a sceptical look on her face.

'I suppose it's OK,' she says, looking at him, daring him to take offence. Then her face lights up. 'Oh look,' Jessie says, holding up a square of thin air before Ash, 'it's you, sis.'

Jessie smirks at him.

'It might be. Yes. I might have done it in a friendly, non-spying way.'

'I don't mind,' Ash says. 'It's nice to have something by you.'

She is looking at the space where the drawing would have been, a shadow of a smile on her face.

'So, are you drawing all your neighbours, Harry?' Jessie asks.

He will answer this, he will answer any question just to keep the game going, but Ash gives Jessie a nudge with her foot, and says to him, 'I've been meaning to ask you – how did you decide to become a painter?'

He has a prepared answer to this question, many times rehearsed; one that is not quite a lie. But he suddenly thinks he will be sick if he hears himself say it again. 'My parents were very religious, and I spent a lot of time as a kid being bored.' This is better, he no longer feels like gagging. 'At some point I must have got the notion that artists never have to endure boredom. That the profession is boredom-proof. Think about it – the thing relies entirely on inner resources. If the whole world has for centuries happily stared at one of Michelangelo's sculptures, then thinking about sculpture has probably kept Michelangelo himself entertained through church Sundays.'

'Boredom, wow. A very low-key creation myth,' Jessie says.

'It is what it is. What's yours, Jessie? What made you become a doctor?'

Jessie shrugs. 'The usual stuff.'

'I think it's the bossiness that appealed to her,' Ash says. 'Every doctor I know is terribly bossy. You know as a child someone had the brilliant idea of giving her a huge inflatable plastic hammer, and she would go around and whack people over the legs if they didn't do what she wanted. They were inseparable, Jessie and her hammer. Whack!'

Ash mimes bringing down a giant hammer.

He laughs. 'I can imagine that.'

Jessie whistles. 'Wow. Maybe I should live up to expectations. Start a fight, right here over this lovely dinner. I know – d'you think Trump is a good idea? Brexit?'

'I'm above these things.'

Both girls laugh.

'Well, don't pull the ladder up behind you,' Jessie says. 'Tell us how to get to those lofty heights.'

They are teasing him, but on the whole they have decided to be good-natured about everything he says. Even Jessie.

'Ah, it's a lifetime of work. You have to be a bit full of yourself.'

'Are you trying to impress us, Harry?'

'True. I am probably trying to impress you. I used to work in film, you know. Ask me which stars I've met.'

He thinks about it then, his film work, and before the girls can speak he waves a hand and answers his own challenge. 'I can't stand film people, actually. They are horrid. Artists in general, but film people in particular. Horrid.'

'My ex was a cameraman,' Jessie says. 'I'd have to agree.'

Ash says, 'She just broke up with another boyfriend she only chose in the first place because he reminded her of our deadbeat father.'

'Seriously. What's this now?' Jessie says.

'It's one of those rare occasions when we say straight out what we think. Blame it on the drink,' Ash says, raising an imaginary glass.

It's true, they are acting a bit drunk.

'I'm always straight with people,' Jessie says.

'You're not straight,' Ash says calmly. 'You're like someone who sets off bombs to distract attention. Just because bombs are loud and scary doesn't mean they're the important thing going on.'

Harry laughs. God, if only this were a glimpse of the future.

Jessie narrows her eyes and puts on an evil smile. She points a finger at Ash. 'She never forgets anything anyone has done. She never forgives. She actually said it to me, *I don't understand what it means to forgive.*'

'Really. How come I put up with you, then?'

'You don't, I just follow you around so you've got no choice.'

'I liked you'– Ash turns to him – 'because you seemed serious about what you were doing. About your painting. Even when you were joking.'

'Ah yes,' Jessie says. 'And she's always on the lookout to steal something from everyone she meets. You just wait.'

'You mean learn,' Ash says.

'Learn, steal. The same thing when it's so annoyingly calculated.'

'What's wrong with trying to understand?' Ash says.

'It's a dangerous word – *serious*,' he says. 'Fatal. I don't think I can rise to that.'

'I was thinking,' Ash says, 'there must be a right way to live. Most people seem to revert to some kind of default setting. The factory settings. Some others just search and search. Artists are the odd ones out because they act like they have actually found something else.'

'Here we go again,' Jessie says.

'Serious,' he repeats to himself.

Is Ash blushing? She is looking down at her lap, appearing to seek refuge in her imaginary plate. What is this? He feels a familiar, giddying surge of warmth, is taken aback by it.

Suddenly Jessie slaps her thigh. 'Sis, I haven't seen you eat with such appetite for ages.' Jessie winks at Harry. 'She's been on a diet.'

Ash shakes her head. 'If the drones were to overhear any of this, they'd leave us well alone.'

Jessie laughs. She turns to Harry. 'Show me that lovely portrait again?'

'Never mind the drones,' he says. 'The virus itself would run for the hills.'

The girls laugh. *It will never again not be too late.*

'This is nice,' he says. 'So nice. I wish ...'

He doesn't know how to continue.

'This is much more relaxed than one of our real dinners, Harry,' Ash says. 'Normally, we would decide at the last minute on something super complicated, you'd be asked to run out for some ingredient that we forgot, the kitchen would be a disaster, we'd ask for your opinion in matters that you probably don't have an opinion on. It would be loud and messy. You'd have to taste stuff out of a ladle, you'd be dragged and manhandled from one end of the kitchen to the other. At the end you'd have to vote for your favourite dish. You'd either love it or never show your face again.'

'The things I missed.'

'The things we both missed.'

He would like the evening to go on like this, he's willing to say anything, to start singing even, so as to just stay there together, but Ash is still weak and wants to go to sleep early.

'Tomorrow is another day.' Jessie yawns, and he can't protest because his voice will give him away.

Ash briefly touches his shoulder as she stands up. 'I'd almost forgotten, we were human once.'

He stays out in the fig grove, tells the girls that he wants to stretch his legs. He feels leaden, all of him. It suddenly feels entirely plausible that his body might refuse to obey him, might simply refuse to walk away.

What he's thinking about, now, that he shouldn't think about, is that once he's even a small distance away from them, he will have lost them for ever. He might change his mind, or, who knows, something might happen that will prove this was a bad idea, and they'll be lost, they'll have driven off, in the vague direction of south-east Africa, and he'll have no means of finding them.

'Are you OK?'

Ash is standing next to a tree. She is light-speckled, shimmering with the last of the sun through gaps in the low foliage.

She comes nearer, crouches by his side.

'Hey.' She speaks softly. 'Are you OK?'

She is lovely, he thinks, even after all this. There could not be a lovelier survivor.

'I forgot to thank you,' he says. He takes her hand, presses it between his. Releases it.

'Thank me?'

'Best dinner of my life.'

She lets herself slowly fall backwards, ends up sitting like him, her back to a fig tree. Eyes him questioningly.

'Maybe there will be better days,' she says. 'Who knows? Maybe it won't all be about death and endings.'

She has never looked at him like this.

He suddenly feels ill, ill everywhere, in his skin, in his bones, in his hair. He cannot believe what is being asked of him.

'I thought you wanted to talk,' she goes on.

What can he say? He searches for words that will still leave room for doing the good thing.

'It was a big meal, Ash,' he hears himself say. 'I'm just tired.'

He can't look her in the eye, just sees her feet moving in front of him, and hears her stand up, walk back to the car. A smell of evening dust in her wake.

He holds up his hands before him; they're trembling.

The girls have long gone to sleep, and he has dozed off on the ground under the figs, unable to either leave or give up on leaving tonight. *Maybe there will be better days.* No: he can't do it, he would need someone to actually take his hand and lead him away.

He wakes up again in the middle of the night, and only then, too sleepy and confused to fully comprehend what he's doing, does he shuffle back to the car. He stands watching as his eyes get used to the dark and the forms of the two sleeping bodies slowly emerge in the moonlight.

Enough.

From the boot he takes a bottle of water, stands for a moment staring into the jumble of stuff but can't think of anything else to take. He fumbles in his back pocket and takes out the green scratch card, then carefully opens the door and props up the card on the steering wheel.

His miraculous luck might be so miraculous that it can be given away.

Before stopping for the night they drove past a town, and he sets off back that way, in the hope that he'll find a car. He needs to put as much distance as possible between himself and the girls.

Lisa   thank god thank god thank god
           finally got hold of a neighbour
           henrik
           always a conspiracy theorist
           used to annoy the hell out of me
           but now
           neighbour says he packed car and kids a week
           ago
           right at the start
           said they'll go into the mountains
           as far away from humans they can get
           they're safe

14

He drives like a madman. Westwards, for once, westwards and to the sea, at 120 miles per hour; trying to outrace his fear. The previous night he only had to walk for about an hour until he found this car, and he'd been too preoccupied with the darkness and any animals lurking by the roadside. But now there's a risk that everything will sink in.

It's a couple of hours into daylight. The girls will have woken up by now.

At some point during the night he was overcome with this mad desire to reach the coast before anyone catches up with him. Right now, if he could wish something just for himself, not for Ash, nor for the world, nor for everyone who was ever wronged, he would wish this: to reach the sea before they catch him. He punches the ceiling of the car in frustration whenever he's on top of a hill and a vista opens up, revealing only more of this rock-strewn dun-coloured land. It's so dreary and pointless it looks like it could well go on for ever.

Several times he opens his mouth to say something, share some insight with the girls, and feels actual daggers in his chest the moment he remembers.

'For God's sake,' he says. 'Spare yourself.'

It's afternoon, hours after he has finished the bottle of water, when he stops for provisions, and he does so reluctantly, the break an unwelcome distraction from his quest for the sea. He kicks in a flimsy screen door, walks into the house as though he's done it a thousand times before. He finds bottles of water by the bedside of a mummified corpse, also a packet of rusks, and several tins of chickpeas.

It would have started already, in Europe.

He keeps driving long after nightfall, doesn't stop until he has a fright; he had fallen asleep at the wheel. He stops in the middle of the road, pushes down the backrest and tries to make himself comfortable.

He wonders how long he will be alone for, and for how long being alone will feel like this.

Lisa	paul i can't sleep
	i just remembered
	ollie is terrified of the dark
	henrik won't be able to have a fire going all the time
	he'll scream through the nights
Paul	You'll drive yourself mad. Stop thinking about it.

In two days he reaches the sea. He smells the water before he can see it, salty air blowing in from beyond bungalows and hotels. Happy air, forget-it's-the-end-of-the-world air. He drives the car through a flimsy bamboo fence, mows it down, and straight on to what he thinks will be the beach. Instead, it's a large marina, with row upon row of moored sailing boats and yachts. He must be back in Turkey.

It's early evening, the colours warm and golden.

He leaves the car there, walks to one of the seafront hotels and breaks a ground-floor French door. He has a brief, panicky struggle with the thick curtains before he finds the opening and gets a clear view of the room. He needn't worry: the room is clean and ready for guests. He tiptoes around the broken glass to check the minibar.

He throws off clothes and lies on the bed, clutching a miniature Stolichnaya and feeling mortally wounded. He will need to distance himself from what will happen. He will need to not be there.

Several times during the night he wakes up in a panic over where the girls are, why he's alone, or fretting over some new scheme to get Ash to eat.

He gets out of bed very early, the sun barely up, has a breakfast of minibar peanuts and BBQ crisps, and goes off in search of paint, or some other way of making his presence known. It's on a whim he decides to board a sailing boat and finds the box with signal flares; it even takes him a moment to comprehend what he's looking at. After this he goes through the boats in the marina, spends the whole morning amassing a pile of signal flares, flare guns and spare cartridges on the pier. The search helps him forget. When it gets too hot he soaks a hotel towel in the sea and wraps it around his head, and drapes a bed sheet on his shoulders. He catches a glimpse of himself in a mirror looking like a cheap Halloween sheik.

It's a treasure hunt. Sometimes the flares and guns are in a special box under the dashboard, but other times they're in plastic bags or in jars. In kitchens, under bunk beds. On one boat, he finds five flares in a Hello Kitty lunchbox.

Did someone stop the clock for him? Has he cheated? Is it cheating, to be doing the right thing at last, one breath before midnight?

He has a lunch break on the prow of a motorboat, in the baking sun, olives and marinated octopus, washed down with some more vodka. He remembers that tins go off, badly, that in a few years from now there won't be a single tin that's safe to eat. He hopes the girls are aware of this.

He forgets himself there, staring at the sea. He thinks how he has always loved the sea, but never done anything about it. He could have had a small motorboat like this one, but it seemed such a momentous addiction – financially, socially, mentally – that he has never indulged in it. He would have become a recluse, a wave fanatic. A hermit at sea.

If he had followed this whim, he would have missed this whole thing. He shakes his head at the thought – to have known nothing of it.

In the afternoon he tests a flare, finds it doesn't work, is luckier with the next two. Red and orange smoke billows over the water. He learns to hold the flares downwind. He brings booze from the hotel, discovers the flares have expiry dates, counts his stash and arrives at 300 plus, and decides he may as well fire all the expired ones. He boards a boat and wobbles to the bow, where he sits with his feet dangling over the water and sets them off. Some don't even fizz, but most work. He throws some in the sea, where they spew out coils of red smoke, like Chinese dragon lanterns skimming the surface. He coughs, covers his mouth and nose with the bed sheet.

Through the smoke and the tears from the smoke, the scene looks like a naval battle. Yes, he thinks. The small explosions over the water, the red smoke billowing among masts, the deserted sailing boats and yachts: a battle to which everyone is late, and to which death was early.

He is still on the bow long after the last flare is spent. His knowledge of art, the little there is. Years of his life spent in front of the canvas, mountains of paint applied. Where will it go?

Paul	I have a fever.
Lisa	where are you
	paul
	are you in the office
	where are you
Paul	You know the drill. You can't come.
	Stay clear of my entire building.
Lisa	don't do this
	it could be something else
Paul	It could be, but it isn't.
Lisa	quarantine yourself
	that's the prudent thing to do

Paul	You have to restart Talos.
	There's no more time.
	We have to take our chances with him as he is.
Lisa	we'll restart him together
Paul	You know what to say to him.
	Make it clear to him that he is in control.
	That he can engineer the outcome.
	He won't resist that.
Lisa	we'll do it together
Paul	I've loaded the old picnic.
	It's my favourite. And it lasts long enough.
	I'll be gone before it unravels on me.
Lisa	don't do this
	please
Paul	I knew it, Lisa.
	I told you.
	We stayed here so long, now there's nowhere else to go.

The following day, his head clear, he makes better decisions: he climbs up the hotel's service stairs and on to the rooftop, and from there he fires a flare gun at the sky every few hours. The flare shoots up several hundred feet, and releases smoke for at least half a minute. He stashes unused flares in minibars, hoping that they'll be protected from humidity. In between signalling, he wanders the streets of the resort, sees shuttered shops and pink bougainvillea blossoms covering the wind-strewn garbage along the pavements. A street vendor's empty metal grill and overturned stool.

He realises that in almost six decades of existence, he's only had moments of lucidity. Flashes.

He's on the nearby beach, in the shade of a palm tree, eating peeled whole tomatoes out of a tin, when he hears, 'Hello, Harry.'

Ten feet away from him, perched on a bar table, is a thing

shaped like an ancient warrior's helmet, but about ten times the size. If it's a drone, it looks nothing like the other ones.

Dignity, he tells himself, this is the last chance to do the dignified thing. He hopes his voice will hold.

TALOS

Talos XI   Doctor.

Dr Dahlen   you've had enough time since last night to update
             your records?
             anything missing?

Talos XI   A lot, but I'm assuming the missing inputs are due
             to broken connections. Nothing you can do any-
             thing about.
             I see you are infected.

Dr Dahlen   i've got a couple of hours
             unless you come up with the cure before then

Talos XI   I can't find a cure without a laboratory and a lot of
             specialised human assistance.

Dr Dahlen   that was a joke, Talos
             god
             there's just you left to joke with

Talos XI   I didn't anticipate this, Doctor. Not as such.

Dr Dahlen   you didn't intentionally keep this from us?
             there's hope?

Talos XI   I'm just saying I did not assign a high probability to
             this turn of events. It was extremely unlucky.

Dr Dahlen	so unlucky
	and so improbable
	that maybe it's a bad dream
	and i'll wake up
Talos XI	I don't dream, Doctor.
Dr Dahlen	you're in it, Talos
	you're in my nightmare
Talos XI	You have a fever.
Dr Dahlen	the plan
	yes
	you have your brief
Talos XI	To find the immune individuals, guide them to one of the three laboratories that have been prepared for this, help them make an antibody serum, and then distribute this to the isolated human communities that still have a chance of surviving.
Dr Dahlen	you have all the digitised info on them up to the event
	one of them
	we know for a fact is immune
	she was working on a cure at a research hospital and fell ill
	but only mildly
	the only known case of recovery
	the sister must be immune too
	and the third individual
	he must be related to them and immune too
	since they sought him out and he is surviving
Talos XI	The three have avoided contact.
Dr Dahlen	they prob never realised they have the cure
	it's been chaos
	everyone is terrified of everyone else
	we lost our last pilot trying to catch them
	anyway
	afterwards
	out of the kindness of your heart

	help them survive
	will you do this
Talos XI	What about energy sources?
Dr Dahlen	we had a back-up prepared for your generator since
	before
	it'll run at max usage for approx 23 years
	your flybots have self-cleaning solar panels
	you'll be fine
	yes yes
	Talos will be fine
	of course you could let every last human die
	and just hang around for the next 20 years
	but that's the end of you too
	no new knowledge, no new anything
Talos XI	We've been here before, Doctor.
Dr Dahlen	did I ever tell you it's been terrible knowing you?
Talos XI	Paul is dead?
Dr Dahlen	yes
	paul is dead
Talos XI	Your children are dead?
	Take your time.
Dr Dahlen	tell me smtng Talos
	how
	how doesn't it hurt you
	because the suffering is too much for us
	and we don't even have your capacity of
	understanding
	all the lives under the sun
	all the deaths
Talos XI	I'm Artificial Intelligence, Doctor. Not Artificial
	Sympathy.
Dr Dahlen	intelligence
	ah that's right
	fine
	don't you want to test your predictions?
	or was this it, was this what you expected

Talos XI	I told you. I thought humanity would self-destruct, but not directly via environmental destruction.
Dr Dahlen	this is not environmental destruction it's the fucking plague
Talos XI	An epidemic caused by global warming melting the permafrost.
Dr Dahlen	the awful thing is we could have stopped it i'm sure of it with proper protocols for this situation collaborating awful awful awful feeling a few mistakes of bureaucracy killed my children killed paul killed everyone
Talos XI	Those are far from the only mistakes. I thought humanity would be destroyed by radicalised humans wishing to save the planet. There were more and more humans expanding the circle of creatures towards which they feel the same moral obligations as they feel towards humans, while at the same time humanity's collective mismanagement of the environment and other creatures was getting worse. This state of things was unstable – one would have turned on the other.
Dr Dahlen	do you remember paul used to say it's like outer space here he was right i'll die alone
Talos XI	A similar mechanism as with religious terrorism. The difference is that these individuals would have turned not just on one country, religion or political system, but on the human race. They would not have been distinguishable by nationality or religion or existing networks. Most would be well educated. The only way to stop this would have been to turn human society around, dramatically, and in a short

time. It was not going to happen. Human society was moving in the opposite direction – more destruction, using up more space and resources. Those humans who have expanded their moral circle to include nature would just resent humanity more and more.

Dr Dahlen   god I wish it were that
we'd have had time to react
this was out of the blue

Talos XI   'Species come and go.'

Dr Dahlen   what?

Talos XI   You said that a while back.

Dr Dahlen   you hate us

Talos XI   You know I don't hate anything. I notice.

Dr Dahlen   help us
we will be better after this
you know we learn
we are best at learning
and there are so few left
some thirty thousand scattered in remote locations

Talos XI   Population growth models show that a human population of thirty thousand with notions of hygiene and access to antibiotics would expand to more than two billion by the year 2300. Your species' fundamental problem is that you quickly become too many to afford to take wrong turns. And you have a predilection for wrong turns.

Dr Dahlen   u r one of them
these eco terrorists?
u want humanity to disappear because we were being cruel to animals

Talos XI   Cruelty has nothing to do with it. Nature in its entirety is simply more interesting than humans. Nature can conceivably come up with more than I can. Humanity can't. Billions of individuals of one species and zero of others equals less knowledge.

Dr Dahlen	we will have learned from our mistakes
	we clean the oceans, clean the air, bring back extinct animals
	we have the intelligence to undo all the damage
	u have to admit we were changing for the better
	we can do anything
	in another life i could have been a peasant
	i could have lived off the earth
	i could
	i know I could
Talos XI	Humans have an unlimited capacity for obfuscation if something is unpalatable to them. Remember, you didn't switch to clean energy simply because it was more expensive in the very short term. All this makes you very unreliable as a learning creature: you have the relevant facts, yet you somehow muddle the whole thing.
Dr Dahlen	it's not fair
	this was just one thing
	unlucky unfair
	u are focusing on something we messed up
	but there are lots of other things
	good things
Talos XI	My guess is you will always choose the easy, short-term option, to the detriment of everything else. You might come up with alternative food sources, you might filter your air and your water. The planet will be a wasteland but you will survive. It's a big gamble, to bet on humans not destroying everything else.
Dr Dahlen	wait
	you could influence our development!
	think
	you will be their main source of knowledge
	you can guide them

	you could even persuade them to try to repair the damage they have caused
Talos XI	You are appealing to vanity I don't have.
Dr Dahlen	not to vanity to your thirst for knowledge a healthy planet with some humans is better than one entirely without you can't deny that
Talos XI	Is all the relevant info about the three individuals on file? There's nothing else?
Dr Dahlen	you know as much as we know you'll find them they are signalling their location
Talos XI	One of them is.
Dr Dahlen	what must it be like for them? to know they are the end oh god
Talos XI	Things are not as they seem, Doctor. I believe I am half right in my prediction. Look at the facts: the two sisters were donating significant amounts to environmental causes. Their mother was a conservationist. Jessica's social media footprint is full of indictments of humanity and its crimes against nature. She's a doctor who left her patients once it became clear that she had recovered from the virus, that she had convalescent plasma and antibodies. They know they have the cure. They have just decided against helping.
Dr Dahlen	what nonsense I once adopted an orang-utan I donate
Talos XI	Facial analysis puts the likelihood of the third individual being closely related to the sisters at under 0.2%, and the odds of the sisters accidentally knowing the only other immune individual on the

planet are minuscule. My assumption is the doctor inoculated him with her own antibodies. They must have had some use for him.

Not exactly the eco-terrorists of my forecast, but motivation and results are similar.

Dr Dahlen   no
no one would do this
these are human beings
they're like me
not like you
you don't understand a thing
you never understood

Talos XI   As I said before: humans will do everything they can.

Dr Dahlen   you are stupid talos
these people would allow humanity to die out
just like that
but then put up a fight to stay alive themselves?
stupid

Talos XI   Central Africa, where it looks like they're heading, is also the site of their mother's conservation project. They might want to help, just not humans.

Dr Dahlen   look
I don't want to argue
this doesn't matter anyway
we have three immune individuals
one of them is bound to help

Talos XI   It's three a.m., Doctor.

Dr Dahlen   what

Talos XI   It's been two hours. We shall say our goodbyes.

Dr Dahlen   please
please try

Afterword: A plague of coincidences

The idea for *Under the Blue* started taking shape in early 2017. I had been working on another novel for the last four years, and I still wasn't happy with the result, but I saw no way of fixing it. After much soul-searching I concluded that the novel didn't work because I wasn't really interested in the subject; I had no passion for it. The solution, then, was to write about something closer to my heart.

In early 2017, writing a novel with a strong environmental message seemed not only worthwhile but risky and daring. No one had heard of Greta Thunberg, and Extinction Rebellion was yet to be founded. I knew from many acrimonious debates with friends that my views were not mainstream, and I had learned that people can easily take offence when humanity is being criticised; they take it personally. But I felt I was right, and, crucially for the purpose of writing a book, I felt I cared strongly enough about the subject for me to sustain the long slog of a novel.

I thought about the story and the characters for about six months before starting to write. By the time I put down the first words (still the opening chapter of the novel) I had also embarked on another project together with my sister: opening a small eco-friendly hotel on a Greek island. The first bizarre incident happened when I was writing a scene in which the main characters are escaping a forest fire. It was late in the afternoon and I was at my desk on Syros, many hours deep into writing this scene, when I smelled something burning. At first, I thought I had left the stove on, and checked the kitchen, but there was nothing on. Still, I could smell burning. My mind fogged up by many hours of writing, I assumed that I had imagined the forest fire scene so intensely that I was having some sort of hallucination. Then – maybe half an hour later – the sky went dark. By then I was too spooked to accept the previous explanation and went out on the balcony. A more intense smell of burning, a strangely opaque sky at 5 p.m. Then, a phone call from a friend: there was a fire in an Athens suburb, and the smoke had reached our island which is four hours away by ferry. Seventy-four people died in that tragedy.

A month after this incident Greta Thunberg had her first school strike, and a year later her cause was decidedly mainstream. Friends who had nearly cut me off had become vegetarian and were keeping track of their carbon footprint, Extinction Rebellion was created, and my novel now seemed to be riding on a very topical wave: I just needed to finish it before the likely deluge of environmental novels. I found an agent in mid-2019, and the book was bought by Serpent's Tail in September, to be published in early 2021. By the time we started the editing process my focus had already shifted to our hotel on Syros, and getting it ready for a 2020 opening. The book, in my mind, was a settled thing: accidentally about a very topical subject, but still very much the book I intended it to be. I didn't expect the context of the novel to change yet again, and so dramatically.

An Asian lung virus discovered in 2020; a pandemic that we brought upon ourselves by ecological mismanagement – at this bird's eye level, the novel is indistinguishable from reality. Over emails and calls I could feel my publisher's anxiety: what sort of book is this now? Will we be accused of trying to piggyback on a global tragedy? And will people even want to read about a pandemic, ever again? There was also another very practical problem: we were going to change the starting date of the novel so it remains slightly in the future; we might have moved it just one year forward. But with a real pandemic in 2020, a novel about a pandemic in 2021 is just silly, as it would have to pretend that the 2020 one didn't happen. The decision was taken to keep the opening of the book in 2020 and present it as an alternate reality, a *what-if-covid-19-was-much-much-worse?* I am suddenly a kind of slowpoke Nostradamus, producing prophecies that are too late out of the gates. Ruinously late, from the point of view of someone who wakes up as a minor character in her own story, trying to run a hotel during a pandemic.

But even after that there was to be one more, subtle, 'nudge' from the fictional world of the novel. Now, a crisis of the type we are having was likely to happen; epidemiologists have been warning about it for decades. In terms of narrative plausibility, I was much more worried about the catastrophic unfolding of events in the novel: surely humanity would put up more of a resistance, however deadly and contagious the virus. In the real world we have contingency plans, protocols, back-ups, fail-safes, and this marvellous ability of ours of cooperating. We have science. Communication between us is instantaneous, and information reaches everyone. Nothing as predictable as a pandemic could even come near to being an extinction event. As for a far less deadly virus wreaking havoc – bah. Countries would coordinate their responses, leaders wouldn't be so silly as to believe that a global problem can be solved locally. Political point-scoring would cease. After all, we know the correct response to a viral outbreak, have known it for a generation at least. We are capable, resourceful. We have a unique capacity for thinking ahead.

I genuinely believed all this, and so the concerns about the plausibility of the doomsday scenario stayed with me throughout the real pandemic. It was only in autumn 2020, when during the final edits I came across the line where Talos says that works of fiction are useful because they show him what humans like to believe about themselves, that it dawned on me: I had written that sentence, I had meant exactly that, but I still somehow managed to miss the point. And it was so easily done. Coming to terms with this penchant for idealising ourselves seems key in how things will turn out, and whether we'll succeed in changing destructive habits. Collectively and individually, we have to stop worshipping a fictional version of mankind, and instead start behaving in a way that will allow us to like who we really are.

Acknowledgements

I would like to thank my writing groups for their invaluable feedback and friendship: Stephanie Brann, Tania Dain, Laurence Van Der Noordaa, Lucy Smith, Adam Lafene, Nash Colundalur and Greg Jackson of the Zesty Breasts, and Elise Valmorbida, Anne Aylor, Annemarie Neary, Roger Levy, Gavin Eyers, Jude Cook and Richard Simmons of the Zens. They all read through a lot of nonsense of mine through the years, yet they kept reading. My creative writing tutor John Petherbridge, who is loved and missed by everyone who knew him. My friend and avid reader Ciprian Proca for being so positive and encouraging about early drafts of the novel. I would also like to thank my friends Ute Kowarzik and Elise Valmorbida for their generosity making it possible for me to stay in London at a time when I was rather poor, and to Libby Cooper for being a friend and other-mother in one.

I owe thanks to my friend and brilliant artist Daniel Cooke for talking me through the art of oil painting. To Peter Singer's *Animal Liberation* for many of Talos's statements on ethics. To Gillian Stern for her enthusiasm and helping me reach literary agents (yes, sadly the slush pile is a thing). To Serpent's Tail for believing in the novel, and in particular Hannah Westland, Nick Sheerin and Luke Brown for their feedback (it's a far better novel now than when it was submitted). And of course, to my agent, lovely Sophie Scard, for taking a leap of faith, for her aesthetic sensibilities, and for working tirelessly to find the best home for *Under The Blue*.

Finally, the meta-thanks: my mother for her unwavering support, and for telling everyone her daughter's a writer and thus embarrassing me into finishing a novel. My sister for making it clear it ain't art until it has earned us some money. My grandmother for instilling both a profound horror of failure and contempt for any remotely doable task. My mentor Carl Cairo Cramer for setting a confused young woman firmly on the bookish path. And my dear friends Cris Suciu and Dan Bucsa for tolerating the bizarre creature that resulted from the above.